THE GIRLS OF

A fair-haired and very pretty seventeen-year old girl sprawled on the sofa, her dark skirt pulled up to the top of her creamy thighs. Her small white knickers were halfway down to her knees and her eyes were almost closed. Her lips pouted and the tip of her tongue was showing. She trembled and sighed – as well she might, for there was someone's hand between her legs . . .

The Girls of Lechlade College

Lucy Cunningham-Brown

HEADLINE
DELTA

First published in 1996
by HEADLINE BOOK PUBLISHING

A HEADLINE DELTA paperback

10 9 8 7 6 5 4 3 2 1

ISBN 0 7472 5408 7

Typeset by Keyboard Services, Luton, Beds

Printed and bound in Great Britain by
Cox & Wyman Ltd, Reading, Berks

HEADLINE BOOK PUBLISHING
A division of Hodder Headline PLC
338 Euston Road
London NW1 3BH

The Girls of
Lechlade College

Chapter One

A fair-haired and very pretty seventeen-year-old girl sat half sprawled on a grey sofa, with her dark skirt pulled up to the top of her thighs. Her small white knickers were halfway down to her knees, showing a patch of wispy light-brown curls. Her eyes were almost closed but her mouth was open and the tip of her tongue was showing. She was trembling and sighing – as well she might, for there was someone's hand up her skirt and between her legs.

Fingertips slid over the soft pink lips that the wispy curls half hid and pressed between them to open her. Her legs shook at the touch – she pushed her own hand further up the skirt of the woman playing with her. She felt the smoothness of nylon and the warmth of flesh through thin knickers. That was as far as she went; the sensations between her own legs were absorbing all her attention.

Annabel – that was the young lady's name – loved being diddled like this and made to come. She couldn't stop herself squealing in pleasure when probing fingers prised her kitty open to expose the little pink nubby inside. Knowing fingertips made sensations soar when they slid inside – those lovely throbbing sensations up through her belly to the pink bobbles of her titties. At these times she told herself that she was being ravaged, and forced to submit – she was being made to come, whether she wanted to or not.

The truth of it was that she always wanted to come, any time of day or night. It was a game she played in her mind, pretending she was being forced against her

1

will – it made everything much more exciting.

There were places and times when the noise of Annabel getting her big thrill – crying out and drumming her heels – might attract unwanted attention. She was incapable of controlling her actions when she came, and so the friend diddling her had to press a hand over Annabel's mouth to muffle her cries. In the throes of pleasure she'd gurgle and moan into the palm over her mouth, her pale blue eyes staring wide open and her fingers clawing at whoever was doing it to her.

This fine summer afternoon, sprawling on the sofa, it was different. The fingers between her legs were not those of a friend of her own age. The sofa was in the combined study and sitting-room of Joy Locksley – one of the teachers at the exclusive educational establishment where Annabel was a first-year student.

Joy Locksley was more than just a teacher. She was the Head of Wexby House, one of four houses that made up Lechlade Ladies' College. She was responsible for the discipline and care of the forty girls in her house.

Lechlade College was for girls whose parents intended them to continue their education and go on to university. It accepted them at the age of sixteen and specialised in getting them through A-Levels with the highest possible grades and guiding them through the minefield of university entrance when they were eighteen.

Joy Locksley was a slender dark-haired woman of twenty-nine. She and Annabel were both surprised by the situation in which they found themselves on the grey sofa. Up till now, Annabel's pleasures had been shared only with friends of her own age – she had never considered the possibility of letting a member of the teaching staff touch her.

There were tales about some teachers. It was said that they took an interest in particular girls and had their knickers off when the opportunity served. Gossip said that Miss Redruth, who taught maths, jumped on any girl who stood still long enough. Apart from tittle-tattle about teachers, there were no secrets about what girls did together. They played with each other when they felt like it.

For Miss Joy Locksley, with her hand between Annabel's legs and her fingers in her warm, wet little kitty, it was very surprising to be in this situation. She'd never considered doing it with a student. She knew, as all the teaching staff knew, that the girls did each other all the time. That was to be expected of sixteen- and seventeen-year-olds who lived in close proximity and were deprived of the company of boys their own age, except in the holidays.

Dark-haired Joy Locksley also knew that women teachers at the college went to bed together, went on holiday together, and that they changed partners each academic year – and sometimes each term. That too was only to be expected of healthy and intelligent women living in a closed community.

There were no hard-and-fast rules about friendships between teachers and students, not in writing, but most of the teaching staff preferred each other to young girls. Eleanor Redruth was an exception. She happily took advantage of any girl who let her. She boasted to her friends that no girl had ever refused her.

Joy Locksley had a different set of rules of conduct – but here she was on the sofa in her sitting-room, with her hand up Annabel Darwen's skirt. She asked herself how it happened that she found herself playing with this very pretty fair-haired girl, who, at that moment, was obviously on the verge of coming?

Nothing like it was in her mind earlier that afternoon when she called Annabel to her study. She had heard a disturbing tale about the girl and as Head of House she was responsible for the moral and physical welfare of all the girls in her charge. She thought it her duty to enquire into the matter.

When Annabel tapped at the study door and came in, Joy got up from her desk and asked her to sit on the sofa. The

3

conversation was going to be awkward and Joy didn't want to make it worse by having a desk between them. If they sat on the sofa it would make their talk less formal and easier to get through. So she thought.

The girls of Lechlade were too grown-up to be made to wear uniform but there were some dress rules. These were to discourage the richer ones or the wilder ones from wearing outrageous clothes to impress. Shirts and skirts were required for day wear, skirts not to be ridiculously short. Annabel was in a pale pink shirt and a navy-blue skirt.

'I suppose you're wondering why I asked you to see me,' Joy began. 'I'll get straight to the point. It's come to my notice that you've been given a nickname by your friends. Plenty of girls have nicknames here, there's nothing wrong in that.'

She looked at Annabel, whose cheeks were turning a pretty pink.

'I've been told,' said Joy, 'that the nickname they've given you is "Anybody's". There's no need for me to spell out the implications of that. What I must ask you is this – is it true?'

'Who told you that?' Annabel demanded, her face bright red now.

'Does it matter?' Joy countered, staring at the girl curiously.

As it happened, her informant was Eleanor Redruth, the maths teacher. They were discussing the first-year students the evening before, sitting in the teachers' common room over a gin and tonic. Joy and Eleanor and Sharon Pomeroy, who taught geography. They talked about the nicknames the girls gave each other. Mostly the reasons were obvious 'Ginger', for a girl with hair that colour, 'Lanky' for a tall thin girl.

'There's a girl in Sawby House they call "Monkey",' Eleanor said. 'You must know her, Rachel Fermor, tall very dark-haired girl, a first-rate tennis-player.'

'Why do they call her that?' Joy asked.

'Yes, why?' Sharon Pomeroy echoed.

'It's obvious neither of you has seen her in the showers,' Eleanor said with a grin. 'She's got an amazing jet black bush between her legs, halfway up to her belly button. The minute I saw it I knew I had to get my hands on it.'

'And have you?' Sharon asked, her eyebrows rising.

'Of course I have. It's so thick and bushy I have to make a parting in it with my fingers before I can slip my tongue into her. She told me she shaves her armpits three times a week, her hair is so dark. She asked if she should clip her bush, but I told her it was too beautiful to spoil.'

They talked about other girls. Eleanor mentioned that a girl in Joy's house had the interesting nickname of 'Anybody's'.

'Who do you mean?' Joy asked at once.

'Annabel Darwen, that pretty fair-haired first-year girl.'

Joy asked if Eleanor had dabbled personally with the girl.

'Not yet,' said Eleanor. 'I've had my hands full so far this term.'

'We can guess what your hands have been full of,' Sharon said, shaking her head in mock disapproval.

'To be candid, Eleanor,' said Joy, 'I'd say that "Anybody's" should be your nickname, not a girl's. You're the one who takes on all-comers. Or so you claim – I never know whether to believe half your stories.'

'My ambition since I came to teach here has been to get through every girl in the college,' Eleanor answered with a happy smile. 'Forty girls to a house and four houses – a hundred and sixty of the young darlings. A hundred and sixty pairs of titties to lick! And a hundred and sixty pretty little kitties to get my finger into – I can feel my knickers going damp at the idea – well, they would if I had any on this evening.'

'You're not serious,' Joy said – she was trying to make light of it but she couldn't entirely suppress a note of dismay. 'A hundred and sixty girls indeed!'

'I don't suppose I'll ever manage it,' said Eleanor, 'though I never stop trying. What happens is that by the time I've got through half or two-thirds of them, the second-year girls have gone on to university and are out of my reach.'

Joy liked Eleanor and never took her wholly seriously. If she played with a girl now and then it didn't matter much. Eleanor did not have the responsibilities of a Head of House and made it clear she never wanted to be one.

'Don't let the Principal hear you talking like that,' said Joy. 'She might think you meant it and report you to the Board of Governors. Then you'd be out on your ear.'

'I am a tireless ravisher of sweet young girls,' Eleanor said with her usual grin, 'but I'm not a fool. Our Principal may suspect what I get up to but she'll never have proof. And if she ever did, I know something about her that will keep her mouth shut.'

'I don't want to know about it,' Joy said. 'Let it be your own secret. But what I would like to know is how you came by this information about a girl in my house. Have you had her?'

'I'm sorry to say I haven't,' Eleanor said with a comic grimace, 'I'd like to get my hand into her knickers. She's very pretty and from all accounts when she comes it's like a bomb going off.'

'How do you know that?'

'One of the other girls in your house told me about Annabel at a time when she was feeling very well-disposed toward me. Penny Carlton – the girl with the big bouncing titties.'

'Naturally you've had your hands on them,' Joy suggested.

'Of course I have. I've done a lot more than that to her. Off-hand, I can't think of anything I haven't done to her. She's very active after Lights Out, in case you didn't know. One of the girls she's active with is Annabel Darwen.'

When Annabel asked who had told Joy about her nickname, it was out of the question for Joy to say it came from Miss Redruth. She insisted that the source didn't matter – the important thing was whether it was true.

'It's a joke on my name, Miss Locksley. They turn Annabel into Anybody but it doesn't mean anything.'

The pretty pink flush on her cheeks suggested that the nickname meant much more than Annabel was ready to admit. Joy turned on the sofa to half face her and stare earnestly into her pale blue eyes.

'You can tell me the truth, Annabel, no harm will come of it. I want to help you in every way I can.'

Joy was wearing a pale green and cream summer dress that day; her dark hair was brushed back and glossy. Annabel's eyes were downcast, as if in modesty or indecision. She looked up slowly to Joy's face. The look in her eyes said all that could be said – Joy's mouth fell open in amazement when she recognised the invitation.

This is absolutely ridiculous, she said to herself, but even while the thought was passing through her mind she was slipping an arm around the girl's waist to hug her close.

'Annabel,' she said uncertainly, wondering what on earth was going on. What was happening to her?

Before the thought could develop further, Annabel pressed her lips to Joy's cheek. The touch was thrilling – she turned her head and kissed Annabel full on the mouth. *This has got to stop*, Joy thought desperately.

During the kiss Joy realised that she'd put her hand up Annabel's skirt and her fingers were pressing against the warm softness between the girl's thighs. *No, this won't do at all*, she said to herself. *Pull yourself together*.

By then it was too late for good intentions. Her hand was inside the girl's knickers and down her smooth belly, fingers feeling for the curls and soft lips. Annabel sighed and trembled in a way that revealed very clearly that this was what she expected to be done to her. Joy saw that the nickname was a fair one. She *was* Anybody's, this pretty fair-haired seventeen-year-old. Scores of hands, perhaps even hundreds of them, had been where Joy's hand was now, between Annabel's legs.

All that term Joy had been having an on-and-off affair with Sharon Pomeroy. Sharon was nice enough in bed but it was more a matter of convenience than of strong desire. They both needed someone they could talk to very intimately, someone to go about with, someone to share pleasure with.

Neither of them was inclined to satisfy her healthy urges with a self-administered finger-wave unless there was no alternative. So once a day they met in Joy's sitting-room, or Sharon's, and did pleasing things to each other.

Last evening, after their drink and chat with Eleanor Redruth in the common room, Sharon had gone with Joy to her quarters. They'd gone straight into the bedroom to undress each other and lie naked on the bed in the warm summer night. They kissed and stroked each other's bodies, they sucked each other's titties, they felt each other between the thighs. Sharon rolled over face down between Joy's parted legs and pressed her tongue into her open chuffie.

All that was forgotten now. The impact of holding Annabel close to her and feeling her drove everything else out of Joy's mind. In two minutes she had the girl lying back on the sofa so she could pull her knickers down her legs and see her wispy-curled kitty while she played with it. The lips were well-shaped and prominent, opening very easily to the pressure of a finger. This was a young lady well-used to being handled and fingered.

Annabel was whimpering in pleasure. She knew this time was different from when she was seen to by her friends. The fingers moving so expertly inside her were not trying to force her to come quickly, nor were they teasing her to make her squirm and gasp in long drawn-out torment. These controlled her.

'So it's true, Annabel,' Joy said softly, 'you really are Anybody's. Not that I mind, at this moment, since I'm the one who's having you. You're so pretty that I don't know whether to give you the big thrill here or take you into my bedroom and strip you naked first.'

'Please . . .' Annabel whispered, 'make me come. I'll go into the bedroom with you afterward and do anything you like – anything . . .'

Joy's fingers worked their magic inside the girl's slippery wet slit. Annabel was sighing and shaking. Under her pink shirt her titties were heaving in time with her rapid breathing. Joy eyed them appreciatively and made a promise to herself that before she let Annabel go she'd have that shirt off and use her tongue on those soft young titties.

'I'll let you come, Annabel, but I shall hold you to your promise. Put your hand inside my knickers and feel me – I want you to have your hand there when you come.'

Annabel was almost delirious with excitement. She felt right up Joy's dress until she could slide her hand down inside her knickers and clasp her soft-haired chuffie. By this time Annabel's mind was reeling and the spasms flickering through her belly had grown so strong and insistent that she knew she would come in two more seconds.

Joy's smooth and slender thighs moved as far apart as her dress would let them, Annabel's hot palm pressed against her moist chuffie.

'Yes,' said Joy in a shaky voice, 'oh yes.'

'I'm coming...' Annabel gasped.

'Of course you are.'

Annabel sobbed in delight and her feet jerked up off the carpet as her belly turned inside out in throbs of ecstasy. When it was all over and they were both breathing calmly, Joy got up from the sofa and held her hand out to Annabel.

'You're going to take me into your bedroom,' Annabel said.

It wasn't a question, hardly even a statement – it was just something that was going to happen and they both knew it.

Joy's bedroom was not large. There was a dressing-table with a mirror, a wardrobe and a bed – a single bed. There were no double beds anywhere in Lechlade Ladies' College. Annabel knew about two people playing with each other on a single bed – it was an experience she had nightly.

In Annabel's opinion it was an experience Miss Locksley knew all about too. She looked at the teacher's bed and guessed that two shared it most nights. The whisper this term in Wexby House was that Miss Locksley and Miss Pomeroy were friends.

They'd been seen going for walks together by the river. Everyone knew what that meant. Annabel was certain the bed she was looking at had two people in it most nights – Joy Locksley on her back with her nightie up to her chin and her long-haired friend Sharon Pomeroy kneeling between her legs and tonguing her.

Annabel stood by the bed to be undressed. Joy kissed her and undid the buttons of her pink shirt. She undid Annabel's plain white bra and took if off then held the girl by the hips and licked her pointed titties.

Their bobbles were firm and beautifully pink. All of Annabel's friends told her how pretty they were, even girls like Penny Carlton who handled them roughly. Annabel liked having them handled roughly. She also liked having them licked and sucked – as Joy was doing now, drawing a firm pink bobble into her mouth and sucking hard while her tongue played over it.

'Oh yes, yes,' Annabel moaned, her whole body trembling.

She was not far from coming when Joy left her titties and fell on her knees to undo her skirt and slide it down her legs. Then her tights and her small white knickers were round her ankles. Soon she was naked, this pretty seventeen-year-old, and Joy was on her knees in front of her, holding her by the cheeks of her bum and kissing her kitty.

'You'll make me come again,' Annabel sighed – she wasn't complaining.

'Mmm,' Joy answered. She couldn't speak in words while her tongue was flicking inside the moist pinkness of Annabel's open kitty.

She'd stopped worrying about what she was doing. It was incredibly exciting to play with Annabel – much more than with Sharon Pomeroy. That being so, the rules Joy had lived by in the past were no longer of the least importance.

It wasn't a question of ravaging every girl in the college, Joy

10

told herself, the way Eleanor Redruth claimed she did. It was a question of this one girl, fair-haired Annabel. Joy wanted her, she was having her, she was loving it.

Annabel swayed on shaking legs and put her hands on Joy's shoulders to support herself as she came, squealing in delight. Joy's fingers clenched tight in the flesh of her bum, pulling her close and pushing her tongue as far up Annabel's slippery-wet kitty as it would go. She was nearly coming herself and she was desperate for it. But she waited for Annabel to recover and made the girl sit naked on the bed while she undressed.

Annabel watched with interest as Joy took off her summer dress and her tights and underwear. She had a long slender body, round titties set high, a flat belly and a neatly trimmed triangle of dark-brown hair. She caught Annabel staring at her and smiled.

'Do you like my body, Annabel?' she asked.

'It's very elegant. Are you going to do me again?'

'You may rely on it,' said Joy, 'but first . . .'

She lay down naked on the bed and spread her long slender legs apart. Annabel knew what to do – she put her hand between Joy's open thighs.

'You want me to give you a thrill,' she said as her fingers slid into Joy's warmth and wetness.

'It won't take much,' Joy said in a trembling voice. A moment later her back arched off the bed and she moaned. Annabel's fingers fluttered faster to spin out the thrill, until with a final moaning sob Joy collapsed back onto the bed.

She grabbed Annabel's wrist and pulled her down on top of her, belly on belly, soft titties on soft titties, wet kitty on wet kitty.

Chapter Two

In her second year at Lechlade, Penny Carlton was one of the acknowledged leaders of Wexby House. Her own view was that she was the natural and only leader. She took her pick of the girls, first-year and second-year, and she did what she pleased to whomever took her fancy. Whenever she was in the mood, which was often.

She was well-liked by the other girls. Her natural assertiveness had something to do with that, because most women prefer someone else to take the initiative. In social activities, in opinion-setting – and most certainly in sexual activity. They might be keen for it – and ready for it – but they liked someone else to make the first move.

Someone else to put an arm about their waist and begin the kissing. Someone else to slip a hand up between their thighs. Then in their minds they absolved themselves from all blame. *Not my fault*, they whispered secretly to themselves when someone else suggested they lay down on their back and spread their legs. *I'm not to blame – she's making me do it*.

Penny was big and beautiful and bold. As a result she was much sought-after by other girls, as a friend as well as for sex games. And she was courted by the few teachers at Lechlade who enjoyed playing with girls. Eleanor Redruth was by no means the only one – she was just the one who admitted her preferences openly.

Among the girls in Wexby House, a particular friend of Penny's was Nesta Wade, a tall girl with long yellow hair. Nesta was also in her second year. In their first year she and

13

Penny had been room-mates, and their many nights together helped make them close friends. In their second year they were separated and each was given a different room-mate – that was one of the rules at Lechlade.

Penny and Nesta still did it to each other, but less often now that they each had another room-mate to kiss and hug and diddle. Not that they'd ever been exclusive, even when they shared a room; Penny had a strongly inquisitive nature that led her to experiment with everything and everybody. The truth was that she was a lot nearer to doing every girl in Wexby House than Eleanor Redruth was ever likely to be.

Nesta took her lead from Penny. She slipped her hand into the knickers of every girl she found attractive and played with what she found there. And she slipped a hand into the knickers of some she didn't much like, just for the fun of it. And to learn more about the variations of sexual pleasure.

Nesta and Penny exchanged confidences, telling each other of the girls they had and the teachers they opened their legs for. When Nesta had a favour from someone new, Penny immediately went and did the same so that they could compare impressions of how it had been. When Penny had someone new, she told Nesta, so she could try her out and see if they agreed on whoever it was – girl or teacher.

In consequence, it was surprising when eventually they quarrelled over a girl. Linda Knight was sixteen-and-a-half, not especially pretty, her figure not out of the ordinary. But Linda had bright ginger hair – and not only on her head. Down between her legs she had a thatch of bright carroty-coloured curls. Penny was enchanted the first time she saw Linda's fiery little bush and clasped it in her hand. She stroked it and combed it through with her pocket-comb, she felt it and rubbed it with her fingers, she pushed Linda flat on her own bed and parted those bright curls to push her tongue into the pink kitty they adorned.

Afterward she went looking for Nesta, to tell her all about her fantastic hour with Linda. Nesta's interest was instantly

14

aroused by the enthusiasm of her friend; the very next day she sought out Linda and took her aside to examine the ginger tuft for herself.

No question about it, Linda's kitty was a wonder and a joy to look at. And to play with! Nesta gave it the full treatment, and in her turn she lay on her back for Linda to do the same to her. Both of them were well-pleased when they parted.

Naturally Nesta rushed to tell Penny about this and they agreed that young Linda was a real find. Then on reflection Penny decided that she wasn't pleased with the situation. Listening to Nesta describe how she'd diddled Linda raised a till-then unknown emotion in Penny – jealousy.

She'd never admit it, because that would be too shameful, but Penny had developed a crush on Linda. She wanted her to herself, and she decided she could not share that ginger tuft between Linda's long thighs with anyone – not even her best friend.

For once in her life Nesta refused to respect Penny's wishes. She too was fascinated by Linda's bright ginger kitty and she saw no reason why she and Penny shouldn't take turns with the girl, as they had shared so many other girls in the past. And so the falling-out began. Neither would give way. Their voices rose. Their faces turned red with anger. Bad feeling grew between them until finally they started to push at each other.

The controversy took place in Penny's room in Wexby House soon after lunch. If Penny's room-mate had not come in just as they reached the pushing and scuffling stage, there would have been a fight then and there on the carpet. The room-mate was Jackie Offord, a pretty brown-haired girl who'd been diddled by Penny more times than she could remember – and by Nesta too. She saw what was going on and tried to calm the situation and reconcile the two friends.

When that proved to be impossible, she suggested that they settle it between them in the gym. This was a recognised last resort way of ending bad quarrels. If it happened more than once a year, that was unusual. Jackie expected her friends to pull back when they realised how far their altercation had gone and what the logical next step was. But they didn't – they glared angrily at each other, each saying it would be a pleasure to half murder the other.

By the time they got to the gym, which was a short distance away behind the main building, the news was all around Wexby House. Penny and Nesta were going to fight each other over Linda Knight! Every girl in the house hurried along to watch.

The gym was large and modern. There were machines on which you could sit or lie to lift weights, machines to row on, machines to pedal on. There were vaulting-horses, parallel bars and hanging rings. There was even a fencing piste, a very popular feature as fencing was said to be effective in preventing weight gain. And there was a large clear area with thick mats, where various martial arts were taught to girls who wanted to learn self-defence.

More than thirty girls gathered round the mats, chattering excitedly to each other, offering opinions on who was going to win. Penny was the favourite, though not by much.

Scowling furiously at each other across the expanse of white mats, Penny and Nesta stripped down to bra and knickers. The onlookers stared and sighed and whispered to each other in pleasure and anticipation. Pairs of girls clung together, arms reaching around waists and hands slyly stroking bums.

Annabel Darwen was arm-in-arm with Orline Ashby. She'd have preferred Miss Locksley, but obviously there were no teachers present. A teacher would have stopped the proceedings at once. This was an affair to be settled between the girls themselves.

Orline Ashby was Annabel's room-mate, a brown-eyed charmer who loved having her bare bum stroked. She usually giggled when her bird's-nest was fingered – but not for long because she was easily excitable and the giggles soon turned to long sighing gasps that came faster and harder as she got closer and closer to coming. When she was the active partner, she had a firm touch that demanded a sensational response.

Like every other first-year girl, and many of the second-years, Orline took advantage of Annabel any time she wanted to. 'You're Anybody's,' she'd whisper in Annabel's ear, hand up under her skirt. 'Everybody knows how much you love being done – how many times have you come today?'

Ginger-haired Linda stood alone, halfway between the two sides, her face flushed with excitement. As well it might be, for it's not often a sixteen-year-old girl is fought over in public. And whoever won, it was certain that Linda would be diddled stupid before the day was out!

Penny's bare thighs were strong and shapely. There was hardly a girl present who hadn't felt the powerful grip of those thighs around her waist. The very thought was enough to make several of them tremble at the knees and feel moist between the legs.

Penny's titties were nothing short of magnificent. She was almost eighteen and would be leaving Lechlade at the end of term and going to Oxford University next September. By general agreement she had the biggest pair of titties in Wexby House, probably in the whole of the college. She adored having them rolled and stroked and squeezed and licked – she often made her friends do it until their tongues and jaws ached and Penny had come two or three times.

She was wearing a white bra and knickers, the bra of the largest cup size, the thin material of the knickers stretched tightly over the cheeks of her full round bum. She knew she was being admired. It was her due, she felt, and she played to it. She raised her arms and clenched her fists and pulled her shoulders back to make her titties look even bigger.

The onlookers cheered her, and cheered again when she moved her bare feet apart and twisted sideways at the waist to show the pull of muscles down the inside of her thighs.

'Such thighs!' Orline moaned to Annabel. 'If she'd let me I'd go down on my knees and lick them in front of everybody. All the way up to her kitty.'

'Yes,' Annabel sighed, 'so would I.'

She meant it, and so did Orline. They'd both done it to Penny before. But secretly Annabel was thinking that much as she adored big strong Penny, she'd rather go down on her knees and lick up inside Miss Joy Locksley's bare thighs, right up to her kitty. She'd done it to her once, lying on the teacher's bed, both of them naked. She'd like to do it again.

Superb as she was, Penny couldn't overshadow Nesta or make her seem insignificant by comparison. Nesta was tall and well-shaped, and very fit from the college's sports curriculum. She stood half a head taller than Penny, with a bright mane of yellow hair. For the fight she had tied it with a ribbon in a long pony-tail that hung down to her shoulder-blades. It would be a danger-point for her, that pony-tail, when the hand-to-hand started – Penny would try to grab it and pull her over backward.

Nesta was long of leg and broad of face, her titties round and set high on her chest. They stood out firmly, not like Penny's much bigger ones, which needed the support of a bra to prevent a slight droop.

Nesta's underwear was pink, with tiny flowers embroidered on the edges of her bra and knickers. Not to be outdone by Penny's showing-off, she held her arms out sideways at shoulder level and kicked upward with one bare foot – higher than her head. The girls watching saw the muscles of her bare belly go taut and her titties bounce as she changed legs very fast and kicked the other foot above her head.

Every girl there who had spread her legs for Penny had also spread them for Nesta. They had pleasant memories of Nesta fingering them and teasing their little buttons to make them shriek in pleasure – including Linda Knight, standing pink-faced and isolated, in whose knickers was the origin of the confrontation.

A collective sigh could be heard as Nesta bent over straight-legged and put her palms flat on the floor. The pose displayed her firm round bum to the girls behind her – a bum most of them had kissed. And more interesting still, the bent-over pose showed off the mound between her thighs, where her knickers were stretched tight.

'You can have me any time, Nesta,' Pru Renwick called out, making the other girls laugh. They weren't laughing at Pru, they were laughing with her in sympathy; most of them would have shouted the same thing if they'd thought of it first.

Penny didn't laugh. Pru's words made her angrier still, much too angry for the ritual bowing that is usual in martial arts contests. She screamed and hurled herself across the mats at Nesta, hoping to get her in a head-lock while she was bent over and kick her legs from under her. But it didn't work. Nesta, quick and agile, stood up straight in time to meet the attack.

Neither of them was very skilled in this sort of contest. They'd been taught just enough to protect themselves from any would-be rapist they might encounter in an alley on a dark night, as the saying goes. Which meant that they'd been shown the kick to the knee-cap, the knee into the balls, the low punch in the belly, the thumb in the eye, the double hand-clap over the ears. They'd also been taught how to counter these attacks in the event a rapist tried to disable them before dragging their knickers down.

Necessarily, with two girls about evenly matched and taught the same moves by the same instructor, the fight was inconclusive. Nesta and Penny shouted shrilly and jumped about on the mats, they countered each other's kicks and hits, but nothing of much consequence was happening. The onlookers had the best of it, their eyes round and hot as they watched the two lithe bodies in urgent motion.

They saw titties flipping up and down, long bare legs flashing out in kicks that never quite landed, the sheen of sweat on bellies and faces. Nesta's long flat belly above the waistband of her brief pink knickers was a beautiful sight to see; drops of sweat trickled into her exposed belly button and half the girls watching would have volunteered to lick the salty drops up, given the chance.

Penny was sweating too – there were streaks of moisture on her chest between her plump titties. The other half of the girls watching would have gladly fought each other for the pleasure of licking the sweat away from those titties. The arousal level in the gym rose so high that there would have to be urgent orgasms all round before afternoon classes could possibly begin.

Penny had been sure she would beat Nesta, but the fight was turning into an endurance trial. The one whose strength lasted longest would be the winner, finally pushing the other over and putting a foot on her chest to hold her down in defeat. But defeat was something Penny would never accept. She side-stepped a kick aimed at her belly and managed to achieve what she'd been trying for since the bout started – she got hold of Nesta's long pony-tail.

Now she had her! She jerked Nesta's head backwards and got a knee up into the small of her back. Nesta screeched at the hard tug on her hair and bent over backward. Eyes were popping in the crowd at the sight of her well-parted thighs and her belly and kitty forced upwards, as if on offer to whoever might run forward and kiss her there first.

Nesta had been anticipating the grip to her hair, however, and knew how to break the hold. She twisted sideways like a cat, turning under Penny's arm to face her, and smacked her titties hard from both sides at the same instant. It was Penny's turn to squeal – she let go of the long yellow pony-tail and was forced back a step as Nesta smacked her titties again, hard and fast.

'Ooh!' said thirty voices at the same time. Penny's bra-strap had slipped off one shoulder, exposing a big heavy tittie for all to see and admire.

20

Penny recovered quickly and danced in on the balls of her feet, hands reaching out to get hold of Nesta and throw her to the mats. But Nesta was just as quick. She whirled, stepped sideways and kicked at Penny's legs, trying to bring her down. Now the onlookers had the satisfaction of seeing the bared tittie swinging and bouncing to Penny's movements. Hands that so far had been content merely to furtively stroke bums now grew bolder and darted up the backs of skirts to probe between hot thighs.

No one said it, because it didn't need saying – it was in every mind at the sight of Penny's big bouncing bare tittie – the two contestants ought to have stripped off completely for the fight, bras, knickers, the lot! Then there'd have been two pairs of swinging titties and two bare bellies being smacked at, two bare bums bouncing about, two curly-haired kitties flashing – and half the girls watching would have come in their knickers without being touched!

Linda Knight, the cause of the dispute, was shaking so hard she looked as if she was coming already. And she nearly was – if she'd dared she'd have slipped her hand up her own skirt and into her knickers in front of the assembled girls of Wexby House, and given herself a quick finger. But it was out of the question – she had to stand and watch and try not to collapse as her legs shook more and more.

Penny was becoming desperate to break the deadlock and win before total exhaustion stopped the fight. She dropped to the floor and rolled underneath a kick aimed at her kitty. Not as fast or hard a kick as when the bout started, for after ten minutes' fierce scuffling Nesta was flagging as much as Penny was.

Nesta's bare foot flicked harmlessly over Penny's head. Then it was easy – Penny rolled hard against the leg Nesta was balancing on and at the same time punched her behind the knee. Nesta fell, but managed to come down lightly on her hands and a thigh, as she'd been taught, already reaching out to get a grip on Penny's arm and twist it against the joint.

But Penny was prepared, and a moment later had Nesta on her back. Now Penny sat on her chest, pinning her arms to the mats with her knees.

'You're beaten,' Penny gasped. 'Give in!'

'I'm not!' Nesta panted, kicking her legs up hard. 'I won't!'

She was trying to get her legs up and round Penny's head from behind and drag her backwards. Before she could, Penny slithered forward to sit on Nesta's face, her feet flat on the mats and her knees up, all her weight bearing down.

She rubbed herself against Nesta's face. There was only the thin material of her knickers between Nesta's mouth and the warm lips between Penny's thighs.

'Got you now!' Penny said gleefully.

The girls standing around the mats were clamouring, shouting Penny's name or Nesta's name. There were screams of 'Finish her off!' and counter-cries of 'Roll sideways and tip her off, Nesta!'

Nesta's mouth was wide open and she was panting heavily. Penny could feel her opponent's hot breath on her kitty through her knickers. 'Lick me,' she said fiercely, 'I've beaten you, Nesta – lick me!'

The onlookers stared glassy-eyed, unable to see all that was going on but their imaginations hotly at work. They saw Nesta on her back on the mats, underneath Penny, her face between Penny's spread thighs. It was not difficult to guess that Nesta was using her tongue. As indeed she was, licking hard against the thin white material of Penny's knickers.

What the watchers could see clearly was Nesta reaching up behind Penny to grip the waistband of her knickers and pull them down over her broad hips until the cheeks of Penny's full-moon bum were exposed. Nesta's fingers were curled like claws into the knickers, tugging at them furiously.

'Oh yes, yes . . .' Voices squealed round the edge of the mats at the sight of Penny's bare bum and the long crease between the big cheeks. There wasn't a soul present who wasn't aching to rub her fingers down that crease, down underneath to

22

Penny's prominent mound and the place where the lips of her kitty started.

Try as she would, Nesta couldn't get those knickers down all the way. Penny's mound was clamped so closely to her mouth that it was impossible to strip her. In frustration Nesta sank her finger-nails into the fleshy cheeks and made Penny scream. But only for a second.

'I've beaten you – admit it!' Penny shouted. 'Say it!'

Nesta said nothing. She continued licking at Penny's kitty through the thin barrier of her underwear. The tight-stretched strip of fabric between her thighs was soaked through now, warm and wet and pressing in between the parting lips. Nesta's tongue began to lap over Penny's sensitive button.

'No . . . Stop! I've won!' Penny exclaimed.

Even as she spoke, her back was arching and her thighs splaying wider apart. Her hands were reaching down to grip Nesta's ears in an effort to turn her head sideways and get her tongue away from its vulnerable target. But it was too late – the exertions of the long fight and the flow of adrenalin had taken both girls so high they were incapable of stopping. Penny's head went back and her mouth opened wide with urgent cries as her bare belly went into spasms.

The girls of Wexby House stared transfixed and silent for a second or two at the sight of Penny coming – then a shrill outcry echoed around the gym as they gave vent to their pent-up emotions. As for Linda, she fell to her knees on the edge of the mats, her eyes bulging and both hands up her own short blue skirt, scrambling inside her knickers to her ginger-haired kitty, the cause of all the trouble.

Penny's muscles had gone slack in the aftermath of her climax. She sat slumped on Nesta, her arms dangling beside her own lolling thighs. Nesta was still keyed-up. She got her hands underneath Penny's bum and pushed hard while she twisted sideways. With only a slight moan Penny rolled off her.

In a flash Nesta was on top of her opponent, her fingers clamped into the soft flesh of Penny's heavy titties – both of them bare now, for Nesta had dragged her bra down to her waist. In the next instant she ripped Penny's white knickers down her legs and threw them at the kneeling Linda.

Penny was naked on her back, apparently helpless. The watching crowd fell silent at this sudden reversal of fortune. They saw Nesta throw herself bodily onto her opponent and use her weight to keep her flat on her back. Nesta lay between Penny's open thighs, ramming herself hard against her enemy's bare belly and loins.

'No ... no ... stop it ... you can't ...' Penny was moaning.

Nesta was triumphant as she forced her hand down between their bellies and probed Penny's wet and open kitty. 'Now who's beaten?' she demanded, rubbing quickly at Penny's button.

Six feet away from them, Linda, still on her knees, snatched up the knickers Nesta had thrown at her and stuffed them up between her legs. Penny's knickers ripped off her in the fight, or Nesta's pink knickers if things had gone that way, it didn't matter to Linda whose they were. She was too far gone in a sexual frenzy.

'Look out!' came a shout from the door. 'Teacher coming!'

There was a collective groan of dismay, then the onlookers turned and fled from the gym, through the changing-room, straight past the showers and out the back door.

The cry and sudden rush brought Nesta to her senses. She scrambled quickly off Penny and dragged her to her feet by a wrist. They grabbed up their clothes from the floor where they'd dropped them before the bout and ran barefoot across the floor after the rest of Wexby House.

'Come on, Linda!' Nesta shouted as they raced past the kneeling girl, her eyes closed and a smile on her face. Linda came out of her day-dream and followed them in a hurry.

Ninety seconds later Miss Monica Howlett walked into the gym. Her attention had been attracted by the noise as she took a short after-lunch walk before classes resumed. She taught modern languages and was not greatly liked by her students.

The gym was empty. There was nothing and no one to account for the shouting and screaming she had heard only minutes earlier. She shook her head in puzzlement and moved through to check the changing-room, but that was empty too.

Safe in the room Penny shared with Jackie Offord – who had sensibly made herself scarce – Nesta and Penny stared at each other warily. Penny was stark naked, her knickers torn off and lost, her bra hanging ruined about her waist. Nesta still had her knickers and bra on, but there was a long rip in the knickers, which plainly couldn't be mended. The two of them had been very lucky to get this far from the gym without being spotted by a member of the teaching staff.

They stood almost glaring at each other, both wondering what came next. Should they carry on fighting till the question of ginger-haired Linda was finally settled? They were both still breathing heavily from the fight and the hectic dash across lawns and paths from the gym. Penny's big soft titties were heaving with each breath; Nesta's face was flushed scarlet.

It was Nesta who made the first move. She took a step forward to put an arm about Penny's shoulders and press her flushed face against Penny's cheek. At the same time her other hand was between Penny's magnificent strong bare thighs, stroking the lips of her kitty.

'Did you fair and square,' she whispered. 'Made you come twice.'

'Only once,' said Penny, 'I was nearly there the second time when you dragged me up and made me run. Did Linda get away?'

'Don't know, don't care.' Nesta's fingers were sliding inside Penny, who moved her feet apart to open her thighs.

'You didn't beat me,' Penny sighed, 'I had you down and on your back helpless. That was the end of the fight really. What you did to me after that doesn't count.'

'Yes it does,' Nesta insisted. 'You cheated by grabbing my

hair. But everybody saw me win in the end – I was the one on top and you were helpless on your back.'

Penny wrapped her arms tightly about Nesta's waist, lifted her off her feet and carried her upright to the nearest bed. There were two of them, one against each wall, separated by the other furniture in the room. It was not Penny's own bed that she chose now, it was Jackie's, but that was of no concern to Penny in the heat of the moment.

She could feel Nesta's titties and belly and thighs pressed very tight against her as she carried her. How hot she was! Her long yellow pony-tail swung across her shoulder-blades like a pendulum and Penny thought of tugging at it again while she ravaged Nesta. She set her down on the side of the bed and bent over to strip off her bra and knickers so they would both be stark naked.

'We'll soon see who's the winner,' Penny said, 'it's not over yet.'

Nesta moaned and shivered as her bare round titties were licked and her belly was stroked. She was pushed down on her back and told to open her legs. She felt Penny's fingers touch the light honey-brown curls between her parted thighs, and then Penny's hot tongue caressing the lips under the curls.

Penny licked quickly and Nesta's fingers hooked over the edge of the bed, gripping furiously as her back arched. Penny's hands slid under Nesta's bum and her fingers clenched taut flesh. She felt Nesta's loins thrusting up strongly against her tongue and knew she had her poised on the edge of a shattering come – one that would release all the tension and aggression of the fight in the gym.

She heard Nesta's scream and pressed down hard on her body while it bucked fast and furiously, seven or eight times. Then the heat and the tenseness seemed to dissolve and Nesta sank down limply on her back, her eyes half-closed, her curls and inside thighs moist and soft.

'You're done for,' Penny said with a smile of victory.

'No, I'm not!' Nesta retorted. 'That makes it one-all. And

you only did it because I let you. You couldn't stop me from doing you when we were in the gym, that's the difference between losing and winning.'

'I'll make you change your tune if it takes all day,' Penny declared. 'You'll beg for mercy before I've finished with you – then you'll know you're beaten!'

She dropped to her knees between Nesta's parted thighs and slid three fingers into her wet and slippery kitty.

Chapter Three

Lechlade Ladies' College was an all-female establishment – the teaching staff, the students, the college servants. It was intended to be a place where clever girls could develop their intellectual abilities without the distraction of the male sex and their hot groping fingers.

This happy state of affairs endured for almost a hundred years, from the foundation right into the 1990s. Of course, there were some changes in all that time – younger teachers were appointed, the curriculum was up-dated. But one thing remained constant – Lechlade was all-female.

Until the day when Miss Maureen Plessy, the Sports Mistress, twisted her knee on the tennis court for the sixth or seventh time and limped away moaning. She was advised by her doctor to give up the job before she did herself a permanent mischief.

The Board of Governors had the responsibility for new appointments – and the Board was constituted entirely of women. Every one of them was a former student of the college and all now held important positions – in the Civil Service or at the older universities, for example, or in merchant banking or the law.

To the astonishment of all, the Board decided to appoint a man to the vacant position – a man! This curious decision came from a sudden need the Governors felt to be seen moving with the times.

The Principal of Lechlade, Miss Enid Uppingham, was astounded when she heard what the Governors had decided.

She was also deeply shocked. The prospect of a man at the college was an outrage, to her way of thinking. However, she had no choice but to accept the decision – and this was how an athletic twenty-seven-year-old named Toby Dundale came to Lechlade.

The Principal refused to let him have the title of Sports Master. The word *master* implied superiority over women. In this she got her way; the new member of staff was given the job-title of Sports Coach.

Naturally, the Principal had it in for him from the day he arrived. No one could take the place of Maureen Plessy in her affections – Enid and Maureen had been very close friends. During term-time they arranged their days so that they could spend an hour together every day, to the great pleasure of both.

Maureen had a marvellous touch. Her fingers sent Enid into trembling delight in no time at all, and kept her gasping and shaking till she practically passed out. In return Enid did interesting things to Maureen – and she did them often, for a particular reason.

Much as she liked and admired Maureen, the thought never quite left Enid's mind that her dear friend passed her working days in the company of pretty girls dressed in skimpy and revealing sports gear. Maureen put her hands on the girls when she was demonstrating the parallel bars or the hanging rings in the gymnasium. She handled the girls when she was teaching swimming in the pool.

Sixteen- and seventeen-year-old girls in sports gear, bare arms and bare legs, bare thighs and bare backs – the thought haunted Enid's mind. Wet, clinging swimsuits in the pool revealing the delicious shape of lithe young bodies, close-fitting leotards in the gym, brief white shorts on the tennis courts, bare thighs flashing as the girls moved like sleek young tigresses to smash the ball back over the net.

Above all, Maureen put her hands on the girls' bodies when she massaged them – her job included physiotherapy for sprains and minor injuries. The college's sports facilities included a treatment room with a massage-table.

Secretly Enid wished she dared handle some of the girls. Have them lie on the massage-table naked except for their brief little knickers and run her fingers over their titties and thighs.

She was no fool, she knew what went on in the college. She was aware that some of her teaching staff did whatever they wanted to the girls – and the girls never complained. Eleanor Redruth, the senior maths teacher, was notorious for her sexual leanings to students and her flagrant use of their bodies for her pleasure.

Enid Uppingham felt it her duty as Principal to behave morally toward her students. So, much as she would have liked to feel soft young titties and get her hand between firm young thighs, she controlled herself. She often dreamed at night about fondling girls and woke up hot and bothered with her nightie up to her waist and a moist feeling between her legs. But she kept her hands off the girls and vented her seething passions on her friend Maureen Plessy.

There was more to ravaging Maureen than releasing Enid's secret lusts for the students. Enid was determined that Maureen must never succumb to the temptation of slipping a hand into a girl's knickers in the changing-rooms. Or standing naked under a shower with any of them. It was known to all in the college, including Enid, that the showers were the scene of more girlish orgasms a day than could ever be counted.

Enid could picture it vividly – two naked seventeen-year-olds under the cascading hot water, soaping each other's titties. Giggling as they rubbed a soapy palm between each other's legs. Wet pink bodies pressed together while fingers were busy . . . moans and sighs as the inevitable happened to each girl in turn.

That, after all, was only to be expected. But Enid was not going to let her dear friend Maureen dabble in the pleasures she had forbidden herself. There was a way to make sure that

Maureen wasn't tempted – Enid diddled her continuously and excessively. She forced her to come half a dozen times a day, every day. She was determined to ensure that Maureen had no sexual desire left when she was with the girls.

The situation had changed dramatically now that poor Maureen had given up her job and gone to live at Bournemouth. A man had taken over – a man was coaching Lechlade's young and pretty students in games and sports – and Enid had even worse fears than when Maureen was in charge. She felt sure that this Toby Dundale was taking advantage of the girls.

Naturally, he wasn't allowed to give them massage – it was utterly out of the question for a man to lay his lustful hands on near-naked girls on the table. An outside physiotherapist came in twice a week to attend to sprains and cricks – a woman, of course.

All the same, Enid said to herself in anger, he was allowed to put his hands on them when he showed them how to dive into the swimming pool. His hands on their waists, positioning them for the dive. Perhaps a hand would slide accidentally down over their pretty bums. And when he demonstrated a backhand smash on the tennis-court, he stood very close behind the girl being coached, pressing himself up to her body, his arms round her and gripping her arms.

A man's hands on these charming young girls – it was a thought to make the Principal's blood seethe. There were nights when she had dreams of Toby Dundale under a hot shower with two or three of the girls, all of them naked together – she saw him stroking their wet titties, while his great long male *thing* stuck out in front of him.

Enid told herself that these were only dreams, that there was probably nothing to worry about. But she didn't believe it. She had proof of Toby Dundale's moral laxity, for soon after he arrived at the beginning of term she had gone down to the tennis courts to see him in action. She pretended that she was passing by casually, on her way to somewhere else.

What she saw stunned her and deepened her fears that the

new Sports Coach was not a man to be trusted near young girls. To be frank, no man was ever to be trusted with young girls, in Enid's view.

It was a sunny afternoon in early summer. Toby Dundale was wearing a short-sleeved sports shirt tucked into the shortest white shorts that the Principal had ever seen in her life. Between his white ankle-socks and the shorts his muscular legs seemed to be yards long – and much of that expanse of male flesh was thigh.

Toby was fair-haired; there were golden hairs on those thighs of his – Enid noticed this particularly. She stood close to the high wire-mesh perimeter of the tennis courts and struggled to get her breath back.

This is unforgivable, she said to herself, leaning for support against the wire-mesh.

Toby's white shorts had hardly any legs at all. His thighs were almost totally exposed. Enid watched him run and turn and return the ball to Nesta Wade with a flick of his racket – his thighs all too evident as he moved. *This will not do*, Enid told herself firmly.

Her feelings of concern were for Nesta and the other girls the new man would be coaching – or so she told herself. The college was crammed with fit and healthy young girls, their emotions strong and insistent. It had to be recognised that if the girls liked and trusted a man they were at risk: he was instantly in a position to take advantage of their natural emotions.

It was very obvious to Enid from the way Nesta Wade was looking at the Sports Coach that she found him glamorous and attractive. Not only Nesta – there were six or seven other girls standing nearby, watching the lesson, and the same gleam of adoration could be seen in their eyes.

At the end of the day Toby was summoned to the Principal's office for a talk. Enid told him that his tennis shorts were unsuitable. He replied that they were standard shorts as worn by the top seeds at Wimbledon and other international tournaments. To which Enid said firmly that Lechlade Ladies' College was not Wimbledon and that his shorts were unacceptable.

Toby shrugged and claimed not to understand her objection. He had half a dozen pairs, he said, all of them identical. There was nothing much to be done about his shorts until the end of term when he'd be in London and could drop into various sports equipment shops to look at whatever alternatives were on offer.

With that Enid had to be content, even though it confirmed her worst fears about the man. In her view he was deliberately flaunting his male body in front of susceptible girls. He had to go, as soon as possible. She didn't want him at the college next term – or any other term.

It was when she went to watch him coaching a class in swimming that she realised how truly urgent the matter was – it couldn't possibly be left until the end of term. Something must be done at once.

The pool was Olympic-size, roofed over and with facilities to heat the water in winter. But on this fine summer day the sun shone in through the glass-domed roof and the scene was one to bring pleasure to any heart except that of the suspicious and hostile Principal. There were only ten girls to a class at Lechlade; three were in the pool with Toby Dundale and seven sat on the edge, dangling their feet in the water and watching his demonstration.

The only rule about swimming costumes for the girls was that they must be one-piece – bikinis were banned. Enid knew that bikinis tended to get smaller and smaller, if girls were given free choice. Soon the costumes would be no more than tiny triangles joined by strings, and in view of the undoubted desires of some of the teaching staff to take advantage of students, near-nudity in the pool would be asking for trouble.

Enid stood just inside the entrance to the pool enclosure, watching with alarm and pursed lips. Toby was standing in the shallow end explaining some point about the racing crawl. Rachel Fermor was floating full length, face down, balanced on his outstretched hand. His hand was under Rachel, Enid noted anxiously, holding her up.

But where exactly was his hand? Under her midriff? Under her belly? *Under her titties?* Rachel was smiling as she turned her pretty face to the side to breathe. The location of that hand worried Enid. The man was very probably *feeling* Rachel under cover of coaching her!

There was no doubt where his other hand was – it was flat on her bare back, pressed to her wet skin. With disapproval the Principal noted that although Rachel's swimsuit conformed to the one-piece rule, it was backless right down to where her bum started! The coach was taking advantage of the girl's nearly naked condition for his wretched male gratification – he was interfering with her young body, Enid was certain of it.

Veronica Jameson, one of the girls standing beside Toby, waiting for her turn to be coached, glanced up and saw the Principal. She spoke to Toby, who half turned in the water and grinned up at Enid. He took his hands away from Rachel, who laughed and turned on her side and did a lazy side-stroke up the pool. Enid could hardly fail to notice how her left tittie came into view at each over-arm stroke – a full round tittie, provocatively emphasized by the thin, clinging wet material of her skimpy scarlet costume.

Toby waded to the side, put his hands on the tiling and was up and out of the water in one long graceful push. He walked toward Enid, dripping.

'Good morning, Miss Uppingham,' he said pleasantly, 'did you want to see me?'

When he was in the pool she couldn't see what he was wearing. But now as he came to her she couldn't take her eyes off his swimming trunks. If they could be called that! In effect, he was wearing a sort of pouch – jet-black and shiny, even when wet, a pouch that did very little indeed to conceal its fleshy male contents. And it was well-filled, this pouch.

Enid dragged her gaze away from his loins at last and stared red-faced into his eyes.

'Mr Dundale,' she said, her voice almost a croak, 'you are indecently and inappropriately dressed to coach young girls. I must insist you put something more suitable on at once and stay out of the water.'

Later that day she called him to her office and repeated with great force her strong objection to his swim-wear. And just as he had over the tennis shorts, he claimed that all his swimming trunks were the same and there was nothing he could do before the end of term.

Enid was determined that something had to be done before then. There was no need to go to London – that was an excuse, there were plenty of good shops closer than that. Toby refused to co-operate, insisting that he didn't know the area and hadn't the time to go chasing about looking for old-fashioned sportswear.

The Principal was still determined to protect her girls from male depravity. The next day she drove to Oxford, where she knew there were perfectly good shops. She came back to Lechlade in the early evening and sent for Toby.

'There you are,' she said triumphantly when he arrived in her office, and she flung her purchases down on her desk – a pair of loose-fitting white shorts with legs long enough to reach any man's knees, and a baggy pair of navy-blue swimming trunks, just as long.

'The trunks have a special lining at the front,' she pointed out. 'It removes any danger of undesirable movement or show through. I'm sure you understand what I mean.'

Toby picked up the tennis shorts in disbelief and held them against himself. He was wearing a light grey track-suit, the zip pulled halfway down to show the golden hairs on his chest.

'Impossible,' he said firmly but politely. 'There's room for two of me in these shorts. I couldn't possibly play a good game wearing them.'

'How do you know when you haven't worn them?' Enid demanded.

The thought came into Toby's mind that the shorts were big enough to fit the Principal herself. She was a generously proportioned woman, with broad hips and a big bum. She must have been thinking of her own dress measurements when she bought the ridiculous garments.

It also occurred to him that as she was so worried about what he had in his underwear she should be taught to mind her own business. And that was easily done. He unzipped his track-suit top and shrugged out of it, pulled the trouser-legs out of his socks, unlaced his trainers and took them off – and then removed his socks and the trousers.

Enid stared in amazement across her desk as he stood practically naked on her carpet. All he had on was a small garment she believed was called an athletic support – a jockstrap in common speech. Her eyes bulged at the sight – it was of transparent nylon and it concealed nothing at all. She could see his complete set of male equipment, all smooth pink flesh surrounded by golden hair.

'What on earth are you doing!' she gasped.

'Trying on the tennis shorts you've bought me,' he said, straight-faced and polite. He pulled on the baggy shorts and shook his head in dismay. To be fair, and Enid Uppingham always tried to be that, the shorts were ridiculous. But that was not the point.

'Very suitable,' she said.

'They're awful and you know it,' he said. 'If I appear in front of the girls looking like this I shall lose all respect and be unable to coach them. Look at this!' He pulled the elastic waist-band of the shorts away from his bare belly to show how much too large they were.

'Nonsense,' Enid retorted, getting up and coming round her desk for a closer look to justify dismissing his silly complaints. If he looked ridiculous to the girls that suited her very well – they would be less inclined to let him put his hands on them.

'They look very comfortable,' she said, smoothing the material over his hips. 'Much better for leaping about than those over-tight shorts you've been wearing.'

Toby saw he was making no impression. He decided to go further, in the interests of teaching her not to interfere with his coaching methods.

'As for the swimming trunks,' he said, his lip curling in disgust, 'no one has worn anything like them since about 1928.'

He slipped the baggy tennis shorts down, not looking at Enid – he knew she was staring at his well-filled and transparent jockstrap. *Yes, have an eyeful*, he said to himself, *you've never seen one like it in your life – and it's time you did.*

He was wrong about that, although it was twenty years since Enid had seen one. She had lost her virginity at Oxford at the age of nineteen, in a punt on the river one summer afternoon, to an undergraduate named Marcus Burlington. It happened almost without her knowing it. He'd moored the punt by the bank and opened a bottle of bubbly from the picnic hamper. They lay side by side and sipped from their glasses, until Marcus slipped his hand up her skirt.

He'd never done that to her before. She'd let him kiss her and stroke her titties often enough – she didn't take any of it seriously. She had a fine big pair of titties – she was big all over, even as a girl – and sometimes when in the right mood she had let Marcus have them out to feel them bare, and even kiss them once or twice.

It was something men did, it didn't mean anything. The afternoon was hot and Enid was in a lazy and contented state of mind. Marcus slid his hand into her knickers and touched her between the thighs – and she didn't stop him. She lay back with her eyes closed, half-dozing in the warm sunshine. After a while he had his finger inside her chuffie – it felt pleasant, not as nice as when her girl-friends did it to her, but you couldn't expect a man to understand how to please a girl properly.

Marcus took her knickers off and Enid sighed and spread

her legs to allow him to feel her thoroughly. Her hand lay against his white trousers, up where she could feel the stiffness under the cloth. At his insistence she'd felt his long hard thing in the past; she thought it rather ugly, but it made him happy to have it stroked. It was very hard against her palm and a moment later Marcus used his free hand to wrench his flies open and out it popped.

Occasionally in the past he'd persuaded her to stroke his dick until he reached his sticky little release in her hanky. She'd do it for him today, she thought lazily. As it happened, that wasn't what he had in mind. To Enid's surprise he rolled on top of her, his legs between hers. She felt her chuffie being penetrated, stretched open – and filled full by his length of hard flesh.

She'd always thought it hurt when it happened to a girl the first time, but not so for her. Over the years girl-friends' fingers had stretched her and relaxed her virgin tightness. Marcus pushed up her and slid in and out to a gentle rhythm for half a minute – and Enid thought it reasonably nice. Then he gasped and jerked and had his wet little pleasure inside her.

For the remaining few weeks of that academic year she let him do it to her whenever circumstances allowed – but with precautions. She found the sight of his stiffie inside a transparent sheath very comical, but he succeeded in making her come with it. The term ended three weeks later and as Marcus was a third-year student he took his degree and vanished from her life.

When Enid thought it over later, she came to the conclusion that sex-games were much better with girls than with boys. They lasted longer and were more pleasurable. With a man there was all that huffing and puffing and ramming and slamming for just one climax. With a girl it was softer and cosier and in half an hour she could come three or four times. Since leaving Oxford she hadn't let a man near her, she'd taken her pleasure with other women. She didn't dislike men, they simply didn't match up to her standards, the poor things.

That most certainly included the new Sports Coach. He took the baggy tennis shorts off while she watched curiously. He slid his jockstrap down his legs. She stared at his full set, pink smooth flesh dangling between golden-haired thighs.

'What are you doing?' she said. 'Have you no shame?'

Secretly she was wondering how big it would be when it stood up stiff. She was also speculating with horror how many of her teaching-staff and students it had been inside.

'I never wear anything under swimming trunks,' he said, still polite and reasonable. 'This has to be a realistic trial or it's pointless.'

He took the old-fashioned garment she'd bought and stepped into it. As he hauled the trunks up his long legs Enid suddenly understood that he was trying to embarrass her. *We'll see about that, my lad*, she said to herself, clenching her teeth. *You're not going to get away with it.*

The trunks were much too big. The fork hung down well below his male parts and the legs more than reached his knees. It *was* a pity to drape so firm and athletic a body in such droopy drawers but Enid was resolute. He had to be kept away from the girls – heaven knows what damage he'd caused already. It was going to be different in the future, she was determined.

As for thinking he could discomfit her by flashing his male thing at her, obviously he didn't know who he was up against. After all her years in the top reaches of the teaching profession Enid Uppingham was immune to embarrassment.

'You might need one size smaller,' she said insincerely. 'Let me see.'

She moved closer to him and put her hands on his hips, pretending to check the fit of the waist. She ran her palms down his thighs and over the firm cheeks of his bottom.

'They'd have to be ten sizes smaller to even start to fit,' Toby said. 'If I went into the water in these they'd fall off me – then what would the girls think!'

'You're exaggerating.' Enid told him. 'All this fuss over nothing. The waist isn't all that bad a fit.'

40

To prove it she slipped her hand between the waist-band and his belly.

'Well, just an inch too loose, perhaps,' she said.

She was moving her hand about inside the baggy swimming trunks, pretending to be checking the fit, though it was something else she had in mind. It didn't take much of that before she felt something thick and hard and hot pushing against her hand. Toby's face was red – he was the one who was being embarrassed now.

'We could have them altered,' Enid murmured, her hand moving deeper inside his shorts as if to check the fit at the fork – but in fact she was clasping a pair of big hairy balls. 'The waist could be taken in. No great problem. Take them off and I'll have them seen to.'

Toby seemed reluctant to take the swimming trunks off. He'd set out to shame her and it had backfired – he was feeling bashful about letting the Principal see his hard-on, but she wasn't at all bashful – *she* was enjoying shaming *him*. She shrugged and dragged the swimming trunks down his thighs and let them slide to his ankles. She stared down at the long thick member poking up at her.

'Gracious!' she said in fake surprise, 'what a state you're in – are you making improper advances to me, or are you trying to insult me?'

'Lord, no . . .' Toby said, his cheeks very red.

He'd have snatched his track-suit bottom from the floor and pulled it on if he'd been able – but Enid didn't let him. She took a firm grip on his twanger and he noticed for the first time that she had large hands for a woman. Her fingers were curled round his thick shaft and she was gripping tight.

She pulled the visitor's chair away from her desk and sat on it, still holding on to Toby firmly, as if afraid he'd try to escape. When she was sitting comfortably she made a careful inspection of the fleshy length in her hand, then jiggled it up and down thoughtfully.

'The mechanics of the male body have always struck me as

41

awkward,' she told him. 'I mean, you're so exposed and vulnerable and easily damaged. Especially someone like you, teaching sports and games, I'm sure it must be a constant worry for you.'

'No ... not really ...' Toby managed to say. To his surprise and against his will he was becoming very aroused by her handling. She knew that and added to his confusion by a rhythmic up-and-down stroke of her clasping hand.

'I've been told that men are tremendously proud of the size of their organ,' Enid said casually. 'The idea seems very strange, but I have no personal experience of male beliefs. Would you say that yours is larger than the average or smaller than the average? Or just average?'

Toby stood with his bare feet apart, unable to take in the question. He'd never considered Enid Uppingham in sexual terms before. She was big and round, she had to be forty, and Toby's taste was for slim young girls. That was why he'd always taught at girls' schools. Now in his state of arousal he began to see Enid in a different light. Any port in a storm, his hormones seemed to be telling him.

Her hair was black and glossy, pulled back smoothly over her head and fastened at the back with a slide. Her face was round and had a cheerful expression he'd never really noticed before. Inside her light grey dress, her titties looked enticingly full and heavy. She was sitting and Toby was standing, looking down the front of her dress. He found himself wishing he could see more. He'd like to strip her naked, he decided, to stroke her broad plump belly and get his hand between her thighs.

It was as if she could guess what he was thinking – she stared up from his throbbing shaft to his face, her expression firm.

'Do not delude yourself with hopes that you will ever become intimate with me,' she said. 'I can see plainly in your eyes that you lust for my body. Put that idea right out of your mind – I have no dealings of that kind with men and never mean to.'

'But ... but ...' Toby stammered, his legs trembling under

him as her hand kept sliding up-and-down, up-and-down, taking him closer to the final moment.

'Why am I doing this, is that what you mean?' she asked, 'I feel some responsibility for the state you've allowed yourself to get into as a result of trying on the shorts, so I am doing the obvious to reduce your highly unnecessary tension.'

She wasn't being honest with him. She was doing it to demonstrate her authority over him. She had no fears that he might report the incident to the Governors and get her dismissed – she could totally deny anything he said and claim he was lying in order to discredit her. She would be believed, he would be sacked.

'Oh, oh, oh...' he gasped. His whacker was straining upwards toward his chin and had swollen to an impressive size. His mouth fell open and he knew this was it – it was going to happen now.

Enid produced a small hanky from somewhere just in time to catch his gush of cream as he came in furious spurts. He was moaning and shaking, his straining shaft being pulled upwards mercilessly by Enid's hand as she milked him dry. Then he was finished and trembling in reaction to the powerful sensations.

Enid stopped pulling his dick upward and pushed down instead, forcing Toby to his knees. She let go of his sticky shaft and put a hand under his chin to turn his face up to look at her.

'There is something you must understand clearly,' she said. 'The girls of this college are out-of-bounds to you. If I discover that you have as much as laid a finger on any of them I shall have you dismissed. Is that plain enough for you?'

Toby's mind was in a whirl. First there was the shock of being handled by this forbidding woman till he shot off in her hanky – now there were threats. He didn't know what to make of her.

'Does that apply to all the other teachers?' he asked cautiously.

'That's beside the point,' Enid informed him. 'You're a man and that can only lead to trouble. If you want my advice you'll resign from your position at the end of this term and move on. If you decide to stay on, then watch out – I shall have my eye on you and at the first sign of misconduct you'll leave in disgrace.'

'The other teachers,' Toby said, 'are they also out-of-bounds to me?'

'You may do what you please with them – but I very much doubt that you will be able to persuade any of the staff to give in to your male lust.'

She took her hand from under his chin and he looked away from her dark and gleaming eyes, still kneeling naked on her carpet. His hard length had gone soft and shrunk – it dangled wetly on his thigh. Enid stared down at it with a little grin.

'Yes,' she said, 'awkward and vulnerable just as I said. Put your clothes on and go. We've had our little chat and I hope we understand each other now.'

Toby scrambled up and got into his track-suit. He said nothing – there was nothing he could think of to say to her.

Chapter Four

Whenever Eleanor Redruth had an hour free from teaching during the day she went to the tennis courts to watch the girls playing. She delighted in seeing lithe young bodies in action – long bare legs, the thrilling flash of thighs as short skirts swirled during cross-court dashes.

It was immensely exciting to Eleanor when a girl strained up high to smash the ball back over the net – her arm and body formed a long graceful shape and her titties rose up with the effort. Or when a girl scrambled to reach a ball on the ground and her legs splayed out, her body bending over to push her bum higher than her head for a moment, offering a quick glimpse of white knickers stretched over firm round cheeks.

Eleanor found all this so arousing that she would unfailingly become damp between the legs. Her face would grow pink from the strong emotions that surged in her, and her breathing become agitated.

Most of the girls knew why she came to watch them play, and the first-year students who didn't guess were soon informed by the others why Miss Redruth took so keen an interest. New girls very often asked the obvious question – *have you ever let her?* – to which there was never any answer.

If the truth were told, an impressive number of the girls of Lechlade Ladies' College had opened their legs for Eleanor Redruth. But no one ever admitted doing it for a teacher, not even the ones who did so regularly. There was a code of honour about it, a tradition which dated back to the earliest days of the college, when mention of sexual activity was wholly forbidden.

On one particular afternoon not long after the fight between Penny and Nesta, Eleanor was down at the courts by four o'clock. She knew from the timetable for Wexby House who would be there at that time. There were six courts. Toby Dundale was on one, coaching. He was wearing the skimpiest white shorts, the Principal's efforts to persuade him to wear something else having been a failure.

Eleanor stared thoughtfully for some moments at the bulge in the front of Toby's shorts. It held no attraction for her, but she guessed some of the girls would be fascinated. If he was as interested in young girls as Eleanor was, there was a possibility that some of those who arrived at the start of term as virgins would go home for the vacation in a different condition.

Linda Knight was playing a good game against Pru Renwick – and it was ginger-haired Linda that Eleanor had come to see. She watched her play and visualised her naked except for her tennis-shoes. That long slender body naked and in rapid motion, her young titties bouncing and swinging, the cheeks of her bum clenching and opening with the vigorous movements of her legs.

The sequence in Eleanor's mind was so exciting that she began to wonder if it might be possible to arrange a naked game between two girls. It would have to be at night, when everyone else was tucked up in bed and the courts deserted. But that wouldn't work – it was too dark out here at night to play tennis, more the pity. Another idea struck her: what about a midnight game of net-ball in the gym? Same effect, two sleek bare girls' bodies in fast action.

A long struggle of a game, pushing the girls to the limit, their hair awry, their bodies gleaming with perspiration. Bare pink shiny skin under the overhead lights, little muffs of dark hair between scissoring legs as the players jumped and reached. Until one beat the other – and then Eleanor would take on the winner.

She'd strip off to show her own body – no longer young but still lithe and desirable. It would be a smasher of a game – she'd hurl the ball over the high net and make her opponent leap and stretch.

The girl would be half-exhausted from her first game, so ten minutes with Eleanor would have her gasping for breath and staggering on rubbery legs to try to reach the ball. One final smash and Eleanor would win the game. The girl would stand panting by the net, her head hanging down, her hair falling over her face. Then Eleanor would go to her and put an arm round her waist.

There'd be no resistance as she pulled the girl gently down to the springy wooden floor. Friendly fingers brushing the hair away from the exhausted girl's forehead, a friendly hand wiping perspiration from her heaving titties. The same friendly hand sliding down over her belly and between her legs ... Eleanor's friendly lips kissing sweat-shiny titties, then her head between splayed thighs, breathing in the arousing scent of a pretty seventeen-year-old on the brink of a shattering orgasm.

Eleanor greatly enjoyed her little reverie. She was actively planning how to make the arrangements to stage it and which two girls she'd ask – it would be nice to choose two she hadn't seen naked or diddled before. But that presented problems. Before she had reached any conclusion, the end of the afternoon's classes arrived and the girls finished their game and made for the showers and changing-rooms.

There was a certain jealousy in the way Eleanor observed how three or four of the girls crowded around Toby Dundale and walked away with him. She didn't wonder now whether he'd had any of them, she was sure he had. The question in her mind was how many of them he had done since the term began. She herself had diddled five different girls that term, several times each.

When Linda came off the court with Pru, she found Eleanor waiting.

'I want a word with you, Linda,' she said pleasantly. 'Run along, Pru, and have your shower. Linda will be along presently.'

Linda looked very pretty in her short white skirt with a tee-shirt tucked into it. Her face was a healthy pink from the strenuous game she'd just played. She eyed Eleanor curiously – she'd heard of her interest in young girls. As a matter of fact, she suspected that several of her friends in Wexby House had been fondled by the teacher, although nobody had admitted it to her – not even big bold Penny, who only winked and changed the subject if she was asked.

Eleanor Redruth was a long-legged woman with dark brown hair. Her face was long and her chin prominent, her cheek-bones high and her gaze direct. She was looking elegant this afternoon in a tobacco-brown silk shirt tucked neatly into a darker brown skirt. Around her waist was a broad, shiny brown leather belt with a big square golden buckle.

'Walk with me, Linda,' Eleanor said, 'it's been ages since we had a little chat. But I've been hearing a very interesting story about you.'

Linda was certain in her own mind that Penny had taken her knickers down for Miss Redruth, and for some of the other teachers too. From that it was an obvious conclusion that Nesta had done the same – they copied each other in everything. It sent a pleasant little shiver all the way down Linda's spine to think that Penny's kitty and Nesta's had both been fingered by Miss Redruth.

Linda hero-worshipped Penny and Nesta. The two of them fighting over her had been the most exciting event of her life. She'd wanted both of them to win because she adored being diddled by them both. She couldn't bear the thought that one had to lose and would never touch her again.

'What do you mean?' she asked the teacher. 'What sort of story?'

Eleanor smiled at the question. Linda didn't realise it yet, but they were heading for the gymnasium. It was empty by now, but there clung to it a faint but evocative odour of perspiring young female bodies. It was an odour Eleanor found irresistible. She couldn't have known it, of course, but Toby Dundale was also affected by that lingering scent – he could never walk into the gym without getting a huge hard-on inside his jockstrap.

Once inside the gym with the doors closed carefully behind her, Eleanor put an arm about Linda's slim waist and held her close – close enough to put her other hand up the girl's very short tennis skirt. Her warm palm slid over bare smooth thighs.

'What are you doing?' Linda asked. It was a pointless question that needed no answer – she knew and Eleanor knew exactly what was happening.

'There's a story going around,' said Eleanor, 'that two girls fought each other here in the gymnasium two days ago. Fought each other tooth and nail, until their clothes were ripped off and they rolled about on the floor scratching and biting like wildcats.'

'Really?' Linda said, trying to sound innocent, which was far from easy when Eleanor was stroking her kitty through her knickers.

'Yes, really,' Eleanor said mockingly. 'There's no point in pretending you haven't heard the same story – it's all over the college.'

'Well ... someone did mention it to me,' Linda admitted reluctantly.

Eleanor's hand was clasping her kitty warmly through her knickers. Her middle finger slid gently along the length of Linda's slit and pushed the thin nylon into it.

'Are you telling me that you weren't here to see the fight?' Eleanor asked. 'The most exciting event this term and you missed it – is that what you want me to believe?'

Linda said nothing – it was obvious to her that Eleanor knew more than she should. Meanwhile the intruding hand beneath her skirt had found its way under the waistband of her knickers and down her belly. Busy fingers were tousling her curls and stroking the soft lips between her thighs.

'As I understand it,' Eleanor went on happily, pressing a

fingertip into Linda, 'the fight was about *you*. The two girls involved wanted you for their plaything, and neither would give way. So they fought it out. What I haven't heard, Linda, is which of them won.'

'I don't know,' Linda murmured, 'I don't know anything about it.' What she said was partly true – she didn't know whether Penny or Nesta had won because it was never finally decided.

'You're not telling me the truth,' Eleanor scolded her. 'It's simple enough – just tell me, which one's been diddling you since the fight? Penny or Nesta?'

Miss Redruth knew exactly who was involved. Linda guessed that meant that someone who'd watched the cat-fight had told her about it. Someone in Wexby House had given their secrets away to a teacher.

'Well, never mind that for now,' said Eleanor, grinning at the girl's reluctance to answer. 'We'll come back to it later on. First and foremost is the even more interesting question of why Penny Carlton and Nesta Wade were fighting over you. Give me a clue, Linda.'

The probing finger in Linda's chuffie was having its intended effect. Linda was breathing fast; little tremors shook her slender body. Eleanor walked her across the polished wooden floor to a vaulting-horse, put her hands in Linda's armpits, and with a strength surprising in such a slender woman, swung her round and lifted her up to sit on it.

Linda gasped and stared open-mouthed as Eleanor reached up with both hands under her skimpy tennis skirt to pull her knickers down her legs.

'You're not going to tell me why?' Eleanor said, eyebrows raised in amusement. 'Not even a little clue why two senior girls like Penny and Nesta fought over you? As it happens, I can guess why because I've been given inside information.'

She dropped Linda's knickers on the floor and flipped her skirt up to bare the girl's long slim thighs – and the tuft of bright ginger curls between them.

'That's beautiful,' she said, almost in a whisper, as her fingertips raked through the colourful patch of hair. 'I can see why they both want you as their plaything, Linda – you must be very popular in Wexby House. Have they all done you by now?'

She was standing up close, between Linda's spread legs, keeping one arm about her waist to support her. The exploring fingers of the other hand pressed inside her.

'Oh,' said Linda as Eleanor's longest finger pushed gently in to the first knuckle and touched her moist button.

The arm around her waist pulled her close, and she leaned forward to rest her head on Eleanor's shoulder. This was something Linda knew all about, a friendly finger sliding over the button inside the lips of her kitty. Something she experienced every night of the week in bed with her roommate. And in the daytime with other girls in her house – most recently with big-breasted Penny and with blonde Nesta.

She was sixteen and a half and she'd been fingered and made to come thousands of times, but this was the first time a grown woman had done it to her – the very first time an adult had slid a finger into her. It was so exciting – there was no telling what Eleanor would do next.

Linda was already very wet and slippery between the legs. She could feel Eleanor's finger sliding into her as far as the second knuckle. She sighed and parted her legs wider. Then the finger went in further, penetrating her to the limit, so that she could feel a warm palm pressed against her ginger curls. The three inches of Eleanor's finger were completely inside her.

Linda had sometimes wondered what it felt like to be done by a man – a question she and other first-year girls discussed frequently. She'd read that men had dicks six inches long. The thought of that much hard flesh pushing up inside her terrified her – but for some reason she didn't understand it made her excited at the same time.

She put her hands on the back of Eleanor's neck and pressed her cheek against Eleanor's. The finger had eased back and was gliding over her wet little button again. She was breathing in short quick gasps and hanging on to Eleanor for dear life as the fingertip rubbed faster.

'Oh, oh!' Linda moaned, then her thighs quivered and her body shook as she came.

'Yes,' she heard Eleanor murmur, 'you're very do-able, my dear. And done you shall be.'

In her quick ecstatic throes Linda thought that it was marvellous to be handled like this by Eleanor Redruth – it was even more exciting than when Penny had pushed her down on her back and done it to her. She wanted it again. Eleanor diddled her until she'd come completely and then held her close, waiting for her to get her breath back.

After a minute or two Linda sat up straight on the vaulting-horse and let her hands rest lightly on Eleanor's shoulders. Sitting on the horse, her head was higher than Eleanor's and she was able to look down closely into her dark-brown eyes. Eleanor was smiling and seemed very satisfied with herself.

'Yes,' she said, 'you are *very* do-able, Linda – and your responses are excellent. Is that the first time you've come today?'

'Yes,' said Linda, a little smile on her pretty face by way of answer to Eleanor's smile.

'You're not telling me the truth,' Eleanor chided her gently. 'Do you take me for a complete fool?'

Her long thin fingers pinched the lips of Linda's chuffie sharply and made her squeal.

'That hurts!' she exclaimed.

Eleanor's face beamed up at her as she pinched her hard again and made her yelp.

'Is that *really* the first time you've come today, Linda?'

'No, Miss Redruth.'

'When my hand is between your thighs you may call me Eleanor. But not at other times, do you understand?'

'Yes, Eleanor.'

Linda was half afraid her lips would be nipped again by those inspired fingers, but instead Eleanor stroked her slowly.

'Look over there,' she said. 'There are the mats where Penny and Nesta fought each other for the mastery of your bright-coloured tuft. I can't call it the mistress-ship of it, because there's no such word. Let's say for the domination of your charming little personal possession. I hope your memory has returned and you can tell me which of them won you.'

'It's not that I don't want to tell you,' Linda said quickly, mindful of the fingers combing through her ginger curls, 'but they had to stop the fight before it was settled because a teacher was coming toward the gym. We all ran away through the changing-room so we wouldn't get caught.'

'Who was winning before you ran away?'

'No one really. Nesta ripped Penny's bra off and slapped her titties, then Penny knocked Nesta down and sat on her face. Nesta tipped her off and jumped on top and lay on her and held her flat on her back. I don't know what would have happened next because someone shouted a warning and we all left in a hurry.'

'Interesting – I wish I'd been there to see the fight,' Eleanor said. 'Did either of them look as if they were going to come when they were on top of each other?'

'They were both very pink in the face. And when Penny was sitting on Nesta's face she was rubbing herself against her mouth – I think Nesta was tonguing her. And after that, when Nesta got Penny on her back, she ripped her knickers right off and rubbed her kitty against Penny's.'

Linda wasn't the best person to question on the fight, for she had been on her knees in a sexual delirium during most of the action. She couldn't be sure whether Penny or Nesta had come, but she herself certainly had. With Penny's torn knickers stuffed up between her legs under her skirt.

'From what you say it seems fairly clear that Nesta won the

fight,' Eleanor commented. 'If she stripped Penny naked that indicates to me she was the winner. That's not what I would have expected – I'd have put my money on Penny Carlton, she looks stronger and she's five or six pounds heavier than Nesta. But there you are, the favourite's not always first past the winning-post.'

The tip of Eleanor's middle finger was gliding lazily up and down the soft lips of Linda's chuffie, as if poised to press inside, but not doing so. Pleasant little shivers ran through Linda's belly; she wanted Eleanor to make her come again.

'So when you tell me you've been diddled already today,' Eleanor said, 'I assume it was Nesta who did it to you.'

Linda pressed her cheek against Eleanor's. 'During morning break,' she said softly, 'Nesta came into the classroom after the others had gone out – she made me stand with my back to the door while she played with me.'

'In the classroom!' Eleanor chuckled. 'What next? Doing it to girls in the classroom is reserved for me.'

'Have you done it to Nesta in the classroom?' Linda asked curiously.

'That's none of your business.'

'After lunch Penny asked me to go into her room with her,' Linda said, wanting to surprise Eleanor. 'She made me lie on the bed on my back with my clothes up round my waist.'

'They've both done you today?' Eleanor was incredulous. 'Nesta and Penny? I'm third in line, is that what you're saying? So which of them won the fight?'

'After we ran out of the gym Penny and Nesta carried on with the fight in Penny's room – I know because Jackie Offord told me, she shares with Penny. She said the room was a mess afterwards and she had to clear it up because Penny told her to. So I don't think either of them really won – they kissed and made up.'

Eleanor was surprised to hear about this second battle, because her own informant had been Jackie Offord. Jackie had described the fight in the gym in detail – and she made it sound so exciting that Eleanor gave her a good tonguing, not once but twice inside fifteen minutes. Then she demanded the same favour from Jackie, who by then was flagging just a little.

In bed alone that night Eleanor hadn't been able to get the thought of the fight out of her mind. She recreated it in her imagination – she'd seen both Penny and Nesta naked often enough that she could easily visualise their superb young bodies grappling together. In this fantasised version of the bout, the two girls ripped each other's bras and knickers off right at the start and fought naked.

While she played the scene in her mind, Eleanor pulled her nightie up to her chin and squeezed her own titties and plucked at her long pink bobbles till they were hard as berries. She imagined Penny winning – she had Nesta on her back on the mats and was sitting on her face – Jackie and Linda both said that had happened. But in Eleanor's replay Penny sat on Nesta's face facing her feet, and while Nesta was tonguing her, Penny reached down and slid two fingers into Nesta's blonde-haired slit and made her come with short fast rubs.

By that stage of the reverie Eleanor's own hand was down between her thighs and she was fingering herself busily. When she came, which didn't take long, her bum bucked up off the bed and she moaned loudly. She tried to settle herself to sleep after that, feeling nicely content, her nightie pulled down decently to her knees. But before long the fight was running through her head again.

This time she changed the script so that Nesta came out on top. Nesta had Penny on her hands and knees on the mats; she had a bare foot on the back of Penny's neck to pin her face to the floor. Big beautiful Penny naked and helpless was a marvellous sight, her plump round bum up in the air and her big fleshy titties squashed underneath her as Nesta held her down. Nesta's hand rose and fell – she was spanking Penny's exposed bum, quick hard slaps that brought squeals of dismay from her victim.

55

When the spanking was over, the cheeks of Penny's bum were reddened. Nesta had two fingers inside her kitty from behind and was diddling her fast.

And in her bed on her back, Eleanor had her nightie up around her waist and had two fingers inside her own wet kitty to diddle herself a second time. She came at the same moment Penny came in the fantasy – harder and longer than the first time.

After that she really did fall asleep, her nightie still round her waist. But the thought of the two girls fighting over Linda had so gripped her imagination that she dreamed about it and woke up in the early morning feeling moist and slippery between her legs. She played the scene in her mind yet again – this time it came out as a draw. Penny and Nesta, their naked and desirable young bodies sweating from the effort, were locked together on the mats.

They were head to foot, arms gripping each other furiously, straining to break free, struggling to break each other's hold. But neither could, they were too well-matched. They'd locked their bare thighs about each other's heads – their tongues were sticking out and lapping rapidly at each other's exposed buttons. They were trying to make each other come and break the hold in that way.

Now they were gasping aloud as tremors shook their rolling, heaving bodies. Eleanor's fingers were flicking lightly over her own wet button as she tried to hold off her own climax until she could decide which one she would let win. But she left it too late – the one who came first was Eleanor! Then she fell back to sleep until her alarm clock roused her at seven-thirty.

She owed that night of fantasy to Jackie Offord and her description of what happened in the gym. But Jackie had said nothing about the fight being continued afterwards in Penny's room. Eleanor made a mental note to ask why – and to question Jackie closely next time she had her alone. *We'll have the truth out of you, Missy,* she promised herself with an inward grin, *besides having your knickers down.*

* * *

In the meantime there was ginger-haired little Linda to be dealt with. Eleanor reached up to put her hands in the girl's armpits and lift her down from the vaulting-horse.

'On your knees, Linda,' she said. 'It's time you kissed me.'

Linda sank slowly to her knees, her eyes fixed on Eleanor's fingers as they undid the square gold buckle of her brown leather belt. She reached up and caught it as it fell from Eleanor's waist – and then Eleanor was undoing her skirt at the side, freeing it so that it slid down her long legs.

'Oh . . .' Linda sighed, 'you've no knickers on . . .'

Stockings, not tights, held up by a scarlet suspender-belt, made a thin band of bright colour across the pale skin of Eleanor's belly. Linda was entranced as she stared from close range at Eleanor's belly-button and her thighs – and the triangle of dark-brunette hair running down between her legs.

'I took my knickers off before I came out to find you, Linda – I knew for certain we were going to play with each other.'

On her knees in front of Eleanor, Linda put her cheek against the teacher's flat belly. It was warm and soft and comforting. And so exciting she wanted to lick it. She put her hand on the dark curls between Eleanor's thighs, which were already spread apart, the lips of her kitty pouting and moist. Linda opened them wider with careful fingers to reveal the little pink button, and touched it with a gentle fingertip.

'Yes, just there, that's it,' Eleanor sighed. 'Kiss me, Linda.'

Linda put her mouth to the lips between Eleanor's legs and pressed her tongue in to lick slowly over the button. She knew very well how to do this – Penny Carlton wanted it done every day and lay on her back with her legs apart while Linda did it for her.

'Ah,' Eleanor breathed in pleasure.

As Linda's tongue began to work a little faster, Eleanor trembled and eagerly offered her warm wet kitty, satin-soft and rose-pink. Her belly pushed forward as she pressed herself against the girl's mouth. Her button was stiff and firm under

Linda's tongue; she made little mewing sounds and squeezed her own titties through her silk blouse.

'Who taught you how to do this so nicely?' she sighed.

She could hardly have expected a reply, as Linda's mouth was too busy.

'I should have had you before, Linda, but I never realised how pretty you are with your knickers off. But now I know, we'll make up for lost time, believe me.'

Linda's hands were stroking the bare cheeks of Eleanor's bum, feeling the firmness, circling the double roundness and squeezing the flesh in delight. Her fingers trailed down the long deep crease, until the tip of her forefinger found the little knot of muscle between the cheeks.

Eleanor moaned helplessly as Linda's finger pressed gently up her from the rear – while the girl's tongue flicked fast from the front and ravaged her. Eleanor's legs began shaking, forcing her to take her hands from her titties and put them on Linda's shoulders to support herself. Her body shook hard eight or nine times as her orgasm jolted her.

When she was calm again she stepped into her skirt, pulled it up her legs and refastened her broad belt.

'Put your knickers on, Linda, it's time we went. You've been delicious and I want you again this evening. Come to my study after dinner.'

They left the gym together and walked back to Wexby house, Eleanor very pleased with her afternoon diversion. But there was something else on her mind that she wanted to ask Linda about.

'The new Sports Coach,' she said, 'is he popular with the girls?'

'Oh yes, some of them are crazy about him,' Linda answered.

'I thought as much,' Eleanor said thoughtfully. 'I've seen him on the tennis court and can understand how some girls would let themselves be fascinated by his little shorts.'

'You should see him in the swimming-pool,' Linda said

innocently, not guessing that Eleanor would be irritated by the information. 'He wears swimming trunks so tiny that you can see everything he's got – specially when they're wet. Orline Ashby says it's like the biology lessons we used to have at school, illustrated in colour 3-D.'

She giggled, but Eleanor was not amused.

'Which girls has he had so far?' she asked. 'Have any of your friends taken their knickers down for him, Linda?'

'No, of course not,' Linda said at once.

Secrets like that only stayed secrets as long as teachers didn't get to know them. Somebody had told Miss Redruth about Penny and Nesta in the gym and Linda's own part in the affair – but Linda herself wasn't going to betray any secrets. Not even to Miss Redruth, who had so fantastic a touch when she put her hand between your legs.

'How about Penny – surely her curiosity has led her to find out what it's like with the Sports Coach?' Eleanor persisted.

'I don't know,' Linda replied. 'She never tells me things like that.'

'Even though she owns you – well, part-owns you, along with Nesta?'

'If anybody owns me, you do,' Linda said.

That wasn't what Eleanor wanted to hear. She'd enjoyed giving Linda a good jiggling and fully intended to give her many more. She didn't want to own her, that sounded too serious. Eleanor liked to keep everything casual, have a girl when she felt like it and have another one when she had the time and opportunity. She decided she'd have to speak privately to Penny Carlton to make sure ginger-tufted little Linda didn't try to make everything personal and exclusive.

'These swimming-trunks the Sports Coach wears,' she said, 'What can you see actually see in them? Has he got a big one or a little one?'

'Enormous,' said Linda, 'a huge great big thick thing.'

'Do you mean it stands up stiff when he's in the swimming-pool?'

'I don't think so,' Linda said, 'it's just enormous anyway.'

Eleanor doubted if sixteen-year-old Linda had enough acquaintance with male anatomy to know whether the Sports Coach's thing was oversized or undersized. To be honest, her own knowledge of men's bodies was strictly second-hand. All that she knew of them was what she had read in books or seen in works of art – 'old master' paintings and statues. And everyone said that Renaissance artists gave their creations under-sized parts for modesty's sake. Whether that was true or not, Eleanor wasn't sure, but it added to the general confusion.

All the same, there was something in Linda's tone when she spoke about the Sports Coach that made Eleanor wonder if she had been shown his male equipment privately. Maybe held it in her hand, as she seemed so impressed by it? Surely she hadn't let the man *do* her, though. Surely she wouldn't go that far . . .

Chapter Five

Lights Out at the college was at ten-thirty, which might seem early for young women of sixteen and seventeen. At home in the vacations they stayed up later, especially the ones who liked discos. If their parents let them, they stayed out until midnight – and the last hour of that was spent standing in a dark doorway, or sitting in a car parked in a quiet place, having their titties felt and kitties fingered by a boyfriend.

The girls told each other about their adventures when they came back to college for the start of a new term. They compared notes about the finger techniques of the boys they knew and they giggled over general male inadequacy. It was rare for a girl to report that her boyfriend had succeeded in making her come when he got his hand inside her knickers.

As for letting a boyfriend get his long hard *thing* up them, that was a non-starter. These were ambitious girls aiming for university and important careers, so they didn't want the complications of permanent boyfriends mooning over them. They certainly had no intention of jeopardizing all their future prospects by risking the disaster of being made pregnant by a teenage boy seeking a quick thrill in the back of a car.

One thing all the girls found funny was to hear that someone's boyfriend had been so carried away that he'd come in his trousers. It was a status point for the girl concerned to be able to tell her friends at Lechlade how she'd sent her boyfriend off home with sticky underwear. It wasn't all that difficult to do – the boys were so desperate for it that after half an hour of french kissing and tittie-fumbling a quick rub on the outside of their jeans often made them come.

One of the best tales was told by Hilary Landor, a fair-haired girl in her first year who intended to read law when she got to university and become a well-paid barrister before she was thirty. At home during the Easter vacation Hilary went to the cinema with a boy named Roddy Brent.

She told her enthralled friends in Wexby House that it had been two hours of groping in the dark with Roddy's hand up her roll-neck pullover to feel her titties and then inside her jeans to get at her kitty. He'd unzipped her jeans all the way down and had his hand in her knickers while she kept hoping that the people sitting in the row in front of them wouldn't glance over their shoulders. Luckily none of them did, because they'd have had a good view of Roddy's hand doing things to her inside her open jeans.

As for the couple sitting behind, she was sure they knew exactly what he was doing, but with any luck they were doing the same thing and had no time for spectating. In retaliation she rubbed Roddy's stiffie through his trousers to see if she could make him come in his underwear. He got very excited and tried to ram two or three fingers up her. He did a lot of sighing and twitching but that was all that happened – he didn't go all the way.

When they came out of the Odeon they went to a hamburger bar for something to eat and a cup of coffee, and then he walked her home. The house was on a tree-lined residential street off the main road – and as she expected, when they reached it he pressed her against the tall, thick green hedge outside. While he was kissing her he unzipped her jeans again and got his hands inside and into her knickers.

If only he knew how to make her come, she thought, it would be so much more interesting. But boys were useless at that. If she'd been with a girlfriend both of them would have come at least twice by now – all it needed was a soft and sympathetic touch on the moist little button.

62

Girls understood each other and knew how to make it happen nicely. All boys thought about was their own satisfaction – they tried all the tricks they knew to get their stiffie inside a girl and shoot off, but they didn't care if the girl enjoyed it or not. Some of them didn't seem to understand that girls came at all.

Roddy played with her for at least ten minutes and it was a waste of time for Hilary. He didn't know that, he thought he'd made her wildly excited and dying for it. He unzipped his jeans and pulled out his twanger – he was going to slip it up her right where they stood in the dark by the hedge!

Hilary stopped him before things went too far. He grumbled and sighed that he *had* to do it; he accused her of not liking him at all, because she was making him suffer for no reason – it would only take a minute if she let him push it in. She said no very firmly – but she left him with the hope that next time he took her out she might let him have his way.

The hour was late and if he missed the last bus he'd have a long walk home. There was a bus-stop just round the corner on the main road, but he dithered and stroked her titties underneath her pullover. She'd made him take his hand out of her knickers and had zipped her jeans up, just to make sure he knew where he stood.

They were standing so close in the dark that Hilary was able to rub her belly against his. Even through his clothes and her own she could feel his thing standing up hard and big. He was breathing fast and playing with her titties when they heard a bus and saw it go past the end of the road.

'That's the last bus!' he gasped. 'I'll phone you in the morning.'

With that he dragged his hand out of her bra and ran hell-for-leather toward the end of the road, hoping to reach the stop round the corner in time. Roddy's luck was right out that night. He hadn't had his stiffie up Hilary as he'd been hoping, and she hadn't even given him a helping hand in consolation, not properly. She'd only rubbed her hand against his jeans and then her belly against him – she'd made him hotter and harder than ever.

As he ran to catch the bus his upright hard-on was rubbing against his underwear. In his over-excited and sensitive condition there was only one possible outcome – before he reached the end of the road he groaned and came explosively in his tight-fitting jeans.

Hilary hadn't gone into the house yet. She was waiting to make sure he caught his bus. He'd run no more than fifteen or twenty steps when she saw him stop in mid-stride and bend over, his hands clutching the front of his jeans. She had no idea what had happened to him – the thought in her mind was that he had been taken suddenly ill. She trotted down the pavement, calling out to him. He was leaning against a tree when she reached him, doubled over and breathing heavily.

'Roddy, what's the matter?' she asked anxiously.

'It's all your fault,' he said, sounding very peeved. 'Now look what you've done!'

She stared in mystification while he dragged his zip down and stuffed a handkerchief into his tight jockey-shorts. Even in the dark she saw the stain soaking through and realised that he'd come by accident. She had to laugh, and that made him even angrier.

The girls of Wexby House laughed too when Hilary told the tale back at Lechlade. The account of Roddy's mishap became a favourite and during that term she was asked to tell it many times.

'Poor Roddy,' she always finished, 'he missed his bus and had a long walk home in wet, sticky underpants.'

Ten-thirty might be the official time for Lights Out, but it wasn't the end of the day's activities. The rules said that students must not be out of their rooms after that time and some of them did indeed stay in their rooms and share a bed with their room-mate. They played with each other for half an hour and then fell asleep.

But some girls wanted more than that; they liked variety and went visiting other rooms after Lights Out. They moved quietly along deserted corridors in their nighties and dressing-gowns, each slipping into her chosen room and closing the door silently behind her. The Heads of Houses knew that this went on night after night. In Wexby House, Joy Locksley could guess who was on the prowl any night of the week. She took care not to hear or see anything that would require her to take disciplinary action.

Hilary Landor shared a room with Marjorie Newmill, a slightly plumpish brunette who disliked sports and games but was highly intelligent and very popular because of her good nature and her liking for games in bed. She didn't open her legs for anybody, as Annabel Darwen did, but she had a wide circle of close friends. She and Hilary got into bed together naked almost every night of the week.

On one of these nights the two girls lay facing each other, pressed together, bare titties against titties, belly against belly, thighs interlaced, hands stroking each other's bums. They kissed and murmured to each other until fingers found kitties and pressed inside. Hilary was eager and impatient, moist and open between the legs. Within twenty minutes she had come twice and done the same for Marjorie. They lay resting after that, their arms around each other, and soon dozed off.

Hilary woke up when the door swung open. It was absolutely soundless, but the movement of the air woke her. It was dark in the room, but not pitch-black because they never bothered to pull the curtains across the windows and some light came in from outside. Not enough to identify the visitor, though.

Hilary raised her head from the pillow and stared into the darkness. She heard the creak of a floor-board and could discern a figure coming toward the bed. There were vague movements and little rustling sounds that suggested someone taking off a dressing-gown and slipping out of a nightie. Who could it be, Hilary wondered, straining her eyes in the gloom.

'Who's that?' she whispered.

'It's me – Orline,' a voice whispered back. 'Sorry if I disturbed you – I thought this was Marjorie's bed.'

'It is.' Hilary sat up and swung her bare legs over the edge. 'I'll go back to mine.'

'What's going on?' a sleepy voice asked – Marjorie was awake at last.

Hilary crossed to her own bed and got in. She heard Orline talking in a low and soothing voice to Marjorie as she climbed into the warm space Hilary had just vacated. She was a very pretty girl, Orline Ashby, but her night-time visit was a surprise to Hilary, who hadn't known she and Marjorie were such close friends.

Hilary could hear little murmurs from the other bed and the rustle of bed-clothes. At least she'd left Marjorie naked for Orline to play with. She turned over on her side, her back to the pair across the room, and tried to go back to sleep. After a while she pulled the bed-clothes up over her head to blank out the little noises coming from the other bed, but even that didn't work.

Hilary's knees were pulled up and her hand was down between her legs. *This is silly*, she thought to herself, *I've come twice tonight already – why can't I go to sleep?*

But she couldn't. She tried to bore herself enough to fall asleep by thinking of the history essay she'd written that day for Miss Claudine Stanhope on the Reform Act of 1884 – but her fingers were touching the soft lips of her kitty, still moist from being diddled by Marjorie. With a sigh that was half exasperation and half surrender she slid her finger in and touched her nubby.

There was a warbling little cry from the other bed – Hilary recognised it at once as the sound Marjorie made when she came. That was too much! Hilary was consumed with desire and with envy of her room-mate; her finger danced over her nubby and she came before Marjorie had finished.

After that Hilary was sure she could sleep. She fluffed up her pillows, rolled onto her back and tried to settle down comfortably – but all too soon there were little murmurs and sighs from the other bed again. Obviously it was Orline's turn – she was being fingered and having her titties sucked by Marjorie.

This went on for a long time, longer than Hilary would have believed possible. Marjorie had been fairly slow to come but that was because she'd been done twice before the unexpected visitor arrived. But there was no reason why Orline was taking such a long time to get there. Not unless she'd been at it all day long with someone else. Whatever the reason, the moaning and sighing and little thrashing movements of Orline trying to come were making Hilary hot and bothered again.

She lay on her back with her legs wide apart, her hands clenched by her sides to keep her fingers away from her wet kitty. *It's too silly for words*, she said to herself firmly, *three times and I'm still wide awake! I refuse to do myself again, I'll be a limp rag in the morning if this goes on much longer!*

She heard Orline come in the dark with a long bubbling wail that almost sent her into a frenzy of her own. She'd had enough, she couldn't bear it for another moment. She slid out of bed, crossed the room in three strides and forced herself into Marjorie's bed.

All beds at the college were singles. Two girls could get into one to play together and it was a bit of a squeeze, but that was all to the good. But to get three into a single bed was like packing sardines into a tin.

'What are you doing?' Marjorie asked. She was on the far side and Orline was in the middle.

'If you're going to do each other all night, I want to be part of it,' said Hilary, her hands exploring under the sheets.

Orline had rolled off her back after coming and was lying face-to-face with Marjorie, her naked back toward Hilary. She giggled and squirmed when Hilary put an arm over her and stroked her titties. They were warm and round and soft – Hilary sighed in pleasure at feeling them. She slipped her hand down Orline's belly and felt between her legs, finding lips that were open and wet beneath her soft downy curls.

'What brings you here tonight?' Hilary asked while she was tickling Orline's nubby. 'Have you got tired of Anybody's? I thought she did it non-stop, just for the asking.'

'It's not that,' Orline said, wriggling her warm bare bottom against Hilary's belly. 'She's gone off somewhere and left me on my own. I couldn't sleep, so I thought I'd come visiting.'

'And you've done both,' Hilary said. 'You've visited and you've come! Marjorie didn't tell me you were such good friends.'

Marjorie seemed to have gone to sleep. She lay still and silent while Hilary stroked Orline's thighs and belly and titties.

'It only started yesterday,' Orline explained, 'in the showers.'

'The showers,' Hilary murmured, fully understanding. She'd had some of the most exciting and satisfying experiences of her young life under the warm cascading water of the college showers. It was in the showers that Penny Carlton had her the first time, less than a week after Hilary first arrived at Lechlade. Lovely big Penny had pushed her fingers into Hilary and made her suck her beautifully big heavy titties.

'Oh, that's nice,' Orline said as Hilary's hands roamed over her body. With care, so as not to disturb Marjorie or push her out of the narrow bed, Orline turned over to face Hilary to return the favour. Her hands touched and felt and soothed and sent long tremors of pleasure through Hilary's body.

Orline wanted to do more than that to her but there wasn't room in the bed for much movement. She slid her warm body on top of Hilary and lay on her for a little while, jerking her loins to push her chuffie against Hilary's. Then she got out of the bed and knelt beside it, threw the bed-clothes off Hilary and kissed and licked her titties and belly, while her fingers fluttered between Hilary's parted thighs.

'I shall come in a minute,' Hilary sighed, feeling as excited as if it had been her first time.

There was a little stir on the other side of the bed; it seemed that Marjorie wasn't asleep after all. Or maybe she'd dozed for a few moments and was awake again. She reached out to put her hand on Hilary's belly and stroke it. Meanwhile Orline's mouth was over Hilary's left tittie, sucking it vigorously.

'Oh, yes, yes . . .' Hilary gasped. She couldn't tell now whose fingers were diddling her, Orline's or Marjorie's, nor did she care as long as they kept on doing it.

In spite of her extreme excitement, she was slower to come this time, which was only to be expected after all the activity of this night. She was on the edge, feverish with sexual arousal, her body throbbing and straining to reach her big thrill. Her bum lifted off the bed and instantly Marjorie pushed a knee underneath it to hold her up. Hilary's legs opened very wide as the fluttering fingers working relentlessly at her nubby drove her more and more frantic.

Marjorie and Orline had her pinned between them, her head on the pillow, her legs splayed and her body arching upward to push her belly and her wet kitty up in the air.

Hands gripped her shoulders, hands grasped her titties and squeezed them. Orline, panting in the dark, had stopped sucking Hilary's titties and had changed position so that her head was between Hilary's thighs and her hot tongue two inches inside her.

'Make her come,' she heard Marjorie gasp to Orline.

'Oh, yes – make me, make me!' Hilary said urgently. She pushed her belly upwards in a high arch, writhing in throbbing pleasure as hands moved all over her shaking body. Fingers were pushed into her open mouth, fingers plucked at the tips of her titties, a long wet tongue was ravaging her secret button. When she came it was like an earthquake inside her belly, sensations so powerful they made her scream in uncontrollable ecstasy.

Her scream was so loud that it was heard in the rooms on either side of hers, where friends in bed with their room-mates stopped their own activities to giggle at the telltale sound.

Hilary's ecstatic cry could be heard even as far away as Joy Locksley's room on the floor below, where the Head of Wexby House was naked in bed with Miss Sharon Pomeroy, her long-haired friend who taught geography. Joy thought Sharon was looking very attractive in the soft light of the bedside lamp with her hair covering part of her face and her cheeks pink from her exertions of a few minutes earlier.

'What was that?' Sharon exclaimed, raising her head.

'Nothing,' said Joy. 'Just one of the girls.'

'It sounded as if she was being murdered, whoever it was.'

'No,' Joy assured her, 'it was only someone in the throes of coming – lots of them make that much noise when they come. They're not children any more, you know, having quiet little thrills, they're nearly grown up. Some of them come really hard.'

Sharon had just made Joy come. She lay curled up on her side between Joy's parted legs, head between her friend's thighs. She looked up along Joy's naked body, over the brown-haired kitty she had just tongued so effectively, over Joy's belly with the small brown mole near the deep round navel, up between her pointed titties to her flushed face. Joy's head was still propped up on the two pillows she had used to raise it high enough to watch Sharon tongue her.

'You didn't sing out like that just now when *you* came,' Sharon said, a hint of reproach in her tone.

'I clenched my teeth to hold it back,' Joy said. 'It wouldn't do for the girls to hear sexual moaning from the House Head's bedroom.'

Joy's affair this term with Sharon was an on-and-off arrangement which lacked passion. They diddled each other pleasantly and satisfactorily, but Joy knew that Sharon could never make her come hard enough to scream as loud as the unknown girl somewhere in Wexby House had just done. She liked Sharon, though, and their arrangement was very convenient. It would be a pity to spoil it by upsetting her with the truth.

To be honest about it, Joy thought, she had never yet made Sharon scream like that, either. When Sharon came she shuddered deeply half a dozen times or so and under her breath murmured '*Darling, darling*'. That was all there was to it. She was always ready for a second go, as Joy was herself, but that was never more for either of them than a repetition of the first.

The truth was that although it had been very nice when Sharon did her two minutes ago, Joy would rather have been in bed with Annabel Darwen. While Sharon had been licking her to climax, Joy had been fantasising about the pretty blonde girl the students had nicknamed Anybody's and pretending to herself that it was Annabel doing it to her.

It had been sheer madness, that afternoon in her study when she pulled Annabel's knickers halfway down her thighs to look at her wispy-curled kitty. Sheer madness for the Head of House to play with a student – but it had been *very* pleasant. Annabel had a pretty kitty down between her slender thighs, with well-shaped lips that opened easily to the pressure of Joy's finger.

There was no mystery about it. Annabel was used to being fingered and diddled – she wasn't called Anybody's for nothing. But that made no difference – the fact was that Joy Locksley, who was almost fifteen years older than the girl, wanted her badly. And she intended to have her, as often as it could be arranged without rousing suspicion.

Joy was sure that Annabel was in bed that night with her room-mate, Orline Ashby. The two of them naked, belly-to-belly, kissing while they fingered each other. During that afternoon of madness in the study, Joy had diddled Annabel three times and been made to come twice herself. And Annabel had still been ready for more after that, but there wasn't the time. At night in bed there'd be all the time anyone could want, Joy said to herself – and she was suddenly jealous of Orline, having Annabel night after night.

The two girls shared a room on the floor above. Suddenly

the thought came into Joy's mind that the long shriek she'd heard a little while ago was Annabel. Joy could easily imagine the scene, Annabel naked on her back and Orline Ashby kneeling between her legs, a hand on each thigh to keep them well apart while she tongued Annabel.

The long ecstatic wail that had sounded through the building – that was Anybody's having an orgasm! The thought made Joy instantly excited again. She gripped Sharon by her long blonde hair and pulled her up the bed next to herself. In another second she was kissing all the way down Sharon's belly to her curls and prising her chuffie open to get at her nubby and do exquisite things to it. She wanted to make Sharon squeal as loud as Annabel had!

She was wrong about all this, of course. Anybody's wasn't in bed with Orline Ashby. In fact there was nobody in the room the two girls shared. Orline was making fair-haired Hilary come, with the help of Marjorie Newmill, and Anybody's was busy elsewhere.

On the floor above Joy Locksley's room, Orline had tried to get back into bed with Hilary and Marjorie. But plumply comfortable Marjorie had rolled onto her back and there really wasn't room for three. Orline threw the bed-clothes down to the foot of the bed and straddled Hilary's bare belly.

'Do me,' she begged.

Her naked body gleamed palely in the semi-darkness. Hilary reached up to handle her soft little titties, then down to the dark patch at the base of her belly, where her straddled thighs met. Hilary's fingers found soft wispy curls and warm flesh, slippery with longing and fulfilment. She opened the lips wide and slipped two fingers inside. Orline gasped as her body jerked to the sensations flickering through her.

She was responding very well to the touch of Hilary's busy fingers – it wasn't going to take long this time. Hearing a sigh from beside her, Hilary reached out with her free left hand to touch Marjorie. She felt the girl's soft round titties under her palm. Marjorie's sighs were coming faster and faster. Hilary felt down Marjorie's body and found that she had her hand between her own thighs. She was diddling herself with fast little touches.

'No you don't!' Hilary said, pulling Marjorie's hand away. 'You're not in bed alone, you'll join in with us or you won't do it at all.'

She pressed two fingers of her own left hand into Marjorie's slippery-wet slit and teased her expertly.

'I've got you both now!' she exclaimed gleefully, her right hand busy with Orline and her left with Marjorie. 'I wonder which one will come first.'

Thirty seconds later Marjorie bucked her belly upwards and moaned in a long climax that shook the bed. Her moan penetrated through the floor and was heard downstairs by Joy, who was just putting the last urgent licks to Sharon's exposed pink nubby to make her come. Again she thought it must be Annabel, and became ever more desperate to finish Sharon off and open her own legs for urgent attention.

Five seconds after Marjorie's climax, Orline went into a long frenzied shuddering, bouncing up and down on Hilary's belly until she almost winded her.

'Got you both!' Hilary announced.

The three of them arranged themselves as best they could for a rest in the single bed. After trying various positions and finding them far from comfortable, they settled with Orline, the slimmest and lightest of them, lying on top of Marjorie, as if she were a man doing her.

'Don't fall asleep here,' Marjorie said with a long yawn.

'I'll go back to my own room in a minute,' Orline promised.

'And I'll go back to my own bed when you do,' Hilary said. She enjoyed the feeling of warm soft bodies pressing close to her and didn't want to go back to an empty bed just yet.

'I've got a secret to tell you,' said Orline importantly, knowing that nobody could resist an opening like that. She sounded strange, her voice slightly muffled because her cheek was resting on Marjorie's and her mouth was almost in the pillow.

'What?' Hilary and Marjorie said together.

'The day before yesterday, I was going past the gym and I saw something you wouldn't believe – well, maybe you will, because it was Miss Redruth.'

'Oh yes – her . . .' Marjorie breathed. 'Who was with her?'

'Linda Knight. They were standing by a vaulting-horse. Well, Miss Redruth was standing. Linda was down on her knees.'

'She never was!' Hilary and Marjorie exclaimed, again at the same time. They were holding hands and their fingers gripped tight at the implication of what Orline was telling them.

'Miss Redruth had dropped her skirt and wasn't wearing any knickers. I could see her kitty as plain as anything.'

'Where were you, to be able to see all this?' Hilary demanded, wondering whether Orline was making it up.

'I was in the little office that Mr Dundale uses. The door has a glass panel and I could see everything through it. Linda and Miss Redruth were only about fifteen feet away from me.'

'What were you doing in there?' Hilary asked.

'Never mind about that,' Marjorie broke in impatiently. 'What were Linda and Miss Redruth doing? Tell us that.'

'She was wearing stockings,' said Orline, 'and a bright red suspender belt. Linda was down on her knees staring at her kitty – she's got very dark-brown hair down below, Miss Redruth. Linda was feeling her and they were talking to each other, but I couldn't hear what they said.'

'Really feeling her?' Hilary asked, 'putting her fingers in her?'

'Linda was kneeling with her back to me, so I can't say for certain – but after a little while she put her mouth down on Miss Redruth's kitty as if she was kissing it. And then she tongued her. I know that for sure because Miss Redruth was facing me, leaning against the vaulting-horse, and I could see the expression on her face while Linda was licking her.'

'Did she make her come?' Marjorie asked in a shaky voice. Suddenly her fingers were gripping Hilary's hand very tightly. Hilary was certain that Orline was doing something to her.

'Yes,' Orline murmured, 'she really did – Linda was squeezing her bum while she did her and Miss Redruth was rubbing her own titties through her blouse. You could tell when she started coming because she dropped her hands down on Linda's shoulders to hold herself up, and then she started shaking.'

'Oh, oh . . .' Marjorie was moaning faintly, her fingernails digging into the palm of Hilary's hand.

'What are you doing to her?' Hilary asked. 'What are you doing, Orline – you're feeling her, aren't you?'

'She's going to come in a second, I've got my thigh between her legs and I've been rubbing it against her. Her chuffie's all open and wet on my leg.'

Hilary pressed closer to the two girls. Orline, on top of Marjorie, was moving her thigh rhythmically – not a big movement, only an inch up-and-down, but the rubbing was enough to excite Marjorie to near-coming. Hilary put her free hand on Orline's bum and then down between the hot cheeks, and further down still until she touched the split of the smaller girl's kitty lips. Hilary pushed a finger inside.

'Oh!' Orline gasped. 'Not again, Hilary – I can't do it again tonight, I'm past it.'

'We'll see about that,' Hilary said, her fingertip touching Orline's wet little nub.

Chapter Six

Even before Toby Dundale joined the teaching staff as Sports Coach, the fact was that Lechlade Ladies' College had never really been the hundred per cent female establishment it claimed to be. The teaching staff were all women, as were the kitchen staff and the cleaners, but the post of caretaker had always been held by a man.

This was because there were hot-water boilers to be attended to, large items of equipment and furniture to be moved about, fuses to be replaced and other maintenance tasks not much to the tastes of women.

The caretaker was residential, but he was not allowed to live in the college itself. That would be to locate a man too close to the young ladies and their bedrooms – an unthinkable prospect. The caretaker therefore lived in the gatehouse, which was five hundred yards away from the main building, at the entrance to the grounds from the road.

One of his daily duties was to close and lock the tall iron gates at ten o'clock each evening and unlock them at eight the next morning. And between those hours no one went out and no one came in.

Needless to say, the caretaker had to be a married man. Legend had it, however, that during the war years the college had been compelled to appoint an unmarried caretaker. Most men able-bodied enough to do the job were either in the Forces or on vital war-work, and there was simply no one else available. The man appointed was exempt from war duties because he had a bad limp, the result of a motorbike accident in his younger days. His name was Harry Rollins, and the memory of him lived on in infamy in the suppressed secret history of the college.

Rollins walked awkwardly because his leg had healed twisted after the accident. All the rest of him was in perfect working order – especially his twanger. That was in first-rate condition, so much so that by the time he'd been caretaker for six months, five girls were taken away from the college by outraged parents because they were in the family way.

Confidential enquiries by Heads of Houses established that another six girls had spread their legs for Harry. They were lucky. The scandal was hushed-up fairly easily because wartime newspapers had other and more important news to report. Rollins was dismissed without a reference and the then Principal was asked to resign.

All that was long ago and the Governors, the Principal and the teaching staff were all determined that nothing like it would ever happen again. Over the years, Governors and teachers came and went but the solemn determination was passed on as a sacred duty – the girls must be protected against the sexual attentions of male staff.

The current caretaker was Keith Mason, a man in his late thirties who was married to a thin blonde woman named Sally. He knew nothing about the notorious Harry of fifty years earlier – he'd never even heard of him, for the simple reason that the incident was never mentioned. It was a piece of unfortunate history, over and done with.

Yet unknown to the Principal or any of the teaching staff or even his blonde whippet of a wife, Keith Mason was an enthusiastic Peeping Tom. What more suitable place could there be for a man of his interests than a girls' boarding school? There were changing-rooms and showers, a gym and a swimming-pool – to say nothing of the bedrooms, some of them at ground-floor level.

There were a hundred and sixty young women, sixteen and

seventeen years old. Dark, fair, ginger-haired, all of them well-fed, healthy and energetic – for Keith it was heaven. As he went about his daily tasks he devoted great ingenuity to finding means of observing as many girls as possible in varying degrees of nudity.

He was as surprised as anyone at the appointment of a male Sports Coach when Miss Plessy left after damaging her knee. Before Toby Dundale had been at Lechlade ten days, Keith decided it was all to the good. One reason was that Toby encouraged jogging as a keep-fit exercise. Keith discovered that if he waited out of sight behind a tree near the gates at six each evening he was in for a regular treat.

Led by the Sports Coach, a straggling line of panting girls would trail past Keith's hiding-place on their way back to the showers. Girls in little shorts and thin tee-shirts. After their brisk jog the girls' tee-shirts were soaked with sweat and clung tightly to their bouncing young titties. The sight never failed to bring a smile to Keith's lips and a hardness to another part of his anatomy.

Another new opportunity he noticed was that when Toby was coaching a class in the swimming-pool, the girls seemed to do a lot of posing. In Miss Plessy's day it had been all water-thrashing and whistle-blowing. Now, though, many of the girls clearly fancied Toby, which made Keith a little jealous but gave him exciting secret glimpses of young ladies pushing out their chests to show off their titties or bending over in swimsuits to show their bare bum cheeks.

All this was for Toby Dundale's benefit, but he ignored the display, as far as the caretaker could see. Keith was the one who revelled in the sight, though from a distance, with a pair of binoculars.

But it was the jogging that gave Keith the best idea he'd had since he first arrived at the college. The evening run-past was a pleasure to watch – but some of the more independent-minded girls went for a jog on their own. Keith particularly waited for these. Out of sight behind his tree, he followed their solitary progress toward him through his binoculars, shifting his attention back and forth between swaying titties and pumping thighs. After a few weeks of this Keith noted that there were times when only one girl would be in the showers after going jogging on her own. He gave a lot of thought to how he could make use of this exciting new possibility.

He was mopping the tiled shower-room floor one evening when the answer struck him. There were lockers down both sides of the changing-room, where the girls kept their running shoes and other gear. There were long benches down the middle of the room, where they sat when they dried their hair. And there was one locker standing on its own, right by the doorway that led from the changing-room into the shower-room.

This locker was for the caretaker's equipment, mops and buckets and whatever else he needed. It was five feet tall by two feet wide by two feet deep, or whatever that might be in centimetres these days. Looking at it carefully, Keith saw that if he put his gear somewhere else there should be just enough space in the locker for him to hide in it.

Some modifications were necessary. He'd want a tall stool to sit on so his legs wouldn't give out if he was in the locker for a long time – as he hoped to be. And the louvres on the door weren't right for seeing out. He spent a couple of hours one evening with his tool-box making small and unobtrusive but useful changes. Besides altering the louvres, he made a covered spy-hole in one side of the locker to give him a view into the shower-room. He took the shelf out, so there was room for him to sit comfortably inside.

After that it was just a question of waiting for the right occasion.

He was hiding behind his tree one evening, counting the girls back in from their jog, when one of them – a ginger-haired girl he knew was named Linda – pulled her tee-shirt up as she ran past and scratched her belly. Keith gaped at the pretty sight – an expanse of smooth creamy skin right up to her bra. His knees trembled and he had to lean on the tree while he got his breath back.

There was a girl coming the other way – jogging on her own. She waved to the Sports Coach as she passed the panting group he was leading, then went out through the gates and off down the road. Keith knew who she was – Penny Carlton, a sturdy brunette who had the biggest pair of titties in the college. Even with a bra containing them, they bounced provocatively up and down as she ran. The effect of watching them almost brought Keith to his knees.

About half an hour was the usual length of time that jogging outings lasted, he knew. He needed to take up his position in the locker after the first group were out of the showers but before Penny got back. All the cleaning gear was out of the locker and had been for days, and the stool was inside, waiting for the right moment.

Keith's big moment had come. He walked unobserved up the drive from the gate and round the main building to the gym and showers in the rear. Toby hadn't gone into the showers with the girls, of course, he'd seen them back safely and gone off on his own with a wave. *Poor devil*, Keith thought with a grin, *I bet he'd like to get under a shower with a dozen girls round him – no chance!*

And come to think of it, jogging alongside all those pretty girls and seeing their titties bounce must give the Sports Coach an enormous stand every time. Keith guessed he wore some type of strong athletic support under his shorts to keep his length tight to his belly so that it wasn't obvious to the girls.

Keith had hiding-places behind the gym; he concealed himself in one now and watched the girls come out in twos and threes. He counted them to be sure they'd all gone before he slipped in by the back door. He installed himself in his locker, sat on the stool and pulled the door shut. It was dark and cosy in there, a warm secret place. He leaned forward and put his forehead against the door by the louvres to make sure that he could see out properly. He slid aside the round metal cover he'd fixed over the spy-hole and checked that he had a clear view into the showers.

He heard Penny come in. She appeared in his field of vision breathing fast, her titties heaving. Keith himself could hardly breathe at all for the excitement that was welling up inside him. She wore a ribbon tied round her head to keep her hair in place, figure-hugging white shorts and a tee-shirt beautifully filled out by what she had inside it.

Keith watched her sit down on the long bench in the centre of the room. He had a good side view and was impressed more than ever by the size of her titties. He'd seen her in the swimming-pool, but only from a distance – it wouldn't do to be caught staring too closely at a girl student in a wet swimsuit.

That was why he'd bought the binoculars. They gave him hours and hours of pleasure viewing the girls' bodies as they dived off the high board or climbed out of the pool. But it wasn't entirely satisfactory – there was always the sense of distance, even though they looked close-up through the powerful lenses. Today, if it worked out right, he was going to see Penny naked, and from only a few feet away!

She half-turned on the bench and put one foot up on it to untie the laces of her trainers. From where Keith was watching, her position could hardly have been better; she'd turned toward him so he was looking along her raised thigh and up the leg of her shorts.

She seemed to be having trouble with the knot – it took her a long time to get it undone. All this time he was looking up her shorts to her groin. He could see the edge of little white knickers and he visualised her plump young mound. He hoped the hair round her kitty was as near-black as the hair on her head.

His twanger had been standing up hard as an iron bar ever since Penny came into the changing-room. It was so hard now in his underpants that it was almost painful. It was twitching against his belly and he put his hand flat over his flies to keep it still.

She'd got the trainer off at last. He thought she'd turn the other way and put her right foot on the bench – he'd lose that perfect view up her thigh and have her back to stare at while she got the other shoe off. Oh, well, he might get a look at her bum in the tight shorts if she bent forward to undo the lace.

As it turned out, he was wrong about what she did next – and he hugged himself in delight when she slid her bum further back on the bench and brought her right leg up alongside the left.

Her left leg was now stretched out straight along the bench, the foot in a white woolly sock, and above that a yard of well-shaped leg – shin, knee and thigh. It almost made him dizzy to ogle that expanse of bare young flesh.

The view from Keith's position was even better than before – one leg out straight and the other knee up. Her thighs were apart, letting him see her little white knickers where her legs met – his hard-on was throbbing furiously. She took the trainer off and sat with her knees up while she removed her socks. She stayed like that for a moment or two, knees up and apart, her mound outlined in the shorts, which were pulled tighter than ever by her position.

This was more than Keith had dared to hope for when he prepared his secret hideaway. He very nearly gasped when Penny raised her arms over her head and arched her back as if to stretch her muscles. A loud gasp would be fatal – without the usual girlish chattering in the room any sound that he made would be heard. He clenched his teeth to keep from sighing or moaning.

She pulled her tee-shirt over her head, her arms crossed. His mouth fell open as her titties came into sight, supported by a white sports bra. He'd been right about them – they were beautifully-shaped and really *big*.

Take it off, he was howling inside his head, *take it off girl – let me see them!*

She stood up, still facing him, and reached behind her back to undo the bra. Keith couldn't help it, he gulped when the bra came off and he saw her bare titties – they were round and heavy and oversized for a girl of seventeen. Keith was wearing only a short-sleeve white shirt and black jeans but he was very hot inside his locker. He could feel drops of sweat running down his chest. He held his breath, fearing his gulp had been heard, but all was well.

In his jeans his hard-on was jerking against his belly, even with his hand pressed over his flies to hold it still. He almost gulped again and stopped breathing altogether when Penny hooked her thumbs into the top of her little white knickers. She bent over to slide them down her legs and her plump titties dangled loosely under her, swinging from side to side, their perfect pink bobbles clearly visible.

Keith sweated and sighed – he wanted to grab two handfuls of Penny's titties and suck their bobbles till they stood firm against his tongue. As things were, he had to clamp his hand more firmly over his twanger to stop it jumping about. His other hand was pressed over his mouth to keep himself quiet; he was terrified he might moan and be heard.

Penny stood upright again, thumbs still hooked in her knickers ready to slide them down her thighs. She was looking round for something. Her titties jiggled as she turned at the hips, forcing Keith to suppress a moan. Then she found what she wanted – she went to her own open locker and took out a big pink towel.

Oh yes, Keith moaned silently in his mind, *oh yes ...*

Her thumbs were back in the waist-band of her knickers, and this time she did take them off. But going to the locker for her towel had turned her body, giving Keith a side view now. He watched her knickers sliding to her ankles, saw her step out of them and throw them on the bench. If he could think of any way of stealing them to keep as a souvenir, he would.

The profile view of her titties was magnificent, but he couldn't see her kitty. He willed her to turn to face him and let him see the black bush he knew she must have between her thighs. It didn't work – she turned away from him and marched into the shower-room. But it was almost as exciting to see the full cheeks of her bum rolling against each other in time to her steps. Feeling safer now that Penny had moved away from his hiding-place, Keith allowed himself a long, hard sigh of delight.

She turned on the shower and hot water splashed down. She stood sideways to him, and when she started to soap her heavy breasts the sight was so exciting that Keith was afraid he'd shoot off in his pants before he got a chance to see her kitty. He was breathing harshly now, and his eyes bulged from his head when she put her hand down between her thighs to lather her curls.

She turned under the gushing water – turned towards him, her hand still between her legs. But what he was panting to see was still hidden from him by a mass of thick white lather. *Let the water wash it off*, he was muttering under his breath. But her hand was still there between her parted legs, and it was sliding up and down in a dreamy way.

In his dark locker Keith almost passed out when he realised what she was doing – she was fingering herself! She'd slipped her fingers inside her kitty and was giving herself a slow rub! He tried to get a close-up view of the action through his binoculars, but it didn't work very well, pressing the glasses against the louvres.

Keith had been absolutely right about one thing – jogging with the girls gave Toby Dundale a most tremendous stand every time. He wore a very tight jockstrap under his running-shorts to keep it under control against his belly and stop it bulging too obviously. He waved goodbye to the girls at the door of the showers and jogged off to his own quarters to shower alone.

Even though he was a member of the teaching-staff, Toby wasn't allowed to live within the college grounds. He'd been put in the gatehouse with the caretaker and his wife. Fortunately it was a good-sized building, dating from Victorian days, when the caretakers typically had families of five or six children.

There was space enough for Toby to have a sitting-room and a bedroom of his own, well separated from Keith Mason and his wife Sally.

Since Toby came to Lechlade, Keith had been far too preoccupied with his observations of girls jogging and girls in the swimming-pool to notice that his wife had also discovered the curious pleasures of peeping. And while for Keith there were a hundred and sixty girls to watch furtively, his whippet-thin blonde wife had only one target – Toby Dundale.

Living under the same roof, she had good opportunities to see him in his little tennis shorts and swimming shorts – those garments which had so outraged the Principal. Sally wasn't in the least outraged, she was impressed by Toby's well-developed physique. In fact, she wanted to see more of it. She'd even devised a way of doing so – by taking him a cup of tea in bed early each morning.

She also looked after his laundry, so she knew that all he wore in bed were pyjama trousers. When she tapped at his door at seven-thirty each morning and went in with his tea, she looked closely at his broad bare chest with the golden hair on it – and even more closely at the outline of his lower body under the bed-clothes.

Men often woke up with a hard-on, she knew, and as it was summer and warm at night, Toby slept with only a sheet over him. When he sat up in bed against the pillows to take the teacup from her, he was naked down to the waist. He'd have his legs apart under the sheet and Sally was usually sure she could make out a long exciting bulge along his belly.

This morning her luck had been in – she tapped lightly on his door and went into the room to find him still asleep. She couldn't have known why, but he'd had a particularly busy evening and needed his sleep. Sally tiptoed up to the bed. He was lying on his side, one hand under the pillow. In his sleep he'd thrown the sheet off and his dangler, having escaped through the slit of his pyjama trousers, was on show for her.

She was disappointed to see that it was soft, not knowing

about the workout it had been given the previous evening. Even so, she noted that it was of a good size – it was exciting to speculate about the length and thickness it could grow to with the proper encouragement. She set the teacup with two arrowroot biscuits in the saucer down on Toby's bedside table, intending to shake his shoulder to wake him.

But her hand irresistibly slid further down and instead of shaking his shoulder she found herself running a forefinger gently along the length of his dangler, from where it was rooted at his blond-haired balls to the plump head. It stirred a little at her touch, and she did it again, fascinated – it was growing as she watched! What she wanted to do next was circle it just under the head with her finger and thumb and give it a friendly up-and-down flicking, but the opportunity passed before she grew bold enough.

Toby muttered in his sleep and moved his hand from under the pillow. Sally stepped back from the bed and smiled at him as his eyes opened and he woke up. Puzzled, he glanced at her, then at the little clock and cup of tea on his bedside table.

'Time to wake up,' she said cheerfully.

He sat up and propped himself against the pillows, not yet aware that his now-hard length was sticking out of his pyjama slit. Sally thought it a marvellous sight – he had only to say the word and she'd kneel down on the floor beside the bed and take it in her mouth. But when he realised he was exposing it he blushed and quickly pulled the sheet up to cover himself.

She thought about it all day, that long hard athletic-looking twanger of Toby's – she couldn't get it out of her mind. She was waiting for him in the afternoon when he came back from taking a dozen girls jogging. Keith was out doing a repair job, or so he'd told her. Sally waited behind the front door of the gatehouse, determined to pounce. Since Toby had been careless enough to leave his male equipment on display that morning in his bedroom, she reckoned that he owed her the use of it.

He'd trotted all the way from the shower-block and was

breathing hard when he opened the door. Sally had stripped to bra and knickers so that there'd be no misunderstanding about what she expected. And just to make sure, the instant that Toby was across the threshold she hurled herself at him, wrapping her arms around his neck and clamping her legs about his waist.

He staggered for a moment, taking her weight, then got his hands under her bum and supported her easily. She was rubbing her kitty against the hardness inside his little running-shorts. Sally was a thin woman with blonde hair fluffed out round her head, long legs, slender thighs and thin arms. Her titties were small and slack. At thirty-one her skinny body was packed with as much energy and sexual appetite as when she was twenty.

'Is that for me?' she demanded as she rubbed against his hard hidden length, 'or has one of the girls been touching you up? Have you had a hand up a pair of running shorts?'

'I've never touched a student,' Toby said quickly, 'I'd never dream of doing such a thing!'

He wasn't telling the truth, not by a long shot.

'Where's your husband?' he asked, sounding slightly anxious. If Keith showed up it would be tricky to explain why he was feeling Sally's bum and she was rubbing her belly against him.

'He's out,' she said. 'He'll be busy for a long time.'

Toby carried her, straddled round his waist, into her sitting-room, his fingers busy under her bum, feeling her warm kitty through the thin material of her knickers. She slid down his body and thighs till she was on her knees at his feet, her hands scrabbling to get his shorts off, then his tight black jockstrap. In seconds she had his hard-on in her mouth and was sucking hard.

Until this minute Toby had never given a thought to having Sally Mason – there were too many young girls urgently seeking his attentions for him to consider a married woman in her thirties. But here she was, demanding it from him, and he was never a man to say no. He slipped his wet length out of her mouth, lifted her up and turned her round. He steered her across the room and draped her over the arm of the sofa, face-down.

'Do me,' she was moaning, 'do me hard . . .'

He dragged her knickers over her bum and down her legs. He could see that she'd been sunbathing in the garden behind the gatehouse because her thighs were golden-brown while the cheeks of her bum were white. He pressed his hands over the soft cheeks and squeezed them, then moved in close to her and guided his hard length into her chuffie from behind. She was a blonde on the head but a brunette between the legs, he saw.

One long push took him into her slippery depths. He undid her bra and gripped her slack little titties while he pumped in and out forcefully.

'I'm going to come,' she moaned almost immediately – she was overwhelmed by his brisk no-nonsense approach. She'd always thought it would be good with Toby but she never expected it to be this good.

I want it like this every day, she said to herself, her belly shaking in the run-up to orgasm. *I want him to give me a fast hard jiggle when he comes in from his jogging with a hard-on from being near those girls. And I want a quickie in the morning when I wake him with his tea – I'll have my knickers off when I go into his room, I'll give him a fast rub-up and straddle him on the bed and do him in thirty seconds flat!*

Meanwhile, Keith in his dark hot locker was so excited he was panting. His legs were twitching out of control and his length had grown so big and hard it was painful in his tight black jeans. He'd had to unbuckle his belt and run his zip down to take the pressure off – his standing dick was jerking convulsively inside his jockey-shorts.

The sight of Penny playing with herself under the shower had done this to him. He'd never been so excited in his whole life as he became while watching her hand moving between her strong thighs. Keith wished he was Toby Dundale – he was certain the Sports Coach had excellent chances of getting girls to drop their knickers for him.

If I was him and could persuade Penny to let me, I'd lay her down on the bench stark naked and lick her kitty till I made her come, Keith told himself feverishly.

She'd turned the water off and was coming back to the changing-room with the big pink towel wrapped round her. She'd put it round her waist, leaving her plump titties still exposed. Keith stared at them as if mesmerised while she walked toward his locker. She was going to finish drying herself – she'd have to take the towel off to do that, so he was going to see her kitty at last!

And he was going to see it close-up! She was standing only a few feet away from his locker door, facing him, giving him such a perfect view of her titties that his heart almost stopped beating. Their tips were big and they were an exciting shade of russet-pink. Keith was nearly drooling as he imagined getting one of them into his mouth.

His hard-on was straining upward so fiercely that he couldn't bear the tightness of his jockey-shorts any longer – he pushed them down inside his open jeans and let it stand free. His sweating face was pressed to the metal door, his eye against the louvre, as he watched Penny start to take the pink towel from her waist. This was it!

But it wasn't what he expected. Just as the towel fell away and Penny's glossy dark bush was uncovered, the locker door was jerked open fast. There stood the tall girl with the long blonde pony-tail – what was her name? Keith had got so carried away watching Penny that he hadn't heard her accomplice edging up to the locker on his blind side.

It all happened with bewildering speed. The door flew open to reveal Keith, his jeans unzipped and his underwear down, at the very moment his leaping twanger shot its cream. He sat on his high stool, his mouth hanging open and his body shaking, caught in the throes of coming.

The two girls were laughing at him. They'd set him up and

now they had a story to tell that was even better than Hilary Landor's tale of the boyfriend who shot his lot running for a bus. By mid-morning tomorrow the story of how Keith the caretaker had been caught would be all over the college.

Every girl in the place would giggle when she saw him going about his daily duties. They'd whisper to each other and stare at him. Through a mist of shame and confusion Keith heard what Nesta Wade – he remembered her name now – was saying to him.

'If you try this again I'll have my instant camera with me,' she said. 'I'll get shots of you in the locker with your *thing* sticking out.'

'He hasn't got much to boast about,' Penny observed, wrapping her pink towel round her waist again. 'I thought they were all at least six inches long – it shows you how wrong you can be.'

Keith covered his shrinking length with both hands to hide it from the scornful look in their eyes.

Chapter Seven

There were no classes on Saturday but it rained after lunch, which made outdoor activities impossible. Some of the girls went to the common room for a chat; some stayed in their rooms and got on with their studies. Hilary and Marjorie stayed in the room they shared, doing more gossiping than reading, or so it seemed to Orline Ashby when she dropped in to see them.

At least, she assumed they were gossiping. True, they were sprawled on Hilary's bed, but they were both fully dressed in blouse and skirt and they didn't seem flustered or flushed when Orline knocked and came in without waiting to be asked.

'Have you heard about the trick Penny and Nesta played on that creepy caretaker?' Orline asked breathlessly.

'Heard it at breakfast,' Hilary said. 'What a laugh – they caught him with his jeans down, shooting off in his hand. I'm going to see if I can trick Roddy Brent like that in the holidays.'

'He's forever lurking about the swimming-pool and the gym, Keith the caretaker, I mean,' Marjorie said with her lips pursed in disapproval. 'He's always trying to see up your skirt. It serves him right, being made a fool of.'

'I don't understand why he does it,' Orline said, her pretty face looking bewildered. She sat down on the bed as Hilary and Marjorie moved apart to make room for her.

'I mean, he must be nearly forty,' Orline went on. 'Surely he's more or less past it by now.'

'Don't you believe it,' said Marjorie, 'they go on till they're quite old – I read in the Sunday paper about a vicar of sixty interfering with a young girl in the vestry. That was besides doing married women when he went visiting his parishioners.'

'The caretaker's got a wife of his own to play with,' Orline objected, 'so why is he so keen on spying on us? Do you think Mrs Mason won't let him do it to her?'

'Men are like that,' Hilary told her. 'They want to get their fingers into every kitty in the world – one's never enough for them. They'll stick their thing up anyone who'll let them, and ten minutes later they'll go chasing after someone else.'

'Just listen to Miss Experience,' said Marjorie, mocking her. 'Have you had so many boyfriends that you're an expert? The one who came in his underwear after he groped you – does he have a feel of other girls when you're here at college and he's at home?'

'I'm certain he does,' Hilary said. 'There's a girl whose father owns a garage not far from where Roddy lives – I've seen the way he looks at her, you can't tell *me* he hasn't had her knickers down.'

'And he's still your boyfriend?' Orline asked, even more puzzled now.

'Why not?' Hilary shrugged. 'He's fun to go out with. And I like to play tricks on him when he gets excited and his thing stands up.'

'You know,' Marjorie observed, 'Keith's wife must be nearly forty, like him. That's middle-aged! And she hasn't got much in the way of titties. That's why he was hiding in the showers to get a look at Penny's – hers are fantastic.'

'Oh yes,' Hilary agreed instantly, 'big and bouncy – I've sucked them and so have you, so we know.'

'I haven't,' Orline said, sounding disappointed. 'She's never shown any interest in me. But the caretaker saw me naked once.'

'He didn't!' Hilary exclaimed. 'When was that?'

'I was putting my nightie on to go to bed when I looked up

and saw a shadow outside the window. I didn't scream – I went to the window just as I was, stark naked – I was to going to stick my fingers in his eyes, the way they teach us for rapists. But he'd gone by the time I got the window open. It was Keith Mason, though – I saw him run away across the lawn. It was dark, but not too dark to recognise him.'

'You didn't bother to report him?' Marjorie asked.

'There'd be too much fuss – I couldn't honestly say I'd seen his face, and he'd be sure to say it wasn't him.'

'If you'd seen something else instead of his face, that would be proof it was him spying on you,' Marjorie said with a grin.

'Do you think he had his thing out while he was gawping at me?' Orline asked, sounding amazed.

'Bound to,' Marjorie said cheerfully. 'They all do, peeping Toms and flashers. If you hadn't spotted him he'd have stood watching you undress and playing with himself until he shot his cream up the wall.'

'I wonder how many of us he's drooled over while we've been undressing for bed,' Hilary said.

'He hasn't seen you or me naked,' said Marjorie, 'because I always draw the curtains at bedtime. You ought to do the same, Orline.'

'No need to, now he's had his lesson,' Orline said. 'He won't try that again, after Penny and Nesta caught him at it.'

'Don't be so innocent,' Hilary said. 'He won't hide in the showers again, but I'll bet anything you like he'll think of other ways of getting a look at us stripped off – you can't change men's nature.'

'Beasts, all of them,' Marjorie added solemnly. 'It's that long thick thing they've got between their legs – when it stands up stiff they turn into wild beasts.'

'There's something I've been meaning to ask you, Orline,' Hilary said, dismissing the question of men's things. 'You told us that you saw Linda in the gym with Miss Redruth.'

Orline nodded, pleased to be the centre of attention.

'That's right. But I made sure they didn't see me.'

'You were in the little office that Mr Dundale uses, you said.'

Orline nodded again.

'I saw everything through the glass panel in the door. Linda and Miss Redruth were only about fifteen feet away.'

'What were you doing in Mr Dundale's office in the first place?' Hilary demanded. 'That's what we want to know.'

The three of them were sitting on the bed, Orline in the middle. She caught a note in Hilary's voice that made her feel at risk, and the feeling was reinforced when she saw Hilary and Marjorie give each other a look of complicity. She tried to stand up and move away from the bed.

Before Orline could make her escape, Hilary pushed a hand under her skirt and gripped her thigh, so tightly that her fingers dug into the soft flesh and made Orline gasp. Marjorie, a smile on her face, put her hands on Orline's shoulders and pushed her down on her back.

'I didn't come here to be diddled, not in the daytime,' Orline protested, trying to stay calm.

'You should be so lucky,' Marjorie said. 'You're going to be tortured, not diddled.'

'We'll have the truth out of you,' Hilary added in a stern voice.

Marjorie held Orline down firmly on the bed while Hilary stripped her naked below the waist. Off came her skirt and her stockings, and then her knickers were dragged down her legs. Orline struggled and pleaded, but she was no match for the two of them.

When Hilary had her naked from the belly-button down, she lay across Orline's legs to keep her still while Marjorie finished the job. With an evil grin on her face she unbuttoned Orline's blouse and pulled it off, and then her bra, leaving Orline completely naked. Hilary and Marjorie both held her while they grinned down at her slim thighs, pointed titties and light-brunette chuffie. Hilary started pinching the lips and making her twitch. It wasn't exactly painful yet, but it could become so if Hilary pinched harder. It could also become very exciting, if Hilary turned her grip into a stroking movement of finger and thumb.

'You'd better tell us everything,' Marjorie said menacingly. She held one of Orline's pink bobbles between her finger-tip and thumb, stretching it upwards – and that too could become unpleasant. Or the opposite, if Marjorie wanted it to.

'I don't know what you mean,' Orline gasped. 'Stop it, please.'

'We'll stop the minute you tell us what you were doing in the office,' Hilary told her. 'Who else was there with you?'

'Nobody – I hid when I heard Miss Redruth and Linda come into the gym. I guessed they were going to play with each other and I wanted to see them do it.'

'Why you were in the gym alone in the first place?' Marjorie demanded. Now she was gripping both of Orline's little bobbles, squeezing them hard enough to make her gasp.

'Turn her over,' said Hilary. 'We'll smack her bum till she tells us what we want to know.'

Between them, in spite of her struggles, they rolled her over face-down on the bed. Marjorie sat across Orline's legs, her weight pinning them to the bed, while Hilary sat astride the girl's back. They had her quite helpless.

Orline's bare bum was a pretty sight. Marjorie felt the small, round, smooth-skinned cheeks with both hands and giggled, then trailed her fingers down the neat crease between the cheeks.

'If you ask me, it's going to be hot work, torturing Orline till she tells us everything,' she said. 'I think I'll strip off for it.'

She was out of her blouse and bra in seconds, her plump round titties bare for Hilary's appreciative stare. In another minute Hilary took her clothes off too – all of them – keeping Orline under control with a knee on the back while she got out of her skirt and knickers.

'Now we're ready,' Hilary announced briskly, raising her hand.

Marjorie giggled again as Hilary's hand swept down and slapped Orline's bum – first one cheek, then the other. Orline wriggled and twitched and moaned into the pillow her face was pressed against.

'Let's get some rhythm into it,' Marjorie suggested. 'You smack that cheek and I'll smack this one.'

Orline squealed as two hands slapped her bum alternately, Marjorie and Hilary, left, right, left, right, left, right. But they weren't smacking too hard because that would have hurt their hands as much as her bum, and after ten or a dozen slaps Hilary decided that the smacking wasn't achieving much. Marjorie agreed.

'From the way she's wriggling her bum and trying to get her legs open, it looks as if she's enjoying it,' she said, her eyebrows raised in disapproval. 'I bet she'd be wet between the legs if I pushed my finger into her.'

'Try it and see,' Hilary said.

Marjorie forced her hand between Orline's tightly clamped thighs and slid a finger into her.

'Wet and slippy,' she said. 'She'll come if we keep on smacking her.'

'Will she indeed!' Hilary exclaimed. 'We'll see about that. Turn her over on her back and we'll soon have her screaming.'

'No, no more!' Orline protested weakly. 'Please don't do me ...'

But they rolled her over on her back in spite of her pleading and in another second they were lying full-length beside her. She was on her side, trapped tightly between them. Hilary slid down the bed and Orline squealed as her top leg was forced up and hooked over Hilary's shoulder. Her brown-haired little kitty was fully exposed for whatever they were going to do to it.

She squealed again when they both slid a finger into her. The lips of her chuffie were stretched open and two fingertips tickled her button. She was scared and excited at the same time. Behind her she could feel Marjorie scrabbling one-handed out of the rest of her clothes, to be as naked as Hilary and herself.

It was a complicated manoeuvre because Marjorie never stopped tickling Orline's little button along with Hilary. But eventually Orline felt a warm belly pressing against her bum, which was still glowing a little from being smacked. And Marjorie's plump thighs were pressing close.

'She's nearly coming,' Marjorie said, very matter-of-fact. 'You can tell from the way she's shaking.'

Hilary's titties were pressed against Orline's warm belly and her head was against her victim's titties – she was nibbling Orline's firm little bobbles. 'Mmm,' she said, then stopped for a moment to answer Marjorie.

'You're right – I can feel her belly trembling against me,' she said. 'Two more seconds and she'll come.'

'Know what I think?' Marjorie said. 'I think she's actually coming at this very moment, but she's keeping quiet about it so we don't catch on.'

'No, she moans and squeals when she comes,' Hilary objected, while her fingertip slid back and forth beside Marjorie's on Orline's wet little button.

'Yes, she *is* coming,' Marjorie insisted, 'I'm sure she is – her bum's jerking against my belly, and she's incredibly wet inside! She's coming and coming and she can't stop.'

At that moment Orline really did come – her body bucked and she shrieked. Hilary sank her teeth into the soft flesh of a tittie, though in her ecstasy Orline didn't even feel the bite.

'Ah, ah, ah . . .' Orline was moaning. 'What are you doing to me?'

Hilary raised her head from Orline's titties and grinned over her at Marjorie, who grinned back.

'I told you she wasn't coming,' Hilary said. 'She always makes a noise like that when she does.'

'She was coming all the time,' Marjorie argued back. 'That

was just the end of it, the last second or two. She's been coming sneakily ever since we started to smack her.'

Their fingers remained inside Orline, stretching her chuffie open, but not moving.

'Orline – the truth now,' said Hilary. 'Who's right, Marjorie or me? Were you coming all that time?'

'No,' Orline said faintly.

'Can we believe her?' Marjorie asked. 'If she tells lies about being alone in the coach's office, she's just as likely to tell lies about this.'

'We can soon find out,' Hilary declared. 'We'll do her again and see if we can tell when her climax comes on. If you're right, it will start almost as soon as we stroke her.'

The two fingertips started touching Orline's button again.

'No, don't!' she gasped. 'I'll tell you what you want to know.'

'Go on, then, tell us,' Marjorie urged.

The fingers continued to tease inside Orline, making her twitch.

'Only if you stop that,' she said desperately.

'All right, then,' Hilary agreed, 'but if we think you're telling us a lie, you'll be diddled stupid.'

They let go of her and with relief she unhooked her leg from Hilary's shoulder and stretched it down straight, her thighs close together.

'The reason I went into the office in the gym . . .' she began, but left the sentence unfinished.

'Get on with it,' Hilary said sharply, prodding a finger into Orline's belly. 'Otherwise you'll be on your back with four fingers up you.'

'If you must know,' Orline said, 'Mr Dundale took me into the office.'

'I knew it!' said Marjorie triumphantly.

'What did I tell you!' said Hilary at the same instant.

'You know we don't tell tales about what teachers do,' Orline went on, by way of excusing herself for keeping silent.

'You needn't think you can get away with that,' Hilary told her. 'For one thing, he's not really a teacher, he's the Sports Coach. And he's a man, which makes all the difference.'

'Exactly,' Marjorie agreed, her hand gliding over Orline's belly. 'The rules don't apply to him. So what did he do to you in his office?'

'Did he undress you?' Hilary asked. 'Were you wearing your sports gear?'

'Just an ordinary blouse and skirt,' Orline said. 'He sat on the chair behind the desk and made me sit on his lap. He unbuttoned my blouse and played with my titties – he got me to undo my bra for him.'

Hilary ran her palm over Orline's pointed little titties.

'So these have been groped by a man, have they?' she asked.

'So have yours,' Orline retorted, bolder now. 'You've told everybody how you let a boy feel you in the cinema last vacation. And I don't suppose that was the first time.'

'She's right,' Marjorie said. 'Stop interrupting her and let's hear what Mr Dundale did.'

'He told me to open my legs,' Orline said, 'and he put his hand right up my skirt. It was ever so thrilling.'

'Did it feel different?' Marjorie asked. 'I mean, when a man puts his hand up your leg and touches you, is there much difference? Say you had your eyes closed, could you tell it was a man fingering you and not me, say, or Hilary? What I mean is . . .'

'Shut up – you're confusing her,' Hilary interrupted, 'and me too. Let her tell it her own way – you can ask questions later.'

'Do you want me to go on or not?' Orline asked.

'Yes,' they both answered at once.

'Toby put his hand inside my knickers . . .'

'Toby?' Hilary and Marjorie squealed together.

'He said to call him Toby when we were alone,' Orline said

with pride in her voice. 'He told me I'm very pretty and very sexy – what do you think of that!'

'Pooh – a man will say anything to get his hand up between your legs,' said Marjorie, as if she knew all about it. 'Isn't that so, Hilary?'

'Certainly is,' Hilary agreed. 'They always tell me how pretty I am, but that's because I really am. And I'm sexy too. Why do you think Roddy Brent came in his trousers after we'd been to the cinema?'

'You're the one interrupting now,' Marjorie complained, 'We've heard about Roddy Brent before – what we want to know is whether Toby Dundale came in his shorts.'

'Did he?' Hilary demanded of Orline.

'I think so,' she said.

'What do you mean, *think* so? It's pretty obvious when they do,' said Hilary, 'or haven't you ever seen a male do it?'

'Well . . .' Orline said doubtfully.

'Go back to where you left off,' Marjorie instructed her. 'You were on his lap and he had his hand inside your knickers. He gave you a good feel.'

'Oh yes, it was thrilling. He knew just the right spot. He must have had a lot of experience to touch the right place straight away.'

Orline had turned to lie on her back. On the single bed Marjorie and Hilary pressed close on either side of her, to avoid slipping over the edge onto the floor. They were facing each other across Orline's small soft titties. Both girls kept a hand lying loosely over their friend's downy little triangle of curls.

They were staring into each other's eyes, Hilary's pale blue eyes and Marjorie's dark brown ones locked in a long look of admiration for each other. They seemed to have forgotten Orline and her tale.

'I'd like to do you,' Marjorie said to Hilary over Orline's titties.

'And I'd like you to do me,' Hilary said.

'Several times,' said Marjorie.

'As many times as you like,' said Hilary.

'Don't you want to hear the rest of what happened?' Orline asked with a plaintive note in her voice. 'First you torture me to make me talk and then you can't be bothered to listen!'

'She's right,' Hilary acknowledged. 'We ought to hear all of it. One day it could be useful to have something on dear Toby that we can threaten him with.'

'Tell us the rest of it, Orline,' Marjorie ordered.

'He made me come ever so easily,' said Orline. 'Sometimes I take the longest time, but with Toby it was only a minute or two.'

'He's good at it, is he?' Hilary asked.

'His stiff thing was pressed against my hip right through his shorts,' Orline sighed, not answering the question. 'It was long and very hard, and I wanted to hold it.'

'Did he get it out?' Hilary breathed, staring fondly into Marjorie's brown eyes and pouting her lips as if to send her a kiss.

'I'd just come,' Orline said, 'I felt lovely and I was wondering what he was going to do to me next – and just then we heard footsteps outside in the gym. I nearly went into total panic, but Toby was strong and calm. He pulled me down on the floor behind the desk and whispered to me to stay still and listen.'

'Miss Redruth and Linda walking across the floor,' Hilary suggested.

'We didn't know who it was then. We sat there under the desk and Toby took my hand and pushed it down the front of his shorts – I had his thing in my hand and it felt very nice.'

'Is it a big one?' Marjorie demanded.

'Enormous...'

'Did you make him come in his shorts?' Hilary asked.

'No, we were worried about who was in the gym and if they'd come into the office. When it went quiet again outside Toby took my hand off his thing and we crawled across to the door. We knelt so we could just see over the bottom edge of the glass panel.'

'It gets better each time she tells us about it,' Marjorie said.

'Linda was sitting on a vaulting-horse,' Orline went on. 'Miss Redruth was standing in front of her. I couldn't see what they were doing, but Toby had a bit better view and he whispered that Miss Redruth had taken Linda's knickers off and was feeling her.'

'Ginger Linda,' Marjorie said with a chuckle, 'the brightest-coloured chuffie at Lechlade. Did Toby Dundale get a look at it?'

'I don't think so – I know I couldn't, because Miss Redruth was in the way with her hands up Linda's clothes. Then she pulled Linda down off the vaulting-horse and turned round and leaned against it herself while Linda got down on her knees in front of her. She undid her belt and dropped her skirt – Miss Redruth, I mean – and she didn't have any knickers on. That really got Toby going.'

'Wait a minute,' Hilary said. 'How could you both be kneeling looking through the glass panel? It's not big enough, as I remember it.'

'I was looking with one eye over the bottom edge of it,' Orline explained. 'Toby was kneeling behind me, close up, looking over my head. He had his arms round me and he was feeling my titties all the time – I still had my blouse open and my bra undone. He was giving me such a thrill that I knew he could do anything he liked to me – I simply couldn't say no to him.'

'Oh dear!' Marjorie groaned. 'Don't tell us you let him stick his *thing* up you and do you with it!'

'If you'd listen more and interrupt less you'd learn some-thing,' Orline said tartly. 'Linda was tonguing Miss Redruth, and Toby was close behind me pressing tight. He was rubbing himself against my bum, that's why I said that watching Linda really got him going.'

'Did he get his thing out?' Marjorie asked.

'Well, his flies were open and he was breathing hard against my ear,' Orline said, 'but he wears a funny little pouch sort of thing under his shorts to stop his thing flopping about on the tennis court, and he still had that on.'

'That's called a jockstrap,' Marjorie informed her.

'He was rubbing his thing on my bum through it and I could feel his body shaking against me. When Miss Redruth put her hands on Linda's shoulders and started shaking all over, he gave a groan and squeezed my titties hard and jerked against my bum – I think he came just then.'

'Did your knickers go wet where he was rubbing?' Hilary asked.

'He'd pulled them down to my knees,' Orline confessed. 'He was rubbing himself against my bare bum. But it felt wet when he started moaning and shaking.'

'He came in his jockstrap,' said Marjorie. 'You knew that all along and pretended you didn't.'

'You haven't been telling the truth at all, have you?' Hilary accused her. 'First you claim you were on your own in the gym, when all the time you were being fingered by Toby Dundale. Then you said you couldn't tell if he came – even though you actually felt him squirting on your bum.'

'Lies, lies, lies,' Marjorie said. 'I thought we were good friends, Orline, but friends don't tell lies to each other.'

'You've offended us both, Orline,' said Hilary.

'I'm sorry, truly I am – don't hold it against me.'

'You'll have to pay a forfeit,' Marjorie told her, 'or we shan't talk to you again.'

'What kind of forfeit?' Orline asked nervously.

Marjorie and Hilary grinned at each other across her naked body, then Hilary winked at Marjorie.

'We'll sandwich her,' Hilary announced.

'What do you mean?' Orline wasn't sure she liked the sound of that.

'You'll soon find out,' Marjorie informed her.

On Hilary's narrow bed they arranged Orline on her side

between them. This time Marjorie was pressed tight to Orline's front and Hilary to her back. Orline gasped in amazement as they went to work on her. They rubbed their titties and bellies and their wet little chuffies against her bare body, while at the same time their hands explored every part of her, stroking and squeezing, leaving nothing untouched. Her little pink bobbles and under her arms, between her legs and over her belly, round her bum and between the cheeks – all these places were attended to.

Common sense told Orline that there were only four hands stroking her, only four titties and two warm, hairy chuffies sliding over her, but it felt as if she were being touched on every part of her body at the same time – it was as if twenty hands and twenty titties and ten kitties were rubbing against her. She came very quickly – the long shuddering thrills jerked her body about on the bed like a puppet on strings.

'Got her – she's coming!' Marjorie gasped.

Now they had her climaxing they wouldn't let her stop. Their hot bodies kept on rubbing against Orline as she trembled and moaned – there was a soft tittie in her mouth and fingers in her kitty, wet tongues probing her belly-button and wet lips moving over her little pink bobbles, over her belly . . . she was too far gone to be able to tell whether mouths or open chuffies were rubbing her.

'Ah, ah, aah!' she sang out, her body wracked from top to bottom and side to side by the strength of the sensations that shook her.

'More, more!' Hilary breathed, fingers plucking at Orline's button.

'Yes, more . . .' Marjorie sighed as her wet kitty rubbed along Orline's thigh, while her plump round titties squashed themselves against her victim's face.

They kept Orline coming and coming until her nervous system refused to take the overload of sensation any longer and she passed out with a long sighing moan.

When she came to she was alone on the bed. The summer

rain was still pattering on the window and they'd put the bedspread over her so she wouldn't get cold. She was lying on her back, her legs apart and her chuffie still warm and slippery. As her senses returned fully she realised that she felt very contented. If that's what paying a forfeit meant she'd volunteer for it any time – she'd been well and truly done.

She soon became aware of little sighs and gasps from the other bed. She lay and listened, trying to decide whether it was Hilary or Marjorie making the sounds of delight. She remembered Marjorie saying that she wanted to make Hilary come – and Hilary agreeing readily to be done. So it should be Hilary moaning.

But Orline couldn't guess how long she'd been passed out. Maybe Hilary had been diddled and was now doing Marjorie, in which case it would be Marjorie who was sighing and sobbing. Orline turned on her side to face the other bed across the room. Hilary and Marjorie were lying facing each other, head to foot, their faces between each other's thighs in a 'sixty-nine' position.

They were tonguing each other and sighing at the same time, their bare bodies shaking. *Oh yes*, Orline murmured to herself, *oh yes, yes . . .*

Watching them closely, she pulled her knees up and slipped a hand down between her thighs. Her chuffie was still wet – her wispy brunette curls clung to her skin stickily. She'd never come so hard in her life before. Her fingers slid between the open lips and found her little nubby, but there was no quick thrill of pleasure this time.

I've been done to death, Orline thought in astonishment – and dismay. But her excitement was soon building again from hearing and seeing the other two girls diddling each other enthusiastically. She heard a long moan from Marjorie and saw her plump bare bottom jerking and bouncing as she climaxed in response to Hilary's tonguing.

A second later there was a shrill squeal from Hilary herself as the big thrill took her as well.

I want to come too, Orline muttered desperately, her fingers rubbing over her nubby to no avail, *I've got to come one more time…*

She stared wide-eyed as Hilary's and Marjorie's bodies shook against each other. After a while they calmed down and pulled their heads from between each other's thighs. They whispered to each other and giggled. Orline jumped up and padded barefoot across the room to climb into the bed with them.

Chapter Eight

As if to make up for the showers that had kept everyone indoors for most of the day before, Sunday turned out to be a perfect summer day. After lunch Joy Locksley sat in the flower garden on one of the long wooden benches, reading a book. At weekends teaching staff and students could wear informal clothes; Joy was wearing cream shorts and a pale blue top with the college coat of arms printed on the front.

The book she had taken from the college library turned out not to be particularly interesting. She was pleased to see Eleanor Redruth stroll into the garden and wave to her. She waved back and waited for Eleanor to join her on the bench. Eleanor always knew the latest college gossip, and was more than happy to pass it on. Telling all the teachers about the fight in the gym between Penny Carlton and Nesta Wade had kept Eleanor happy and busy for days.

As for the story of caretaker Keith being unmasked in the locker-room spying on naked girls with his sticky twanger in his hand, Eleanor revelled in it and told it with gusto.

'There the wretched man was – trapped in a locker with his binoculars hanging round his neck, his flies undone and his ugly long *thing* shooting off at the very moment they pulled the door open,' she said. 'He was squirting in his hand while they watched – can you believe it!'

'I've never trusted that man,' said Joy. 'He has a shifty look about him. There was a face at my bedroom window a few weeks ago, when I was lying on the bed resting without any clothes on. It must have been him, though at the time I thought it was one of the girls spying on me.'

'It might well have been him,' Eleanor agreed. 'We know now what he's been up to. As a matter of interest, who was with you at the time?'

'I was alone,' Joy said, 'it was the middle of the afternoon and hot so I lay down for half an hour to rest.'

'Naked?'

'I told you, it was a hot day. I saw a pinkish blur at the window and grabbed my knickers to cover myself up. But he must have seen what he wanted.'

'If you were lying on the bed without knickers on he had a good look at your kitty,' said Eleanor with a grin. 'I suppose he had his thing out and stiff in his hand at the time – how long do you suppose he was watching you before you noticed him?'

'That's a problem,' Joy said, her cheeks turning pink. 'I'd shut my eyes, so he could have been standing there looking at me for ten or fifteen minutes.'

'In that case, he certainly got what he wanted,' Eleanor said with a broad smile. 'He went off home with sticky underwear, you can bet.'

'You think he did himself...' Joy said in shocked tones.

'Resign yourself to the thought,' Eleanor chuckled. 'Your body has been raped and defiled in Keith's imagination – he's shot his little lot all over your titties in his thoughts.'

'Oh, my god...' Joy exclaimed in dismay.

'You said you lay down for a rest in the afternoon and took your knickers off – not a very likely story. The truth is you were playing with yourself, weren't you?'

'None of your business what I was doing,' Joy said. 'I don't expect to be spied on by shifty caretakers, whatever I do in private. I'm sure it *was* him now I think about it – have Penny and Nesta reported him to the Principal to be got rid of?'

'I doubt it,' Eleanor told her. 'Now that the senior girls have got the better of him, I think they've talked it over and decided they can have more fun humiliating him if he stays.'

'That's very wrong of them,' Joy said immediately. 'There's no telling what mischief could result from it.'

'Exactly what I say,' Eleanor agreed happily, 'but I'm looking forward to as much mischief as they can devise. I can't wait for them to pull their first stunt with Keith as their hapless victim – it will be something atrociously perverse, I hope.'

'You know more than you're telling,' Joy accused her. 'I truly believe you encourage the girls in their waywardness.'

'I do,' Eleanor chortled. 'They look to me for guidance.'

Joy decided it would be better if she didn't know what the girls were planning by way of humiliation for the unlucky caretaker. She was indifferent to men as a group and didn't care what happened to this one. As far as she was concerned the girls could gang up on him and strip him in the courtyard and pour bright blue paint over his thing. But as a Head of House she preferred not to know officially what they were up to.

She was more interested, anyway, in hearing about the hand-to-hand fight between Penny and Nesta than the exposure of Keith the caretaker. Like everyone else at Lechlade, except the Principal, Joy had heard whispers and was keen to know whatever details Eleanor could fill in. Eleanor had inside information now that she'd interrogated ginger-haired Linda.

'The way I hear it,' Eleanor said, 'Nesta ripped the underwear from Penny's body, whereupon Penny knocked her down and sat on her face. They say she gave Penny a tonguing from below and made her come in front of them all.'

She related events in the gym as vividly as if she'd been there to see them – but whereas Eleanor took it all as a joke, Joy felt that she had to be disapproving.

'What a way for intelligent girls to behave!' she said. 'I can't

111

see why they felt it necessary to resort to brutality to settle a quarrel. As teachers we are supposed to implant in them a balanced and civilised outlook. It seems to me that we are not succeeding very well.'

'Absolute rubbish,' Eleanor said briskly. 'Intelligence has nothing to do with it when we're talking about sex. And those girls can be as civilised as you like, but when it comes down to a question like which one has Linda for her personal plaything, it's every girl for herself.'

'I find that appalling,' Joy said sniffily.

Eleanor gave her a wicked grin. 'Strangely enough,' she said, 'I heard it rumoured that you take a private interest in a certain girl in your house. What if that interest was threatened by someone else – wouldn't you react strongly?'

'I don't know what you're talking about,' Joy said untruthfully.

'A fair-haired girl in Wexby House named Annabel Darwen, that's what. She is very pretty,' Eleanor said with a knowing smile. 'They call her Anybody's – but you know that already.'

'What do you mean?' Joy demanded, her face pink again.

'We were talking about nicknames one evening recently – your friend Sharon was there at the time. I told you about the girl in Sawby House – the one whose friends call her Monkey because of the thick black bush between her legs.'

'You say so many outrageous things that I can't remember all of them,' said Joy, looking away.

'You remember all right,' Eleanor said with a chuckle. 'You asked me if I'd had a feel of Monkey's chuffie.'

'I certainly did not. It was Sharon who asked you.'

'There you are – you do remember,' Eleanor said in triumph.

'It came back to me,' Joy mumbled, slightly shame-faced. She was not prepared to admit doing anything a Head of House ought not to do. Even though she played with Annabel every day, she was still of the firm opinion that Heads of Houses should not have sexual dealings with students. This made her position inconsistent, and that in turn made her uncomfortable.

Eleanor was watching her closely and understood why she was blushing. She decided it would be entertaining to make dear Joy feel even more uncomfortable. It was very easy to do.

'You ought to find some reason to get Monkey on her own and have her knickers off,' she said slyly. 'Believe me, she has such a wonderfully thick bush you have to comb through it with your fingers and make a parting before you can stick your tongue up her.'

'Eleanor, what you are suggesting is perfectly disgraceful,' said Joy, getting a grip on herself and trying to turn the conversation away from the dangerous subject of tonguing girl students. 'I'm certain you make these stories up to shock the rest of us.'

'Nonsense,' Eleanor retorted. 'Every word I say is the plain truth. And if you doubt that, just slip into the showers sometime when the Sawby House girls are there and have a good look at Monkey. She's only sixteen and a few months and she has the sexiest black bush I've ever seen on a girl. Once you've seen it you'll be dying to get your hands on it.'

'I shall do no such thing,' Joy said firmly.

'I know you won't. And why you won't. You are too occupied with Anybody's to be interested in another girl. If you want my advice you'll extricate yourself from too close a friendship with her before it leads to trouble. Take it from me – the nicest way to loosen the link is to start dabbling with other girls.'

'What makes you think I need advice?' Joy asked. 'What do you imagine is going on?'

Eleanor smiled and turned on the wooden bench to put her hand on Joy's bare knee.

'Let me tell you something,' she said in a friendly manner. 'I've been teaching here at Lechlade for five years. In that time I've touched up dozens of girls. Maybe hundreds, I never bothered to keep count. You've been here as long as I have, but this is the first time you've had a girl's legs apart. Don't make a fool of yourself over it.'

'What makes you think I might do that?' Joy demanded.

'Girls talk. This place is full of whispers. Everybody knows you have Annabel day after day. Well, everybody but the Principal – nobody tells her anything.'

'Annabel talks about it?' Joy exclaimed in horror. 'Surely not – that would be a dreadful breach of confidence.'

'Why do you think she's called Anybody's?'

'You've had her – she's talked to you,' Joy accused Eleanor.

'No, I haven't, not yet. She's on my list and I'll get round to her before the end of term, I hope.'

'I was right before.' Joy sounded annoyed. '"Anybody's" is a better nickname for you than any of the girls. Take your hand off my thigh, please.'

Eleanor chuckled. Instead of removing her hand, she stroked up the inside of Joy's thigh, over her shorts.

'No need to go coy,' she said, 'you're too old for me, Joy. Sixteen to seventeen is what really gets me going. When they have their eighteenth birthday I start to lose interest. Your little playmate Anybody's is a month short of seventeen, but I expect you knew that already.'

'Look here,' sad Joy, anxious to end the conversation. 'You can think what you like, I don't care. Annabel is a special sort of girl and I've made friends with her. It doesn't matter to me what other friends she has, so long as we preserve our friendship.'

That made Eleanor grin.

'What you're telling me,' she said, 'is that you don't mind who else she opens her legs for just so long as you get your share – is that right?'

'That's very crude,' Joy rebuked her.

'I'm a crude sort of person,' Eleanor grinned. 'Maybe it's because I've had my hand up so many young girls' skirts. All I ever think about is feeling a warm sweet young kitty – I dream of it constantly. These high-minded and civilised ideas about special friendships never enter my head.'

Joy knew she was being laughed at, but she didn't know how to retaliate.

'I've said all I have to say,' Eleanor said, and she took her hand off Joy's thigh. 'You can take my advice or ignore it, it's up to you. I'll never mention the subject again.'

'I'm pleased to hear it,' said Joy, much relieved.

'It's a lovely afternoon,' Eleanor said, as if to make the point that she'd never mention Annabel again. 'Come for a little walk with me, down by the river.'

Joy eyed her thoughtfully. And well she might – 'down by the river' was where many of the girls went for privacy when they wanted to play with each other in the daytime.

'I know what you're thinking,' Eleanor said with her knowing smile, 'but you're wrong. If I wanted you to lie down with me I'd ask you to my room. I've no designs on your body, elegant though it is – I've already told you that you're ten years over my age limit.'

The river was really not much more than a slow-running stream across broad green meadows, with trees and bushes marking its course. These were the cover that girls made use of to conceal their activities when they came out here to lie down together. Joy and Eleanor strolled along, chatting and pretending not to see girls lying half-hidden behind dense shrubbery.

Eleanor nudged Joy and nodded her head to the left. Joy pretended not to stare as they walked past a particular clump of greenery. Underneath lay fair-haired Hilary Landor on her back, with her legs wide open and her black mini-skirt up to her hips. She'd taken her knickers off – or someone had taken them off for her – and was being diddled by two girls at the same time.

Joy recognised one of them as Orline Ashby, but the other had her head well down between Hilary's legs and was not instantly identifiable from behind.

'Now there's a young lady worth your trying,' Eleanor

murmured as they went past, 'that Hilary – I've had some lovely times with her. She comes like an express train hitting the buffers.'

Joy took no notice of gasps and little cries that reached their ears from behind almost every tree and clump of bushes they passed, although she and Eleanor couldn't help grinning at each other.

'I'm trying to work out how to stage a naked net-ball game in the gym one dark night,' Eleanor confided. 'The idea came to me one afternoon when I was watching some of the girls play tennis. I think I shall ask Hilary to be one of the competitors. Any suggestions about who the other one might be? A girl with biggish titties, I think, so we get the bounce.'

Joy was listening for the long wailing orgasmic cry she had often heard echoing through Wexby House. At first she'd taken it to be Annabel, but afterward she decided that it wasn't. She'd made Annabel come times enough to know what sounds she made. She'd nicknamed the as-yet-unknown girl the Phantom Wailer and had started prowling Wexby House after Lights Out to listen at doors and hopefully identify her.

'Don't you find it interesting that though they've all got rooms to do it in, they come out here by the river?' Eleanor said with a smile. 'It shows you that there's a difference when you do it in the open air.'

'Oh, there is,' Joy answered earnestly. 'You know I went on holiday to Rhodes last summer with Claudine Stanhope. We went for long swims in the sea every day and afterward we used to find secret places to lie in the sun topless and dry off.'

'And then you gave each other's titties a nice long feel,' Eleanor suggested.

'We licked each other's bobbles for the salt-sea taste,' Joy agreed, 'and we slipped a hand down each other's bikini bottoms. We got the most fantastic thrills – I'm sure it was the open air and the hot sun that did it. I've never come so many times a day before or since.'

'You surprise me about Claudine,' Eleanor said, 'I've been

told she's the least popular teacher at Lechlade. And she's so serious all the time that most of us find her boring. You're the only person I know who's had a hand between her legs.'

'I know what you mean. But she's a different person on holiday – she's laughing and happy and she can't get enough of it,' Joy said. 'We shared a room at the hotel and she woke me up every single morning with a hand between my legs. She insisted she must have a thrill before breakfast – and if she did, I had to. After that we'd get up and have breakfast and go swimming.'

'It goes to show you can't judge by appearances,' Eleanor said with a thoughtful expression. 'Do you remember a girl named Deborah Hughes at all? She was here the first term I taught at Lechlade – a tall thin girl with long straight brown hair and tiny titties. Not pretty, not even attractive. The sort of girl I'd normally never notice.'

'I remember her,' said Joy in some surprise. 'Her father's a politician – he had a minor Government post at the time.'

'I'm not certain now how I came to do her the first time,' Eleanor confessed. 'Just one of those things, something to do on a wet winter evening. But this plain and unattractive girl turned out to be a real raver once I'd got my fingers into her kitty. It became embarrassing when she wouldn't leave me alone, I was having to diddle her ten or twelve times a day. And she was doing the same to me. It was a mercy she was in her last term when we started to do each other, because she'd have worn me to a shadow if it had gone on much longer.'

'This is why it's so unwise to tamper with girls,' Joy said prissily, 'there's no telling what it can lead to.'

'You're so right,' Eleanor agreed readily. 'Oh, dear – what have we here?'

A large weeping willow grew close to the river's edge, its fronds long enough to trail down to the ground. On the river side of the tree, under its cover, two people were lying on the ground. Joy stood still and stared at them with her eyes bulging – the two were Sharon Pomeroy and Annabel Darwen.

Seventeen-year-old Anybody's, the pretty plaything Joy was
obsessed with, was cuddled close to long-haired Sharon, the
geography teacher who was Joy's bed-friend and companion in
sex games.

Their lips were almost touching. Sharon was whispering to
Annabel, who was wearing a tee-shirt and blue jeans. The flies
were unzipped and Sharon had her hand inside, where a
glimpse of bare smooth belly and a little patch of wispy curls
was on view. Annabel's eyes were closed, her mouth open and
the pink tip of her tongue showing.

She was trembling – Joy visualised what the fingers inside
those open jeans were doing to her. Sharon's fingers, feeling
and stroking the soft pink lips half-hidden by wispy brown
curls. In her mind's eye Joy could see Sharon's finger
pressing into Annabel's kitty, Sharon's fingertip touching
Annabel's nubby, Sharon making Annabel come with a wild
ecstatic cry.

Joy stood transfixed – she was unable to look away. This was
betrayal, complete and utter betrayal by both of them.

'Come away,' Eleanor whispered. 'You've seen enough.'

Joy couldn't move. She was shaking with fury – an emotion
that she was reluctant to acknowledge. Not fury, she told
herself, it couldn't possibly be that because a civilised person
never allowed anger to consume her. And not jealousy either,
that also was inadmissible.

Eleanor slid her arm around Joy's waist. She tugged at her
until she was able to turn her back the way they had come and
ease her along with slow and uncertain steps.

'I can't believe it.' Joy found her voice at last, shrill and shaky.

'I did try to warn you,' Eleanor said.

Eleanor steered their steps away from the river and across a
meadow toward a gate that gave onto a meandering lane. The
afternoon sun was hot and Joy was red of face. She was still
shaking when they reached the hedge bordering the lane and
Eleanor made her sit down in the shade of a big oak tree.

'You knew Annabel and Sharon would be there,' Joy accused her. 'That's why you asked me to go for a walk with you.'

'I happened to see the two of them walk out of the college together in this direction,' said Eleanor. 'I guessed where they might be going – I've taken girls along the river bank myself.'

'You took me there to see them,' said Joy bitterly.

'You said you didn't mind how many others had Anybody's as long as you got your share,' Eleanor countered with a shrug, 'so why are you fretting about Sharon diddling her? After all, Sharon's your friend, it's not as if you'd seen a stranger doing it to Annabel.'

'I was wrong to say that,' Joy confessed with a grimace, 'I mind a lot and I should have listened to you. I've learned a lesson and I won't let myself be caught like that again.'

'That's the way,' Eleanor said, 'Try a little dabble with Monkey – it will do wonders for your morale. Or if you prefer to keep it among your own girls in Wexby House, I can recommend Linda Knight.'

'The ginger-haired girl – you've had your hand between her legs too?'

'My dear, I had to find out why Nesta and Penny thought she was worth fighting for. I mean, she's a pretty girl, but she's not so pretty that you'd risk getting a black eye and bruised titties over her.'

'Did you find out?'

'I most certainly did – Linda has the most gorgeous bright ginger hair round her chuffie that you're ever likely to see. I've borrowed an instant camera from one of the girls so I can take colour pictures of Linda's little treasure.'

'And that's all?' Joy was puzzled, 'They kicked and punched each other because Linda has a ginger-haired kitty?'

'There's a bit more to it,' Eleanor confessed. 'Linda is experienced far beyond her years. When she pushes her tongue up you it's utter bliss. I think Linda's a twenty-five-year-old midget nympho pretending she's a schoolgirl.'

'Eleanor – you're impossible!' Joy said, trying to smile.

They sat side by side, their backs against the tree-trunk and the tall green hedge behind them. Eleanor's hand was on the inside of Joy's thigh again, stroking it gently. Gradually her fingers eased up into the leg of Joy's cream-coloured shorts, after a while touching the smooth silky material of the little knickers she wore underneath.

'What do you think you're doing!' Joy complained. 'You promised that you weren't going to try it on with me.'

'I know I did, but I've changed my mind.'

'You said you only went after seventeen-year-olds – but that was a lie, wasn't it? An outright lie.'

'Not entirely,' Eleanor soothed her. 'Usually I only play with young girls, but sometimes I meet a grown woman who makes me wet between the legs. Just the opposite to you – you usually play with grown women like Sharon and only occasionally dabble with a young girl like Annabel.'

Eleanor's fingers were inside Joy's knickers now, stroking the warm lips of her kitty.

'Not a question of occasionally,' Joy murmured, 'Annabel is the first student I've ever been interested in. And see what it's got me – a slap in the face!'

'Yes, but you had your fun with her first. Nothing lasts forever – look at all the other pretty girls you can play with.'

'I know you mean well but I want you to take your hand off me,' Joy said, as Eleanor's fingers glided expertly. 'Even if I felt that way about you,' she added, 'after what I've seen I've lost all interest. You're wasting your time.'

'You don't understand,' Eleanor told her. 'I'm not trying to thrill you. You couldn't possibly want that after the shock you've had this afternoon. I'm doing this to soothe you and to relax you – you're all tensed up. Lie back and let me stroke you for a minute and it will make you feel much better.'

Joy didn't know whether to believe Eleanor or not, but the emotional upheaval of seeing her trusted friend Sharon with her hand in Annabel's jeans had exhausted her. She leaned back against the tree trunk and let Eleanor do whatever she wanted, feeling too lethargic from shock even to argue about it.

Before long, in fact, what Eleanor was doing to her became pleasant and relaxing. Those were skilful fingers pressing into the warm cleft of Joy's chuffie – fingers that moved with exquisite delicacy against her little nub.

Eleanor heard Joy sigh and felt her body tremble. Her fingertips told her how slippery her friend was becoming inside.

'There, you're starting to feel better already,' she told Joy. 'You can trust me, I know what's best in this situation.'

She had the whole front of Joy's shorts undone and wide open, her silky little white knickers pulled down to bare her belly and her dark curls. Joy sighed and spread her knees apart.

'You're a monster, Eleanor,' she murmured weakly. 'You're taking advantage of my emotional collapse – you're behaving disgracefully and you ought to be ashamed of yourself.'

'Oh, I am,' Eleanor said in a cheerful tone. 'Every time I slide my fingers into a nice warm wet slit I have these overwhelming feelings of shame and guilt. But I resist them and I carry on doing the friend who is parting her legs for me.'

'I can't come,' Joy sighed. 'It's impossible after what I've suffered. You may as well give up now – it will be a long time before I'm in the right mood for sex-thrills again.'

'That's not what this is about,' Eleanor assured her. 'It's a form of therapy. I'm trying to calm your emotional turmoil.'

Having stated strongly that she wouldn't be able to come, Joy moaned and did so – a long shuddering climax. Eleanor held her close and gently rubbed her wet nubby.

'You beast, you beast...' Joy was moaning, 'you've made me do it and I didn't want to...'

'Whether you wanted to or not, you needed to,' said Eleanor, with a grin Joy didn't see. 'You'll feel much better now.'

'I'm so tired,' Joy murmured. 'It's the shock...'

'Lie down and have a rest,' Eleanor suggested, arranging her on her side on the ground. She put Joy's head on her own shoulder to make her comfortable and held her close.

'So tired . . .' Joy whispered, her eyes closing.

She dozed off with one arm around Eleanor's neck and the other between their bodies. Her hand was trapped and squeezed between Eleanor's hot bare thighs – bare because Eleanor was wearing neither tights nor stockings under her short skirt on that summer day. Nor was she wearing any knickers, though Joy had fallen asleep without learning that.

Carefully, so as not to disturb her, Eleanor arranged Joy's hand further up between her thighs so that it lay against her dark-haired kitty. Truth to tell, stroking Joy for the first time had made Eleanor very excited. There was a throbbing sensation in her belly and between her legs, a sensation she intended to make last as long as possible.

She didn't want just a quick thrill. She was planning a long, slow, triumphant ascent toward a distant orgasmic peak.

Eleanor lay still, concentrating on the touch of Joy's hand between her thighs and against her hot wet chuffie. She imagined what it would be like to put her hand up Joy's pale blue top and inside her bra to feel her titties. To take off the bra and lick them. They weren't big, seen through her clothes, but Eleanor was certain they'd be elegant and sexy.

I'm going to come soon and you'll never know about it, Eleanor thought, her lips touching Joy's forehead.

To help things along Eleanor was clenching and unclenching the muscles of her belly in a steady rhythm, sending little tremors of pleasure through her body. It was an exercise she had been taught when she was a young girl – one she did at night in bed to give herself a thrill before she fell asleep.

The woman who had taught her how to do it was a teacher at the school where Eleanor was a pupil. Mandy Wright, her name was, at the time a twenty-nine-year-old divorcee with big round titties. She demonstrated to young Eleanor how it was done and made her practise daily. She would slide two fingers up Eleanor's slit, just like a man's thing doing her.

Mandy would keep her fingers there while Eleanor worked her inner muscles in a steady tempo, encouraging the girl with murmurs of *Yes, yes, stronger now – harder, that's nice, yes, yes!* until Eleanor moaned and came.

After that Mandy would spread herself on her back and get Eleanor to lie between her legs, put her tongue inside her teacher's kitty and lick her nubby. Then she'd roll Eleanor over on her back and lick her till she came with a shuddering rush. Eleanor looked back on her schooldays as truly the happiest days of her life, and at Lechlade she was recreating them.

She wanted to put her tongue into Joy, she wanted to feel Joy's tongue inside herself. All in good time – she must take her back to the college first so they could lock the door and strip naked and make each other come again and again.

You will *know I've come while you were asleep, Joy, because when you wake up I shall tell you,* she said to herself. She felt the tremors in her belly grow stronger. Wonderful little sensations that darted up from her chuffie to the firm tips of her titties and back again.

Now we've started together we'll go on the same way, she thought. *You and me, Joy, we'll do each other regularly. And in between times I'll go on diddling every girl I fancy – I'm going to have Annabel now you don't want her. And even if you did, I'd still have her.*

Eleanor felt the thrill start between her legs – fast strong jolts of pure ecstasy that made her body convulse as if struck by surges of electricity.

I'm coming, Joy, she whispered faintly, her eyes closed as she twitched in spasms of delight, *I'm coming...*

Chapter Nine

The physiotherapist who came to the college twice a week to deal with minor sporting injuries was named Debbie Gregson. A good-looking woman in her late twenties, she had generous-sized titties under the white uniform she wore. When the students heard she was a Miss and not a Mrs they assumed her interests were the same as their own.

They felt they could look to her for the same comforts and pleasures that Maureen Plessy used to provide when she was Sports Mistress, before she damaged her knee and had to resign. Of course, they all understood that the only reason Debbie was there was because a man had been appointed Sports Coach.

They knew the Principal's views on this had been over-ridden by the Governors. But Enid had partly got her way – she declared that it was not acceptable to consider allowing a man to perform body massage on young girls – and in this the Governors agreed with her.

The mere thought of a man laying his lustful hands on near-naked girls was enough to send the Principal into shock. She knew she was not being entirely reasonable about this, however, since her own secret and dearest desire was to massage the bare body of every girl in the college – to tenderly stroke and caress their round young titties, their smooth flat bellies, their long graceful thighs.

On many a night after Maureen Plessy left, the Principal lay alone in her bed with legs apart and nightie up around her waist, diddling herself slowly while in her mind's eye she visualised one favourite girl or another lying naked on the massage table to be stroked all over.

Enid Uppingham wanted them all, every one of them, all of the hundred and sixty girls in the four houses of the college. Naturally, there were some she fancied more than others. The girl she most wished to lay her gentle and loving hands on – her absolute number one choice – was Nesta Wade, a second-year student in Wexby House.

Enid had seen Nesta in the skimpiest possible gear a student dared wear for swimming, tennis and jogging. She admired Nesta's splendid titties through her swimsuit, leotard or tight tee-shirt, yearning to feel them and lick them. She studied the hidden mound between Nesta's thighs, certain that the curls down there must be as blonde as her long pony-tail. Just thinking about kissing those curls could send Enid's emotions soaring toward a hot wet climax.

And to tongue Nesta – to hold her kitty open with fingers trembling with excitement, to lick her until she shook and moaned – this was the final image that drove Enid herself over the edge into ecstasy. If Nesta only knew how often she figured in the Principal's night-time fantasies she would have been flattered. Though whether she would have been flattered enough to let Enid put a hand down her knickers and give her a feel was a different matter.

Another girl who had caught Enid's fancy was almost the opposite of Nesta in appearance – Marjorie Newmill, who was shortish and very dark-haired. For Enid the thought of feeling Marjorie's plump young bouncers was irresistible. But to imagine hot and lustful *male* hands on her sweet young flesh was altogether different – Enid found it impossible to explain to herself why the idea of a man laying his hands on a near-naked girl on the massage table was repulsive, but the idea of her own hands on a girl's body was madly exciting.

She rationalised her inconsistency by telling herself that a man only wanted to get his *thing* into a girl and the stroking of her body was only a preliminary to getting on top and forcing it into her. And that activity was not worth bothering with, at least not for the girl, as Enid knew from her own experience in her student days.

Whereas if she had Nesta naked on the table, massaging her titties and belly would be a wonderful prelude to parting the lips of the girl's kitty and gently, artfully tonguing the pretty little pink nubby she would find there. And furthermore, she told herself, if *she* laid her hands on a girl they most certainly would not be hot and lustful, as men's hands were – they would be gentle and affectionate, they would be loving hands that would give the girl a kind of pleasure no man could ever give.

Enid had no clear idea of the techniques of physiotherapy, beyond the fact that hand-massage was included. She had been on the table herself lots of times for her dear friend Maureen Plessy – but that was not to relieve aches and pains. It was a special sort of treatment with another purpose altogether, the sort of massage where Maureen concentrated on stroking Enid's heavy titties and between her spread thighs.

For a very full-bodied woman Enid was attractive naked. When she took her clothes off in the treatment room and sat on the edge of the table, her over-sized titties hung heavily. Maureen slipped her hands under them, lifted them, jiggled them. She rubbed the balls of her thumbs lightly over the big pink bobbles to stiffen them. Then she hoisted those big soft titties as high as she could and bent down to suck their bobbles.

Enid sat with her bare feet dangling and her plump thighs splayed. She had a thick pelt of very dark-brown curls over her prominent chuffie – the hair grew well down into her groins and up over her belly to the crease that ran across it when she sat down. After Maureen had done enough to her swinging titties to make her gasp and shake, she slipped her hands under Enid's thighs and raised her legs up to help her to lie on the table.

127

Bouncers as large and soft as Enid's had to spread sideways when she lay down on her back. They were two plump cushions of warm flesh under Maureen's manipulating hands, which rolled them and kneaded them and slapped them lightly to make Enid shriek with pleasure even before the hands moved down over the soft dome of Enid's belly and between her well-spread legs.

The way Maureen performed her massage on Enid made it last longer than any ordinary massage ever did. Maureen had strong and clever fingers and they didn't confine their attentions to Enid's outside. Eventually the manipulation was extended to that most sensitive little part inside her chuffie. Maureen knew how to spin out her friend's pleasures through endless shudders and cries of delight – she often had Enid on the table for three-quarters of an hour before she induced a final shattering thrill.

All this was strictly between friends. Maureen was never allowed to do it to the girls – Enid as Principal made that very clear to her.

'You must always behave professionally, Maureen,' she often said. 'Put it out of your mind that they are attractive young girls in their underwear. You must see them as patients who need your expert treatment for their aches.'

'There is no need for you to remind me,' Maureen would reply, sounding a bit sniffy. 'I fully understand the ethics of my profession. I would never, never, never take advantage of a young person in my care.'

'I'm pleased to hear that,' Enid would retort. 'Keep your emotions firmly under control and never let your thoughts stray when you are giving treatment. I earnestly advise you to confine your touch to ankles, knees and arms – do you follow me? Never allow your hands to wander toward bare titties.'

'Really, Enid!' Maureen would snort.

'Needless to say,' Enid would go on, undismayed and relentless, 'it would be dishonourable in the extreme if you touched a girl anywhere near her kitty. I suppose there are times when you are required to deal with thigh-strain. This is dangerous, morally speaking – there is no telling what might result from putting your fingers in a girl's groins. I assume they keep their underwear on at all times.'

On several occasions Enid had the effrontery to say this sort of thing immediately after Maureen had massaged her to a moaning climax on the table. Needless to say, it annoyed Maureen that even while the Principal lay naked with her legs apart she would deliver a lecture on the evils of touching a chuffie.

'It's not practical for them to keep a bra on if I am attending to a strained back,' Maureen would answer crossly, 'but to put your mind at rest, I can assure you that they wear their knickers at all times, even when I am massaging a sprained thigh.'

'That's very sensible,' Enid would reply as she reached up to stroke Maureen's titties, which had been bare and swinging while she massaged Enid. Since one good turn deserved another, she'd put her mouth to Maureen's titties as they dangled over her and give them a good sucking.

But the truth was that Enid was not reassured by words alone. Knowing the force of the desires she suppressed in herself, she assumed that Maureen felt much the same toward the girls. She would not let her dear friend dabble in the pleasures she had ruled out for herself. So to make sure Maureen wouldn't be tempted Enid diddled her five or six times a day. She intended Maureen to have no sexual desire left.

Before Debbie Gregson was appointed part-time physiotherapist, Enid interviewed her rigorously. She wanted to be convinced that Debbie was not interested in taking advantage of the students.

Enid had been right about Maureen Plessy being attracted to the girls, however often Maureen denied it. She never really believed Maureen – it was asking too much of her not to give way to the temptation that was all about her every day. But the fact was that Enid's efforts to diddle Maureen to a standstill and keep her hands off pretty young kitties were not effective at all.

Exactly as Enid suspected, her dear friend Maureen did at least two girls every day of the week, flat on their back on the massage-table, the very same table where she did Enid whenever she asked.

Maureen's skill and willingness to oblige made her very popular with the girls. They arrived at the treatment-room complaining about ricked backs, twisted knees and strained thighs. Maureen nodded and smiled and asked them to strip completely naked and get on the table.

The girl of the moment would smile back and do so. Maureen's repeated assurances to Enid that her patients kept their knickers on were false, a total fabrication.

'Which knee is it you've twisted, Connie?' she would ask. Or Nesta or Jackie or Pru or Marjorie or whoever it was lying on the table. 'This one – I see. Try to relax all your muscles while I examine it and see what needs to be done.'

She would run careful fingers over the supposedly afflicted area and then announce her diagnosis. 'We can soon settle the problem,' she'd explain. 'A good massage *here* will put it right in no time.'

Naturally, *here* was where she put her hand at that moment, invariably between the girl's legs. And that was where she massaged, a delicate procedure that lasted five or ten minutes and ended with Pru or Jackie or Nesta or whoever drumming her heels on the table as she achieved full relief.

'Does that feel better, dear?' Maureen would enquire when the girl got her breath back.

'Much better, Miss Plessy,' the grateful patient would sigh.

'Just to be sure,' Maureen would say with a professional smile, 'come back tomorrow about the same time and I'll repeat the treatment.'

The physiotherapy services Maureen provided were much appreciated by the young ladies of Lechlade College. When she was forced to leave her job they had a collection and bought her a large bottle of expensive perfume. They were sorry to lose her – but they looked forward eagerly to the arrival of her replacement when it was announced that an outside consultant had been appointed part-time.

Debbie Gregson proved to be a disappointment. She didn't seem to understand what was expected; she took the girls' complaints of bruised thighs and pulled muscles seriously – she actually believed them and fussed about with heat-pads and other unwanted treatments. Nor did she understand why her patients always stripped naked before they got on the table, even when they claimed they'd twisted an ankle or banged an elbow.

All was made clear to her in her second week at the college – by Anybody's. Annabel arrived late one afternoon at the treatment-room and said she'd hurt her thigh on the tennis court. Before Debbie even had time to ask any questions, Annabel had taken all her clothes off.

She lay on her back on the table with one hand touching her own right tittie and a look of expectation on her pretty face. Debbie looked at the thigh in question, kneaded it gently a few times, and said with a puzzled expression that she could find nothing wrong with it.

Annabel smiled up at her and parted her long slender legs until her kitty was completely exposed.

'It really does hurt, Miss Gregson,' she said. 'Higher up from where you're touching me – much higher.'

Debbie was trying not to look at Annabel's kitty – she was staring fixedly into the girl's pale blue eyes.

'How high?' she asked, letting her hands slip upward an inch or so.

'Higher,' Annabel directed her. 'High as you can go.'

Debbie's fingers were almost touching Annabel's kitty.

'You feel a strain here in the groin?' she asked.

'I want to come,' Annabel announced calmly.

At this moment Debbie understood and blushed scarlet.

'Then you must do it yourself,' she said sharply. 'Put your clothes on and leave at once, Annabel.'

Word spread round the college so fast that by Lights Out everyone knew that the routine of Miss Plessy's day was not going to be re-established under the new physio. Disappointed girls met in small groups after dark and began to plot together. Two days later representatives from each of the four houses got together in secret to discuss ways and means.

After lengthy debate a decision was reached – an experiment would be tried with the new Sports Coach to see if he was any good to them. It was known that he had a qualification in sports physiotherapy because the personnel files in the Principal's secretary's office had been raided in the middle of the night by two girls chosen for the job. They found Toby Dundale's file and made a copy to take away on the photocopier.

So far, so good – but the first approach to him needed to be planned carefully. A very thorough enquiry in all four houses ascertained that several girls had been touched up by the Sports Coach – and when asked they had no reluctance about describing what he did to them. Mostly it was a sly feel of their titties in the swimming pool.

They all told the same story – while he was groping them there was the most tremendous bulge in the front of his swimming trunks. If you could call them that, when what he actually wore for swimming was hardly more than a pouch.

'Thick as my wrist, it was,' said Wilma Harrington, 'and so long that I thought it was going to pop out of the top of his pouch.'

'He's definitely interested in girls,' Penny Carlton said, 'same as all men, he can't keep his hands to himself. But he's timid because he's afraid of being found out.'

Sophie Maitland of Sawby House had an interesting experience to relate. Toby had got her alone one afternoon behind the pavilion, and she made no objection when he put his hand up her skirt and fondled her bum. He was wearing his very brief tennis shorts at the time, and again there was the big bulge in the front that everyone talked about.

'He grabbed my wrist and pushed my hand down the front of his shorts,' Sophie told her friends – and anyone else who would listen. 'I had it in my hand,' she said, 'it was hot and very hard.'

'Sometimes in the pool you can see it jerking inside his pouch,' said Susie Wilton-Warrington. 'Did it jump when you were holding it?'

'Oh, yes,' Sophie agreed, 'it was like holding a live animal, the way it jumped in my hand. I really thought he was going to come.'

'In your hand!' Wilma shrieked, 'you wouldn't let him, would you?'

'I think I might have, just to see what it felt like,' said Sophie, 'but we heard someone heading toward us round the side of the pavilion and he pulled my hand out and walked away very quickly.'

When all the available stories of Toby Dundale's exploits with girls were compared and considered, what emerged was that he'd gone furthest with Orline Ashby of Wexby House. She claimed he'd had her down on her knees in the gym and rubbed himself against her bum till he came in his shorts. There was some disbelief at first but Orline stuck to her story when she was questioned closely.

In the circumstances, Orline was the obvious choice to sound Toby out to see if he could be persuaded to give her massage. It was agreed that the best time would be after the evening jog and Orline was given her instructions. So the next day, in the last five minutes of the trot back to college, Orline developed a bad limp. Toby dropped back to see what was the matter.

Orline said she'd pulled a muscle in her calf and it was so painful she could hardly walk. She was wearing loose jogging trousers in bright green, with elastic round the ankles. Toby squatted down on his haunches and felt her calf – and she yelped convincingly. There was nothing he could do but help her hobble back to college – he got her arm over his shoulders and put his own arm round her waist to help her along.

By the time they got back the other girls were in the showers. Orline begged Toby to massage her leg to relieve the agony. Perhaps it was a cramp, she suggested, and easily cured. Toby shook his head and told her what she already knew – that he wasn't allowed to treat students.

'Why not?' Orline asked, pretending not to understand.

He didn't even try to explain because he was sure she knew the reason already – the moral dangers of a man's hands on a young girl's innocent body and all that sort of thing. Instead he simply said that he would be dismissed if it came to light that he'd touched one of the girls for any reason.

Orline said she could see why he wasn't allowed to put his hands on her bosom – she nearly said 'titties' but remembered in time – but surely there weren't any rules that said he mustn't massage her calf?

'I mustn't touch any part of you,' he said sadly.

Orline looked at him with pleading blue eyes and she reminded him he hadn't said that when they were in his office watching Miss Redruth and Linda through the glass panel.

Toby's twanger always stood stiff in his shorts when he took the girls jogging – it was the sight of so many young titties bouncing under tight tee-shirts that did it to him every time. Holding Orline's hot and sweating body close to him while he helped her limp back to college had excited him even more.

He'd had a hand in her armpit to support her, and it had strayed to her tittie – by accident, of course. Or maybe not. But accident or not, he'd had her neat little right tittie cupped in his palm for part of the way home and now his hard twanger was throbbing furiously against his belly.

The main thing on his mind was finding time for a dash back

to the gate-house to rattle the caretaker's wife on the doormat. Assuming that Keith was out and Sally was on her own. Oddly enough, Keith hadn't been out and about as much as usual in the last day or two – Toby had no idea why he was behaving differently.

Orline or any of the other girls could have told him why, of course – could have explained how the caretaker had met his doom in a locker with his hard-on diddler in his hand.

Orline repeated her plea for treatment for her injured leg while Toby looked at her doubtfully.

'I'd like to help you,' he said, 'truly I would – but it's more than my job is worth. The Principal was very strict on this point.'

'I never said a word to anyone about what you were doing to me in the gym that day,' she lied with a perfectly innocent face. 'If you treat my leg I won't mention it to a soul, I promise.'

That was a promise she had no intention of keeping. The whole of Wexby House was waiting for her to return and tell them if she'd succeeded in persuading Toby to break the rules. Not just Wexby – the entire college was waiting for her.

Toby hesitated a moment too long. He looked into Orline's blue eyes, he looked at her pretty seventeen-year-old titties, closely outlined by her clinging tee-shirt. She wasn't wearing a bra – her pert little bobbles were completely visible through the thin cotton. Toby's stiffie twitched in his tight jockstrap – he smiled at Orline and took her to the treatment-room.

Naturally, before he could examine and massage her injured calf her baggy jogging trousers had to come off. He watched her untie the draw-string round her waist and let the trousers slip down her legs. To his astonishment she was not wearing knickers under them. And her tee-shirt ended an inch or so below her hips – her bum was bare when she dropped her trousers and kicked them off.

Not wearing knickers was her own idea when the girls chose her for the task of seducing Toby and discussed how she could

135

get him going. She faced away from him while she dropped her trousers, but it was not from modesty – she did it to remind him that he'd rubbed himself against those bare cheeks of hers in the gym.

He'd given himself a thrill with her then and the memory should make him hope for another thrill now. Not that he stood any chance of getting his *thing* up her. That wasn't the plan. In fact, all the girls insisted that they would never, never, never allow themselves to be done by a man. Maybe it was true and maybe not – but what they wanted from Toby was the same facility they'd had in Miss Plessy's day: an expert hand-massage whenever they felt like it. As Debbie Gregson refused to oblige, there was nobody else except Toby – it had to be him.

Orline sat on the edge of the massage-table, with her legs apart to give him a good view of her kitty. She was a fair-haired girl and the curls between her legs were very light brown. Toby was down on one knee to handle the leg she said had a pulled muscle. He tried to look up into her face while he kneaded the calf lightly, but he wasn't strong-willed enough – after ten seconds his eyes dropped to her pretty young chuffie.

He was still keeping up the pretence of treating an injury, although he realised by now that Orline had been putting on an act. As she sat on the side of the table with her legs apart, her blondish-haired kitty was on the level of his eyes and only twelve or fifteen inches in front of him. The throbbing in his shorts had become so insistent that he was sure he was going to come in a fast splurge at any moment.

Although he could see that Orline had set him up, the situation was beyond his control. His hands massaged up her calf, over her knee – and along her bare thigh. She watched what he was doing with a coy look on her face and the tip of her tongue showing. His face turned pink and when he pushed a fingertip into her and touched her nubby, she knew that her mission was a success.

'This tee-shirt is so sweaty,' she said as she stripped it over her head. As Toby already knew, she had no bra on. She rubbed round her titties and then in her armpits with the wadded-up tee-shirt.

His eyes were staring when he saw the wispy blondish hair in her armpits and she wondered if he'd like to lick her there. Pru Renwick loved to do that to her – it tickled at first and then it felt very sexy.

Toby was more interested in her chuffie than her armpits. 'Orline,' he sighed, resigning himself to the urges he couldn't fight any more. He knew she was teasing him but he no longer cared.

She leaned forward to put her hands on his shoulders, a blissful look on her face now as his fingertip slid back and forth over her moist little nubby.

'That's marvellous,' she whispered, 'I'm going to come now.'

He heard her sudden intake of breath and felt her legs shake as she went into a long quivering orgasm. He continued teasing her nubby while he counted in his mind how many seconds her orgasm lasted. Then she was calm, breathing a little faster than normal, but smiling at him now she'd got what she came for.

He was desperate to push her down on her back and jump on top of her, but knew he mustn't because young girls like Orline fell into the family way the instant a twanger slid up them. Orline knew what he wanted to do to her and she also knew he daren't. She grinned slyly at him, enjoying his predicament.

Moaning under his breath, he suddenly stood up and grabbed her by the hips. In a flash he turned her over, face-down on the massage table, and pulled her toward him until her belly lay flat on it and her legs were dangling down toward the floor. He was standing between her open thighs, close up, his fingers kneading the soft flesh of her bum.

Orline thought he'd gone right over the top and was going to force his twanger into her kitty from behind. She squealed and struggled – she was a virgin and wanted to stay one. She was only a virgin in the technical sense, of course – no male had been allowed to slide his *thing* into her kitty. Other girls' fingers didn't count – that was just a little game she played every day with her college friends.

Toby was tempted beyond endurance by the sight of her blondish-haired chuffie so very close to him. He wrenched his shorts open and pulled his jockstrap down to free his hard-on. He clasped it in his hand and rubbed the purple-pink head against the lips of Orline's kitty – he very nearly pushed it in, but stopped himself at the last moment. He was breathing in long gasps now, hardly aware of what he was doing when he parted the cheeks of Orline's pretty bum and rubbed the swollen head of his stand lightly between them.

'What are you going to do?' Orline gasped, trying to look over her shoulder. She was scared he might ram it in her back door – she'd heard about men who did that and she didn't like the idea at all. But strain her neck as much as she could, all she could see was Toby's face, flushed with passion, close to her own.

She felt his hand pounding up and down, a hard beat against her bum. She realised what he was up to and gave a long sigh of relief – he was doing himself by hand – the only safe way he could think of to relieve his bursting passion. He was pressing himself close against her thighs and she felt his teeth nipping at her bare shoulder.

'Oh,' she gasped, beginning to enjoy what was happening.

She'd succeeded beyond expectations. She'd persuaded Toby to give her a finger-massage against the rules – and she'd also reduced him to abject slavery. He wanted her sleek young body and knew she wouldn't let him have it; by diddling himself he was simply confirming his enslavement.

The girls would adore her for going first and discovering the best way to handle him to get what they wanted. They'd all insist on having a go. With forty girls in Wexby House alone, to say nothing of the rest of the college, Toby was going to be worked hard for the rest of his time at Lechlade. Orline giggled to herself at the thought.

She exclaimed *Oh!* and giggled again when Toby gave a

great jerk and shot spurts of warm cream over the cheeks of her bum. He too was panting *Oh oh oh*, but not in the same amused tone as Orline – for him this was a serious moment.

He's done it all over my bum again, Orline thought, *just like that day in the gym when we watched Linda on her knees tonguing Miss Redruth.*

Chapter Ten

Debbie Gregson thought for a long time about her encounter with Annabel. At home that night she turned it over in her mind until she came to the conclusion that it was her duty to report what had happened. So on her next visit to the college, two days after the incident, she asked to see the head of Annabel's house.

'What can I do for you, Miss Gregson?' Joy Locksley asked.

She was sitting at the desk in her study; she gestured toward a chair and Debbie sat down. Joy could see that she was not at ease and gave her a smile of encouragement. It had to be a complaint about one or other of the girls of Wexby House, Joy was sure of that.

Debbie was wearing her usual crisp white coat-dress buttoned all the way down the front, with white shoes and black stockings. Her dark-brown hair was cut in a neat fringe over her forehead, and the impression she made was nurse-like and competent. Joy liked the look of her.

Although Debbie had thought a lot about what she wanted to say, now that it was the moment to speak she felt awkward about it. She took a deep breath and plunged in.

'I want you to know it's not a question of telling tales,' she started hurriedly. 'I'm a member of the staff here, though only part-time, and I feel a responsibility to pass on something you might want to take action on.'

Oh dear, Joy thought, *one of the girls has really upset her – what can it be about?*

'Annabel Darwen came to me for treatment for a pulled

141

muscle in her thigh,' said Debbie, 'or at least that's what she told me. But it turned out to be just an excuse to strip naked and get on the massage table...'

The mention of Annabel's name secured Joy Locksley's full attention – and not in the most cordial of ways. Since that unforgettable afternoon when she saw Annabel and Sharon diddling each other under a tree down by the riverside, Joy had broken off her friendship with both of them.

Sharon was not invited to share Joy's bed any more. In fact Joy hadn't spoken to her since that day, except to inform her she was a poor friend and a treacherous bitch. As for Annabel, Joy understood now why she had been nicknamed Anybody's. So let her go with anybody and everybody, Joy told herself with a shrug, I want no more to do with her.

Evidently Annabel was doing exactly that, going with everybody. But it seemed that her approach to the new physio had gone wrong.

'Naked on the table?' Joy said, raising her eyebrows in an expression of displeasure. 'I see no need for that.'

'Neither do I,' Debbie said quickly, anxious to clear herself from any suggestion of blame, 'but the fact is that all the girls do it when they come for treatment, whatever I say.'

'Strip themselves naked? Do they indeed?' Joy's eyebrows rose even higher as she considered the implications of what she had been told.

'Every one of them, without exception,' Debbie confirmed. 'I tell them there is no need to remove their underwear, but they merely giggle and ignore me. I can only think that my predecessor encouraged them to take everything off, in accordance with some theory of her own.'

'Very possibly,' said Joy, who had known Maureen Plessy well enough to suspect that she dabbled with girls. 'Please go on.'

'I could find nothing wrong with Annabel,' Debbie said, 'and she soon made it clear that her story of a strained muscle was an excuse.'

'She admitted it?' Joy asked.

'There was no need, because she opened her legs and told me that she wished to be sexually manipulated. I was flabbergasted.'

'She said it outright?'

'Her actual words were "I want to come".'

'I see,' said Joy, thinking hard.

If all the girls stripped naked in the treatment room and lay on the table to display their bodies to the physio, then the only possible conclusion to be drawn was that they were all after the same thing as Annabel – a 'finger-wave'.

As Head of Wexby House, Joy saw the danger at once – this incident with Annabel might turn into a scandal in the newspapers. Debbie Gregson was not really a member of the college staff, even if she claimed to be. She was an outsider with no real loyalty to the college. A Sunday newspaper would pay a lot of money for an inside story of hanky-panky between girls at a prestigious establishment such as Lechlade Ladies' College.

Joy was horrified by the idea of the college featuring in a tabloid. Debbie must be side-tracked at once before any such thought occurred to her.

'What did you do?' she asked Debbie, trying not to sound too worried.

'I told her to put her clothes on and leave at once.'

'Very wise,' said Joy, wondering how to save the situation. She wished Debbie had taken her inconvenient tale straight to the Principal instead of herself. But she hadn't – and it had to be dealt with.

'Have you mentioned this to anyone else?' she asked, her calm voice belying her agitated thoughts.

'I felt it best to come straight to you,' said Debbie.

'You did the right thing,' Joy assured her with a pleasant smile as she got up from her desk and moved round it toward the physiotherapist.

'We must talk off the record for a minute before we get into

143

the area of official action,' she told Debbie. 'Come and sit over here with me.'

'Over here' meant the grey sofa. She sat down on it and Debbie joined her there. It was ironic, Joy thought to herself, that they were about to discuss Annabel's misbehaviour on the very sofa upon which Joy had put her hand up Annabel's skirt and felt her kitty.

'Let's try to decide if there was a reason why Annabel came to you with her suggestion,' she began.

'What do you mean?' Debbie looked very surprised.

'There must be an explanation why she chose you instead of another of the staff,' Joy said carefully. 'It can only be because she is attracted to you sexually, don't you think?'

Debbie's cheeks blushed pink at that. 'I hope you're not suggesting I'm that way inclined,' she exclaimed indignantly.

'Of course not,' Joy soothed her. 'I'm simply trying to find out why Annabel chose *you*. It's hard to believe that it came out of the blue.'

'It did as far as I'm concerned,' Debbie insisted. 'I was absolutely stunned when she said it – I stood by the massage table with my mouth hanging open while that girl lay with her legs apart and everything she's got on show.'

'You're an attractive woman,' Joy commented, 'and you're not married, though you're about my age. Could Annabel have drawn a conclusion from that and acted upon it?'

'I'm twenty-seven,' Debbie said, 'not old to be unmarried, and I've got a boyfriend. I've given Annabel no reason to think I'm interested in her in that sort of way.'

'I'm sure you didn't. But she obviously felt that you did. We must talk frankly if we're going to get anywhere, Debbie, please don't take offence. When you say you have a boyfriend, does that mean there's a man you go to bed with regularly?'

'I don't see why you're asking me these questions,' Debbie said, her broad forehead wrinkled in a puzzled expression. 'It's as if you blame me for what Annabel did.'

'Certainly not,' Joy said. 'I'm sure you behaved properly.'

'I can't be responsible for what the girl was thinking,' Debbie insisted, 'and since you ask, my boyfriend does take me to bed regularly. I'm perfectly normal – in fact he doesn't do it as often as I'd like him to. But he can't always get away.'

'Get away from what? Is there a problem?'

'The fact is,' Debbie admitted, 'he's married. He manages to be with me twice a week, that's all.'

'I see,' Joy said in a sympathetic tone. 'How long has this love affair been going on?'

'We went to school together, Lawrence and me. We've been lovers since we turned sixteen,' Debbie said.

As a Head of House, Joy had long experience of winning the confidence of girls and advising them. Debbie was a grown woman but evidently she felt comfortable about confiding her secrets to Joy.

'We were engaged to be married at one time,' Debbie went on, 'but when I was away studying for my diploma in physiotherapy he started going out with someone else. We had rows about it and I told him I never wanted to see him again. He went off in a big huff and married this girl, Lorna – she's a cousin of mine, actually.'

'Very distressing for you,' Joy murmured sympathetically.

'Lorna had twins four months after the wedding,' Debbie went on, outrage in her voice. 'Lawrence must have known she was pregnant when we broke up, although he never said so. By the time the twins were born, he was seeing me again.'

'You took him back, a married man, after the way he treated you?' Joy was astonished and didn't try to hide it.

'He was waiting for me one afternoon in the car-park of the clinic where I was working then. I was very surprised to see him, and naturally I was furious with him.'

'You weren't very furious if you let him talk you round that easily,' Joy said. 'He must be a very persuasive man, this Lawrence of yours.'

'He is,' Debbie said fervently, 'and it wasn't only what he said. He pulled me into his car and kissed me till I was right out of breath. By then he'd got his hand up my clothes and I couldn't help myself.'

'You let him maul you about in a car-park?' Joy couldn't believe what she was hearing – she'd conveniently forgotten that she herself had allowed Eleanor Redruth to diddle her in a meadow, not so long ago.

'It's the effect he has on me,' Debbie explained, 'I was nearly coming just because he was feeling me. What could I do but take him to my flat and let him do it properly?'

'And it's been like that between you ever since?' Joy asked in amazement.

'I love him,' Debbie said, as if that explained everything.

This is ridiculous, Joy was thinking, *the woman's an idiot to let a man take advantage of her like that. She doesn't have to be his doormat – she's very attractive, if you like women with heavy titties and broad hips.*

In the past few weeks Joy Locksley's outlook had undergone a very considerable change. She had always been opposed to the idea of sex-games between teachers and girls. A mild affair with another teacher had satisfied her. But that was before she let herself go with Annabel Darwen. Playing with the girl day after day had brought a new perspective into Joy's life.

The shock of finding Annabel being diddled by Sharon could easily have confirmed her old belief in the unsuitability of relations with a girl – but before that happened Joy had been taken over by Eleanor Redruth, who had awakened her to a more intense kind of sexual pleasure than she had thought herself capable of.

'It's far from satisfactory, your affair with Lawrence,' she told Debbie. 'It goes nowhere toward explaining why Annabel was attracted to you, except that she may have sensed something in you, perhaps a feeling of dissatisfaction or lack of fulfilment, that aroused her. Leaving aside this married man you allow to abuse you, have you ever at any time had a sexual experience with another woman?'

'Certainly not!' Debbie protested, her cheeks pink.

'Not even when you were very young – before you started to let Lawrence do what he likes with you?'

Debbie was silent for a little while, her cheeks becoming pinker. Joy waited patiently.

'Well, you can't really count that,' Debbie finally said hesitantly. 'Young girls play with each other when their titties start to grow. It's only curiosity.'

'Of course,' Joy agreed at once, convinced now that she held Debbie in the palm of her hand and could have her when she chose to. 'How old were you when those lovely round titties started to appear – eleven, twelve?'

'Twelve,' Debbie confided, a note of pride in her voice. 'I had this friend called Franny who lived next door, and she was so interested in them that she'd never leave them alone. There was an apple orchard at the bottom of our garden where Franny and I used to go together and lie on the ground under the trees. She would have me on my back for hours with my blouse open while she stroked my titties.'

'You enjoyed that?' Joy asked sympathetically.

'I loved it, especially when she licked them. She used to make me come two or three times, but I was so young and knew so little about it that I didn't realise I was coming. All I knew then was that it felt very nice when she did it to me.'

'And you did it to her in return, of course,' Joy suggested.

'She had little titties, firm and pointed,' Debbie said. 'I loved sucking them and making her wriggle about on the grass and gasp out loud when it happened to her. We had been playing about with each other for months before we found out about having a climax. There was an older girl at school who told us what it meant to have a climax – after that we couldn't keep our hands off each other, Franny and me.'

'You must have played with more than each other's titties,' Joy said in an understanding way. 'I mean, one thing leads to another. At least it did for me when I was about that age.'

Debbie's cheeks were a bright pink by now but she felt secure enough with Joy to reveal the secrets of her childhood. 'We put our hands down each other's knickers for a feel,' she confided with a little smile that showed embarrassment. 'We played about and tickled each other's kitty – you know what young girls do – we put our fingers up each other and gave each other a thrill.'

'All very natural,' Joy encouraged her.

'It was just curiosity,' Debbie insisted, anxious for Joy to believe her. 'We didn't think of it as sex, it was just our own little game we played together – tittie-kissing and kitty-feeling. We were curious about the hair growing between our legs and looked at each other every day to see who had the most.'

'I understand perfectly,' Joy assured her. 'How long did this friendship with Franny last – till you left school?'

'No, something else happened before then,' Debbie said. 'Not that we ever fell out – we were the best of friends for years. My titties kept on getting bigger and Franny swore that was because she played with them so much. But I never believed that because I used to play with hers just as often and they stayed small and pointed.'

'So in fact your friendship lasted till you took up with Lawrence, did it? How did that happen, Debbie?'

'He asked me out to the cinema one Saturday afternoon when I was sixteen. I agreed, thinking nothing much of it, but he had big ideas. As soon as the lights went down he'd got his hand up my sweater and was feeling my titties. It felt just as nice as when Franny did it to me, so I let him carry on.'

Joy was fascinated by Debbie's story. She leaned closer to her on the sofa until their thighs were just brushing.

'You can guess what happened,' Debbie said with a grin. 'I came in about three minutes flat. Lawrence told me later that he couldn't believe it when I started moaning and twitching. But he knew how to take advantage of the situation – he got his hand up my skirt and inside my knickers while I was still coming.'

'Which led on in due course to lying down and parting your legs for him,' said Joy thoughtfully.

' "Due course" was that same afternoon, straight after we came out of the cinema,' Debbie said with a chuckle. 'It was winter and dark by four in the afternoon. He talked me into taking my knickers off in the car-park behind the Roxy and he stood me against the wall with my feet apart and shoved his hard-on up me. I felt it stretching me – I'd never had anything thicker than Franny's fingers inside me before, and it hurt a bit. I gave a yelp and he smothered my mouth with his own while he rammed away. You wouldn't believe it, but I came before he did!'

'Debbie,' Joy said with an encouraging smile, 'I'm glad you trust me enough to speak frankly. It's clear to me that you've been treated badly by your boyfriend. I shall do everything I can to help you.'

It was an indication of how much Joy had changed that she was unashamedly assessing Debbie's sexual potential. Those big plump titties might be very pleasant to handle, and they probably had long soft bobbles to lick. And inside that white coat-dress Debbie had a broad belly that would be worth stroking and kissing.

Obviously she came very easily when she was felt, if all she said was true. Joy had formed a desire to watch Debbie thrash about in a big climax, and she wanted to push her tongue into Debbie's gasping mouth while she was coming.

'What do you mean, help me?' Debbie asked uncertainly. 'How can you . . . I don't understand.'

Joy put a hand on Debbie's shoulder and pressed her gently back on the grey sofa.

'You have fantastic emotional and sexual potential, Debbie, which is being wasted on a man who can't begin to understand you. Surely you know that already, deep down inside.'

'That's true,' Debbie said. 'In all the years we've known each other Lawrence has never really understood me.'

Joy held Debbie under the chin and turned her face upward

while she kissed her mouth. It began as a friendly kiss that implied nothing, but it steadily grew more passionate. Joy's other hand slid over Debbie's left tittie, stroking it through her clothes.

Debbie gurgled and struggled a little. Joy's grip tightened on her neck, just under her chin, forcing her head up and stopping her breaking off the kiss – which had become hot and insistent. Debbie trembled and tried to peel Joy's fingers from her throat, but by then Joy was undoing the top button of her white dress. A moment later she slid a hand inside it.

Debbie's titties were very round and chubby. Joy's fingers forced their way inside her large-cup bra to clasp a full soft tittie. 'Nnnn,' Debbie protested, pulling at the hand under her chin and trying to turn her face away from the long kiss.

The attempt worked against her, for as soon as she opened her mouth to protest, Joy's tongue pushed inside. Debbie gulped and shook as she felt her mouth being filled with Joy's warm wet tongue. She struggled, but the hand inside her bra was taking liberties – there was a fingertip rubbing lightly over the little bobble and making it stand firm and upright.

When Joy ended the lingering kiss and moved her mouth away, Debbie gasped, almost breathless, and stared into her face wide-eyed as if she didn't understand what was happening. Joy released her throat and with both hands free began to unbutton Debbie's crisp white dress all the way down, from neckline to belted waist.

'No . . .' Debbie was murmuring, 'this isn't right.'

Joy didn't bother to answer. She smiled at Debbie while she unbuckled the belt and carried on unbuttoning her dress to the hem. When it was completely undone, the dress fell open to expose the large-cup white bra containing Debbie's titties and white briefs under fine black tights.

'It would be different if you were a man,' Debbie moaned, holding on to Joy's wrists to stop her touching her body.

'Don't be silly,' Joy said softly. 'If I were a man I'd be trying to get a big hard *thing* into you for my thirty-second thrill – just a cheap thrill, that's all men ever want. But I'm going to love you as it should be, for *your* satisfaction, Debbie.'

The white bra soon hung unclipped and loose round Debbie's neck while Joy ducked her head and licked the red-brown bobbles of her titties. They were not as big as she'd imagined they'd be, considering the size of Debbie's fleshy mounds. But they were exciting to lick and they stood up proudly under Joy's wet tongue.

'No – you'd better stop . . .' Debbie gasped urgently. 'I don't want you to do this to me . . .'

Joy was unable to answer in words. She had sucked one firm bobble into her mouth and was lapping the tip of her tongue over it in quick little butterfly-wing strokes. She had the other between forefinger and thumb and was rolling it gently. It took hardly a minute before Debbie came with a long gasping moan.

It was over very quickly, Joy noted – *easy come, easy go*. Debbie was slumped on the sofa, her body almost horizontal, trembling in the aftermath of her big thrill. Joy turned her attention from her new lover's titties to the insides of her sturdy thighs and began to stroke them slowly and gently.

Debbie's knees drifted apart as soon as her thighs were touched. She sank lower when Joy's hand glided up her thigh all the way and cupped the warm mound over which her knickers were stretched.

There was a puzzled look on Debbie's face. She couldn't have been in any doubt over what Joy was doing to her – all she could be puzzled about was why she was letting her do it. The answer was simple enough, even if she hadn't reached that point in her thinking yet: she was letting Joy play with her because it was very pleasurable.

More so than it was with Lawrence, though Debbie wasn't ready to admit that yet. Joy smiled down at her and slid forward off the sofa. She knelt in front of Debbie on the carpet and with both hands pulled her black tights down to her ankles, slipped her flat-heeled shoes off and removed the tights completely.

'Oh,' Debbie sighed, staring at Joy in bewilderment, 'oh, do you really think we should be doing this . . . ?'

'Yes, I do,' Joy answered confidently. 'I really do think so, Debbie. You've been misused for years by your boyfriend – it's time now you were shown a little tenderness.'

She ran her hands up Debbie's strong bare thighs and started to pull her knickers down. Debbie's face turned bright pink with embarrassment at this exposure of her ultimate secret. With the knickers halfway down, Joy stopped and stared, her mouth open in surprise.

Debbie's kitty was shaved smooth and bare. Joy put a hand between Debbie's legs to feel it – its total lack of hair made it look young and girlish, virginal – except that the nudity also made the kitty appear to be bigger and more prominent.

The long lips were firm to the touch and they parted easily when Joy pressed a finger between them to find the nubby. It was slippery and still firm from coming, and when Joy touched it Debbie trembled and sighed, 'Yes'. But the next moment she murmured, 'We really shouldn't . . .'

She was sprawled with her feet on the floor and her knees apart. Joy used the fingers of both hands to hold her kitty open while she rubbed the balls of her thumbs gently over the little pink nubby she had uncovered. Debbie twitched about on the sofa, eyes staring, and came again almost at once.

'How lucky you are, Debbie,' Joy said softly, 'to be able to come like that – no long struggle and strain for you, eh?'

'I can't help myself,' Debbie sighed, 'I've always been like that – it's a nuisance at times.'

She made it sound like a disadvantage, which Joy couldn't at first understand. Then realisation dawned – it was because of Debbie's extreme susceptibility to stimulation that her boyfriend could so easily take advantage of her for his own pleasure.

Joy left her new friend's nubby alone for a while to let her recover and instead stroked her sturdy thighs and nude groins. Debbie was sighing softly all the time and Joy guessed that she hadn't experienced gentle, sensual lovemaking for a long time, if ever. This Lawrence person who had been ramming his twanger into her since she was a sixteen-year-old schoolgirl very probably never bothered to do more than fumble at her kitty for a few seconds before he slid into her and shot his little lot.

'Why do you shave your kitty, Debbie?' Joy asked, trailing her finger-tips lightly up and down the long smooth lips. 'Do you do it because Lawrence wants you like that?'

'Yes, he tells me to do it – he says it makes him think that we're still kids at school and that turns him on.'

'Does he kiss it? Does he tongue you?'

'He'd never do anything like that. He just likes to look at me when I've got my knickers off. And feel me.'

'Only your knickers? Why don't you strip naked, as this happens at your flat, or so I imagine?'

'We don't actually get into bed together,' Debbie confessed. 'Lawrence can never stay long enough. I take my knickers off and sit on the table, he stands between my legs and puts his thing in. He feels my titties while he's doing me and when he's come he wipes himself with my knickers and kisses me Goodbye.'

'This is monstrous!' Joy exclaimed. 'You may think you love him but that's no reason to let him use you as a convenience.'

'You don't understand,' Debbie said stubbornly. 'He loves me, too – he tells me so every time and he wants to be with me all the time, but he can't leave Lorna because of the children. We meet when we can.'

'Children? Just the twins – or are there more?'

'Lorna's had five so far,' said Debbie. 'He can't desert them, can he?'

'Lorna didn't have them all by herself,' Joy pointed out. 'Lawrence seems to be attending to her very seriously.'

'Well, she's his wife,' Debbie said in explanation. 'She's got her rights, I understand that.'

Joy could hardly stop herself smiling at this.

'Poor abused Debbie,' she murmured, 'you've been victimised for years by a man you trusted. But I'm going to change your life.'

She laid both hands flat on Debbie's thighs and bent down until she could kiss the long bare lips of her kitty. Her tongue lapped up and down their whole length, wetting them.

'Oh!' Debbie moaned, 'oh, no!'

Joy slid her hands under Debbie and gripped the full bare cheeks of her bum. The soft flesh was warm and welcoming – Joy sank her fingers deep into it and squeezed and rolled.

'I'm going to come...' Debbie moaned.

A moment later she dissolved, gasping and twitching, as a tide of orgasm swept from her wet open kitty up through her broad belly to her titties, to their standing pink bobbles and back down again through her heaving belly to her kitty.

Her eyes were staring, her back arched – she came and came as if she'd never stop. Joy pressed her tongue between the loose lips and flicked it fast over the hot little nub inside. Debbie was screaming and jerking in a frenzy, until finally she collapsed and lay limp with her mouth open.

'There,' said Joy, raising her head, 'that's how you should be done. You'll never meet a man who can do you as I can.'

'I can't believe you did that to me,' Debbie sighed, 'I thought that was only for young girls playing about together.'

Joy lay forward over Debbie's soft belly so that she could kiss her mouth and hold her titties at the same time.

'That's how it's going to be for you from now on, Debbie. Forget those thirty-second bouts sitting on a table for a man to take his pleasure – that's all a bad dream from the past. I'm going to give you very special love and attention.'

'I can't just break up with Lawrence, not after ten years with him,' Debbie said. 'I love him, surely you can see that.'

'You won't have time for him,' Joy assured her. 'When he

calls round to misuse your wonderful body for his lust you won't be there – you'll be with me.'

Her fingertips were roaming over Debbie's plump titties, making the little pink bobbles grow bigger.

'Well, I don't know . . .' Debbie said doubtfully.

'Don't worry about it,' Joy told her. 'Leave everything to me. I'll take good care of you.'

Debbie's brown eyes were starting to close; exciting little sensations rippled through her from Joy's manipulation of her titties. No need to worry about scandal and Sunday newspapers now that Debbie had joined the circle, Joy decided.

'I think you should come again, don't you?' she murmured.

'Yes, yes . . .' Debbie sighed.

Chapter Eleven

After his misadventure in the locker-room, Keith the caretaker became wary. Being caught hiding in a metal cupboard to get a good look at Penny Carlton's naked young body – with his flies undone and his twanger in his hand – had been the most shameful experience of his life.

Or so he thought at the time it happened. For days afterward he went about his duties at the college with downcast gaze, staring at the ground. He avoided eye contact with any of the girls, because he was certain Penny and her friend Nesta Wade had spread the story round the college. He knew he'd blush scarlet if he saw a girl grinning at him.

He heard giggles behind his back from time to time and he knew they were talking about him and pointing. But he daren't look round to see who it was. They'd be whispering about him shooting off at the moment Nesta jerked the locker door open.

There was another result of the nasty shock to his nervous system: his flopper hung down limply between his thighs and refused to raise its head. Nothing Keith could do to it made any difference – it dangled lax and surly, as if it were just as ashamed as he was. For Keith this was the most worrying thing of all – he began to wonder if he'd ever have another stand in his life.

But as the days passed, the sense of shame faded and his confidence began to return. The old urges stirred and he felt he wanted to look at girls again – just a sly look at their bobbing young titties when they were jogging beside the Sports Coach

157

on the evening run. Or a view of long smooth thighs on the diving-board over the swimming pool.

He wanted to lurk by the tennis courts for a glimpse of little white knickers when skirts swirled up in an energetic match. And he wanted to stand silent at windows after Lights Out and see bare young titties when girls were undressing to go to bed. He wanted to watch them take their knickers off and hope for the supreme prize, a clear view of naked bums or kitties.

Sometimes a girl getting ready for bed took her time before slipping a nightie over her head, giving Keith the chance for a good long ogle. Some girls went to bed in pyjamas, and when he saw one of those he had a bet with himself whether she'd put the top on first or the bottom. He'd more than once wondered what it would be like to get into bed with a girl wearing pyjamas he imagined himself giving her kitty a feel through the thin trousers instead of putting a hand up a nightie.

Whether the girls wore pyjamas or short nighties, he knew what they did to each other when they got in bed together. He'd never actually been able to *see* them doing it because they turned the lights off, but he'd heard their little gasps and shrieks of pleasure.

There'd been one time he'd been very lucky at a window – when it wasn't even bedtime. It was the middle of the afternoon and on the off-chance he'd looked into one of the teacher's windows on the ground floor. What he saw astonished him. It was the thin dark-haired woman who was Head of Wexby House – having a nap on her bed stark naked.

Keith's true and abiding interest, though, was young girls. This was a passion he shared with Eleanor Redruth, although he had no way of knowing this. Sixteen was the ideal age, he and Eleanor both believed. At that age girls were at their most lusciously *do-able*. Even seventeen was still acceptable, though by then their chuffies had been handled more.

At eighteen they were more or less grown up. Boys' twangers had been up most of them. It was Keith's belief that the average young woman of eighteen was done by a different boyfriend every week – and that was off-putting for Keith, because what excited him was the idea that he was the first man to feel a soft young kitty.

By nineteen, according to him, girls had not only been done, they'd been practically done to death. He was convinced that after they'd left Lechlade Ladies' College and arrived at Oxford University they were pounced on by male students. He'd seen them lounging about the streets of Oxford – superior lads in long striped scarves who jumped on girls night and day, in between reading books and rowing boats.

Nevertheless, when he looked through Joy Locksley's window one afternoon and saw her stretched out naked on her bed, it wouldn't have been true to say Keith wasn't interested. She was ten years over the age that really excited him, that much was true. But on the other hand, he knew that she wasn't being done night after night by a man. Like all the teachers at Lechlade she was unmarried. She had no boyfriend he knew about. And he wasn't going to let an opportunity like this go to waste.

He pressed his face up to the window and gloated over her naked body. She had small but well-shaped titties and a dark-haired chuffie. Her belly looked smooth-skinned and lickable, with a deep round button Keith would like to get his tongue into. At the same time he would be pressing his fingers into her.

Keith couldn't be sure what she got up to in the vacations. He'd heard of unmarried women who went abroad for their holidays to Spain with the avowed intention of getting themselves done non-stop by waiters and guitar-players. To Keith's way of thinking that was a sad waste – he would have been happy to do it for any of the staff at Lechlade and save them the expense of going abroad.

As to how Joy Locksley managed for sex during term, Keith's guess was that she did what many of the other teachers did – diddle a girl or two. He'd seen girls coming out of teachers' rooms, pink-cheeked and contented, and he could put two and two together.

He knew that some of the teachers did each other, and he'd once caught Miss Howlett, the modern languages teacher, and Miss Stanhope, the history teacher, right in the act. Monica Howlett was perched on a desk in a classroom one lunchtime, after the girls had gone. Claudine Stanhope was standing with her hand up Monica's plaid skirt. The woman being felt had a pop-eyed look on her face as if she was going to come at any moment.

There was every chance, Keith considered, that Miss Locksley had tonguing-sessions with other teachers or diddled a girl when she fancied one. She had a nice body for it, he told himself, looking in at the window as she lay seemingly asleep, uncovered and naked. He could do a lot for her, given the chance. He saw that she wasn't asleep when her hand rose from her side and moved over her belly and between her legs.

She uncrossed her ankles and moved her feet apart, still keeping her eyes closed – and Keith almost moaned out loud when he saw that she was diddling herself with a long slow middle finger.

He glanced around to see if there was anyone in sight. At this time of the day classes and games were in full swing and everyone was occupied. Except Miss Locksley, who apparently was taking the afternoon off. And except for Keith the caretaker, who had forgotten what maintenance job he was supposed to be doing in the excitement of watching her.

Naturally he was hoping to see her make herself come. He had his stiff twanger out in his hand and was stroking it. But she opened her eyes and caught sight of the face outside her window. A pair of pale-blue French knickers lay beside her on the bed, though Keith hadn't noticed them. She grabbed them and held them bunched against her chuffie to hide it.

Keith turned and fled, stuffing his hard-on into his jeans as he ran. He was afraid she'd recognised him, although he'd darted away from the window fast when her eyes opened. But he heard no more about it, so he apparently had got away in the nick of time.

Now that he was getting over the scare he'd had in the locker-room, it was in his mind that he'd like to see Joy do herself again. And he'd like to hide near the tennis courts and the swimming pool to watch the girls. He hoped the sight of their smooth young bodies would be a cure for his worrying problem of limpness between the legs. But he daren't play Peeping Tom in case he was caught again.

A week after the locker-room misadventure, Keith woke up one morning to find he'd been dreaming about Penny Carlton. Where but in the locker-room! The start of his dream had been as on that fateful day, with Penny sitting on the bench to take her trainers and socks off. Keith was inside the locker watching her, staring through the louvre to get a flash of bare thigh.

She pulled her tee-shirt over her head to reveal plump young titties in a white sports-bra. She reached behind her to undo it and Keith gulped when it came off to expose her oversized titties. His twanger was jerking hard in his jeans and he put his hand over his flies to hold it still.

At this point the dream began to diverge from what had taken place in reality. Penny stood up and hooked her thumbs into the waist-band of her little white knickers, and this time she bent over and slid them down her legs immediately. Her titties were swinging loose under her and their pink bobbles made Keith's mouth water. He wanted to reach out and grab handfuls of plump tittie to squeeze and suck.

Penny sat down on the bench again, totally naked and facing the locker in which Keith was hiding. Her knees were spread and he had a full frontal view of her brown-haired kitty. She knew he was in the locker, she looked straight at the door and grinned at him. She beckoned; he pushed the door open and climbed out with his hand on his flies to control his pulsating length.

She spread her legs and told Keith to kiss her chuffie. He went down on his knees on the hard floor with a grateful sob and licked the soft warm lips. He was sure he'd fallen in love with her and he wanted to show her how he felt. The best way he could think of was to give her the ultimate thrill. For himself he wanted nothing. He'd never ask her to lie on her back for him while he slid his hard-on up her – never!

He woke up at this point. It was early morning and he was in bed with a big throbbing stiffie. He was lying on his back and Sally was pressing herself close to him, her hand round his twanger jerking it up and down. As Keith reached full consciousness he found that she'd pulled her nightie up round her neck and was rubbing her hot and hairy kitty against his thigh.

'It's been a fortnight since you did me,' she scolded him as she handled his stiff length. 'Have you been interfering with any of the girls, Keith? I'll kill you if you have!'

'No, course not,' he said in a hurry, 'I'd never dream of touching a young girl – what makes you say that?'

He was worried that she might have heard the rumour that was going round the college. It wasn't only the girls gossiping about him – some of the teachers also had heard that he'd been caught in a locker diddling himself.

'You're always staring at girls when you're supposed to be working,' Sally said. 'Have you had *this* up any of them?'

'No, I haven't,' he said, trying to sound convincing. And it was the plain truth, he *hadn't* had his stiffie up any of them. Though given the chance he would.

Worried as he was about what Sally might have heard, he was grateful that dreaming of Penny had cured the limpness of his flopper. It stood hard as iron, and the vigorous way Sally was wanking it made it even harder.

'Get on top,' he sighed, 'I want to do you.'

Sally needed no second invitation. She rose up, threw a long lean leg over him and sat on his belly, her fist still clenched round his hard-on. Keith slipped his hands between her thighs to feel her warm kitty and she spread her knees wider to let him get his fingers well into her.

162

They were both breathing hard and shaking as they manipulated each other's hairy parts. Keith was staring at the bedroom ceiling and fantasising that it was big-tittied Penny sitting astride his belly and jerking his twanger up and down in her hand. He was going to come in a minute and shoot his lot on to Penny's bare belly, right up to her titties. Higher than that even – he was going to shoot his cream up into her face!

But Sally decided she needed something more satisfying than a couple of fingers in her. She slid down his belly till she was squatting over his thighs, without ever relaxing her grip on his swollen length for a moment. He watched wide-eyed and panting as she pulled her chuffie open and steered the head of his throbbing shaft into it.

'Do me,' she was moaning, 'do me really hard, Keith . . .'

But it wasn't like that at all – she was too busy doing him to let him do her. She sat down hard, driving his shaft all the way up into her hot, slippery slit, and before he could reach up to clasp her slack little titties she was bouncing up and down and making him slide in and out smoothly.

Her blonde hair was fluffed out untidily round her head from sleeping. Her long slender thighs were splayed wide apart to let him penetrate her to the very limit. Her titties flopped up and down in his hands as she bounced – Keith was being well and truly done and he loved it.

'I'm coming,' Sally moaned.

Keith could say nothing in reply except *Ahhh* as his belly jerked and he squirted his lot into her clinging chuffie.

It set him up for the day, that early morning quickie with Sally. He went about his work cheerful and whistling and not afraid to look girls in the face any more. He passed by the tennis courts twice during the day and dawdled as long as he dared, for a look at bare thighs. He stood by the swimming pool for ten minutes, out of sight, eyeing lovely young bodies in clinging wet swimsuits – and his twanger stood hard upright in his jeans.

About four in the afternoon he decided to take a look behind the main pavilion, where girls sometimes sunbathed on the grass, out of sight of the teachers. He could hear voices, so he approached in a roundabout way until he was lying on his belly in tall grass with a perfect view of the area.

He drew in a long breath of appreciation at what he saw. There were four girls lying on the grass sunbathing – and they were topless! He stared at their lithe bodies, golden-brown from the sun. And their fully displayed titties, their bare bellies and their smooth thighs. The only parts hidden were their untouched little kitties in bikini bottoms.

Untouched, that was the key word in his thoughts, although he guessed that they diddled each other all the time. What he meant was *untouched by a man.* Girls feeling each other didn't count. If he ever got his hand down any of those bikini briefs he'd be the first man to have a feel between their legs – it was a thought to make his hard-on bound in his jeans as if to force its way out.

He'd brought his binoculars with him. He focused them on a pair of pert young titties, making them look so close that he felt he need only stick out his tongue to lick their pink bobbles. Next he trained the glasses on a girl lying on her back, focusing on the mound between her slightly parted thighs. He visualised the lovely sun-warmed kitty under the thin blue bikini bottom, and this time he stuck his tongue right out, making believe he could touch the hidden kitty with it.

His twanger was twitching so strongly while he eyed all those bouncy young titties that he couldn't bear the tightness of his jeans, it felt as if they were strangling him. He reached underneath his belly, intending to run his zipper down and give his constricted length more freedom.

It was the disaster of the locker-room all over again. Keith was so lost in his dreams that he didn't hear the rush of feet on the grass behind him. The first he knew of his desperate plight was when the weight of three girls' bodies thumped down on his back and legs. A bath towel was wrapped round his head to blindfold him and his arms were dragged behind his back and tied at the wrists.

'Got him!' a girl's voice sang out. 'Come and see.'

In seconds he heard more voices around him, as the sunbathers he'd been watching arrived. They'd been the bait, though poor Keith was too dumbfounded by his capture to realise that immediately.

He was rolled over on his back by hands and feet, and none too kindly, leaving his bound arms trapped under him. His legs were dragged apart and a girl sat heavily on each knee to pinion him – it was very uncomfortable.

'What have you got to say for yourself?' a girl's voice demanded as she prodded his bulging flies with her bare foot. Flabbergasted though he was, Keith thought he recognised the voice as Rachel Fermor, a dark-haired girl in Sawby House.

He'd once watched her exercising in the gym and had caught a dick-stiffening view of her round young bum when she bent over to touch her toes. She had an unusual nickname – he'd heard other girls address her as 'Monkey', though he had no idea why. Now he came to think about it, all four girls he'd spied on sunbathing were from Sawby House.

'Let me go,' he said, trying to sound commanding, but his voice came out muffled through the towel. 'You're hurting me.'

His plea was ignored. The same bare foot was prodding again at his bulging flies.

'Why do you walk around the college with your hand in your pocket?' Rachel demanded – if it really was Rachel.

'I don't,' Keith protested.

'You do,' several voices said. 'We've all seen you.'

'On cold mornings,' he said. 'I haven't got any gloves.'

'It's summer,' Rachel said. 'We've been watching you nearly all day. You play with your *thing* while you're walking about – you make it stand up stiff in your trousers.'

'That's not true,' Keith protested. He was blushing a bright red, but happily for him the towel round his head hid that.

'See what I mean?' Rachel addressed the other girls. 'He's telling lies. You can see he's got a stand now – look at that bulge in his jeans.'

'I haven't,' Keith protested.

He yelped as her foot ground his hard-on against his belly.

'What's that, then?' she asked.

'Leave me alone,' he said, both excited and alarmed by what he thought the girls might do to him.

'Let's have a look at it, now he's our prisoner,' a voice suggested. 'Get it out, Rachel.'

A knee dug into Keith's belly and then he felt his flies being unzipped. His jockey-shorts were pulled down and he heard giggling all around him as his stiffie jumped up like a Jack-in-the-Box.

'On the slack, are you?' Rachel asked derisively. 'Doesn't look like it to me. What do you think, Loraine? You wanted to see what he's got.'

'You did that to me,' Keith defended himself. 'I *was* on the slack till you lot jumped on me and started to mess me about – it's all your fault.'

'Listen to him,' Rachel said scornfully to the others. 'Did we make him sneak up on us and hide here to stare at our titties through his binoculars while he played with himself?'

'I didn't,' Keith protested weakly, 'I was just having a rest on the grass and I didn't know you were there.'

'We know all about *you*,' Rachel said. 'You were hiding in a locker in the shower-room to spy on girls from Wexby House.'

'I wasn't doing anything,' he muttered through the towel. It sounded feeble even to him.

'When they pulled the door open they found you holding your *thing* in your hand,' Rachel accused as she kicked him in the thigh two or three times. 'They saw you shooting your cream – everybody's heard about it.'

Keith groaned inwardly and said nothing. There was nothing he could say – his worst fears were coming true.

'Is that as big as it gets?' another girl asked curiously. 'I thought they were bigger than that.'

'I don't really know,' Loraine answered. 'If we had a ruler we could measure it. It looks about six inches to me. What do you think, Rachel?'

'About six inches,' Rachel agreed.

'Less than that,' said another voice. 'Five inches, maybe.'

'It might get bigger,' Loraine said. 'They swell up to their full size when you pull them – I've done it to a boyfriend at home. Rub it up and down and see.'

'Not me,' Rachel said. 'You do it.'

'I'll do it,' another girl offered. Keith felt a hand clasp his hard-on and joggle it up and down. He gasped and his legs started shaking under the weight of the girls sitting on them.

'I think it's getting bigger, Tessa,' he heard Rachel say.

'It feels harder,' Tessa agreed.

'Do it to him faster – it won't drop off – and we'll see if it gets any longer,' Loraine suggested.

'Yes, but be careful,' Rachel advised, 'you don't want him shooting off in your hand – think how messy that would be.'

Her words struck a chord in Keith's mind. His fear vanished and he was in seventh heaven. He couldn't actually see any of the girls, because of the towel they'd wrapped round his head, but he visualised them around him as he lay helpless on his back with his wrists tied.

He guessed there were seven of them at least – the four he'd seen sitting together sunbathing and three more who'd jumped on him from behind. They were topless – the four sunbathers, anyway – just little bikini briefs to cover their bums. In his fervid imagination he could see their bare young titties swinging above him as they knelt round him on the grass.

They were staring at his hard-on, fascinated by its size and strength – he could almost feel the intensity of their hot gaze on it. And one of these lovely young girls was holding it in her hand. This was not a bad dream, Keith realised, and he grinned sheepishly inside his blindfold – not a sweaty night-mare at all. It was more like his wildest dream suddenly come true. Half a dozen near-naked young girls were admiring his stiffie!

The hand holding it slid up and down vigorously. Which one was it who volunteered? Ah yes, they'd called her Tessa. In fact he'd heard the names of three of them – it wouldn't be difficult to track them down when he wanted to. What he'd do to them when he'd found them, well, that was another question.

Would this Tessa show him her bare titties and play with his stiffie if he got her on her own? He doubted it. Would dark-haired Rachel rub the sole of her bare foot over his hard-on if her friends weren't there to back her up? Not very likely. But that was something he could think about another day – just now he was too occupied by the thrills he was getting to guess about thrills in the future.

'Yes, it's definitely grown bigger,' he heard Rachel say. 'Just keep it like that while I take a few snaps.'

'Oh, my god . . .' Keith moaned inside the towel.

The thought was thundering through his mind – the sexy young ladies were taking photos of his hard-on, while they held him down on his back helpless. It was just like being raped and he loved it. He started to mumble *Sit over me, Tessa, and slide my dick up you while Rachel takes a snap of you being done – I promise not to come in you* . . . But the girls were chattering away and nobody heard what he said.

Not that it mattered in the least. Keith was almost frantic with lust and he was rolling his body from side to side. His captors thought he was trying to break loose. They laughed at him and bore down harder with their weight on his legs and shoulders to hold him still.

The camera was being pointed at his twanger at that moment. It was focused on Keith's pride and joy. He heard the *click-whirr* of a photo being taken and couldn't stop himself bucking his hips upward in fast thrusts, as if he were driving it up a kitty.

'Hold him still,' Rachel said.

'Move over and let me sit on his head,' he heard a girl say.

He howled in delight as she sat on his face – there was only the towel and her thin bikini briefs separating his mouth from her chuffie. He felt her knees gripping his sides, squeezing his ribs. He burrowed his face up between her thighs, trying to get his mouth closer to the warm girlish lips there.

It was difficult to breathe with her sitting over his face. His mouth was open and he was panting while he tried to push his tongue right through the towel and lick her. His belly jerked rhythmically, driving his hard length up and down through Tessa's encircling hand. Up till now she had been diddling him in an amateurish sort of way, but Keith had taken the initiative and was diddling himself by means of her clasping palm.

'I said hold him still,' Rachel complained. 'The snaps will come out blurred, the way he's jerking about.'

A bare knee pressed down hard on Keith's belly and almost winded him. Other knees pinned his thighs painfully – and the tighter the girls held him and the more helpless he became in their hands, the more ecstatic were the sensations that surged through him.

In his imagination he wished they'd raided the croquet lawn and brought four big hoops and a mallet with them. They could have held him down on his back with his arms and legs spread out while they hammered hoops down over his wrists and ankles to pin him to the ground. *Yes, yes, hammer all the hoops in* he was moaning deliriously to himself. *Hammer them in tight on my ankles and thighs and over my wrists and elbows so that I'm really pinned down and can't move...*

He wished Tessa had been wearing knickers so she could take them off and use them to blindfold him. Thin nylon knickers, warm from her young kitty, tied over his eyes. Dark-haired Rachel should have worn knickers too, so she could have taken them off and stuffed them in his mouth to gag him – it would have been like tonguing her...

The girl sitting on his head was almost stifling him, her

chuffie bearing down on his nose and mouth. Keith was gasping and groaning, only moments away from coming.

'That's better,' he heard Rachel announce. Then she said, 'Move your hand away for a minute, Tessa, it's hiding too much of his *thing*.'

When her hand released him, Keith's twanger strained upward, vibrating like a plucked guitar string. He moaned to think of the instant photos that were being taken – they'd be shown all round and his stand was going to be the talk of Lechlade Ladies' College.

When Penny and Nesta had set him up and caught him in the locker-room they threatened to take photos to pin on the college notice-board. It had scared him when they said that, because of the enquiry that would be sure to follow – but the idea had also made him very excited.

It was only a threat that time and didn't really mean much. But now it was actually happening! Snaps of his twanger were going to be handed round from girl to girl throughout the college. And he hadn't posed for them of his own free will. The fact was that he'd struggled against them, or so he told himself. But there were too many girls against him – if there'd been two, or even three, he'd have been able to break loose. But seven of them? No way!

They made me do it he told himself, gasping. *I couldn't help myself. I was minding my own business when they all jumped on me and ripped my flies open and ravaged my helpless body.*

'Got it,' Rachel said, sounding pleased with herself. 'Move your knee out of the way, Miranda, while I get a close-up.'

Close-up? Keith moaned, pressing his nose hard as he could up into the soft warm kitty on his face. *She's taking close-ups of my dick! I can't stop them . . . I'm going to come . . . I can't help it . . .*

'Will it grow any bigger, Tessa, or is that it?' Loraine asked.

'We'll soon find out.' Tessa's hand gripped Keith's twanger again and jerked it up and down boldly.

Oh, oh, ohhh Keith moaned unheard.

He couldn't help himself – this was it! He felt a thrilling surge inside his belly. The gang of bare-tittied girls had taken him all the way! He came abruptly, jerking and heaving. Through ecstatic sensations he could hear the girls laughing to see his cream shoot high into the air.

Chapter Twelve

There was no continuing friendship between geography teacher Sharon and Anybody's, even though Joy Locksley had seen the two of them lying under a tree with Sharon's hand inside Annabel's jeans – for which Joy called Sharon a treacherous bitch. That afternoon by the willow on the river bank was the first time Sharon diddled Annabel. After the row with Joy over it, she decided it caused too much trouble to play with girls.

The end of term was only weeks away and so Sharon resolved to remain chaste until the vacation – when nobody would know or care what she did. 'Chaste' didn't mean giving up sex entirely – when the mood took her she treated herself to a finger-wave. She also played tennis every day, fast and furious games, to burn up her energy.

She was in a doubles game with three girls when the accident happened. A backhand smash by Hilary Landor sent the ball skimming very low over the net at dazzling speed. Sharon raced for it, arm and body stretching out as she swooped down to get to it before it hit the ground. She missed her footing, missed the ball and went down on her knees with a shriek.

'Game!' Hilary sang out cheerfully. 'That's two to us.'

'Are you all right, Miss Pomeroy?' Orline Ashby asked anxiously. She was Sharon's partner and saw she was in pain.

'I can't get up,' said Sharon, white-faced. 'I've ricked my back. Give me a hand.'

Orline called to the other pair to come and help. They ran round the net and the three girls got Sharon on her feet – but she was bent over double and said it hurt her too much to stand up straight.

'We'll get you to physiotherapy right away,' Orline said. 'It might be a slipped disc.'

'That won't help,' Sharon said, tight-lipped. 'This is not one of Debbie Gregson's days to be here. You'd better get me to my own room and call a doctor.'

'Mr Dundale is a trained physio,' Orline told her. 'He could treat you just as well as Miss Gregson could. Maybe better.'

'That's right,' Hilary said. 'I've heard he's got a diploma. And he's got strong hands, I should think.'

'I can't go to him,' Sharon said ruefully. 'You know that.'

'He's not allowed to give treatment,' Marjorie Newmill said. 'I mean, you can't let a man fool about with young ladies like us. You never know what he might get up to.'

Her tone was so insincere that it penetrated Sharon's agony. She turned her head sharply to stare at Marjorie, then gasped at the pain the sudden movement gave her. Hilary and Orline were helping her to walk slowly off the tennis court, her arms over their shoulders and their arms about her waist.

If the truth were known, Marjorie was one of the girls who'd taken full advantage of Orline's successful scheme to persuade Toby Dundale to massage her. In fact a lot of them had gone to him with imaginary twinges after they'd heard of Orline's success. When he got over his initial misgivings, Toby accepted his new role. But he remained cautious about it, for if the Principal ever got to know he'd ignored the rules set for him, he'd be sacked.

With two or three girls turning up for treatment every day that Debbie wasn't there, Toby's life became full of fun and variety. But it wasn't easy to hold himself back from jumping on top of the pretty young girls who lay on the table with their legs apart to be diddled. How he managed to control his urges was a mystery to him, but somehow he kept his nearly perpetual hard-on inside his tight little jockstrap and himself out of trouble.

That first time with Orline, he'd relieved his feelings by turning her face-down so he could stand between her thighs and diddle himself between the cheeks of her bare bum. Now that so many girls were practically queueing outside the door for his attentions, he couldn't do that every time or he'd be a nervous wreck in a fortnight. It was enjoyable to hold back and let his twanger get harder and stronger through the day.

Sometimes the pressure became so intense that he came in his shorts. There were two girls who had that effect on him every time they opened their legs on the table. Fair-haired, long-thighed, slim-bellied Hilary Landor was one of them. Twice a week she'd lie naked on the massage table and smile up at him while he played with her kitty.

She liked to tease him while he was stroking her.

'Your *thing* is standing up stiff,' Hilary would say, smiling. 'I can see a big bulge in your shorts. You want to put it in me and you can't, because I won't let you.'

'One day,' Toby would gasp, his finger-tip dancing over her slippery little nubby, 'one day I *will* have it up you...'

'That's what you think,' she'd say, 'but you won't, you'll always be just a sex-slave... I'm coming now...'

Her long slender back would arch off the table in quick spasms, while Toby clasped his free hand over his flies and gasped at the wet surge of his cream shooting into his jockstrap.

The other girl who had the same fantastic effect on him was Linda Knight, the proud possessor of the ginger-haired kitty. Toby found it very exciting and he liked to tease Linda when she spread her legs on the massage-table.

'Are you still a virgin, Linda?' he'd ask her while he was stroking gently inside the open wet lips of her kitty. 'Is it true you've never let a boyfriend slip his hard-on into this lovely little chuffie?'

'Never,' she'd sigh, wiggling her bare little bum on the table. 'I'll always stay a virgin – I'm never going to let any horrid big *thing* get into me to stretch me open like an old handbag.'

'Grown-up girls love the feel of a hard-on up inside them,' Toby would say while the ball of his thumb glided over her nubby and made her sigh and tremble with pleasure.

'Not me, though,' Linda would gasp, little ripples of delight pulsing through her, 'I'll never let a boy shoot his sticky stuff into my belly.'

'You won't let a boy,' Toby would murmur, his twanger throbbing inside his shorts, 'but you'll let *me*, Linda – one day I'm going to shoot *my* sticky stuff into your ginger-haired kitty...'

'Never...' she'd moan as she came under his manipulating hands. Seconds later Toby would moan with her as his twanger bounded inside his shorts and shot his load wetly into his tight underwear.

Except when he massaged Linda and Hilary, Toby could usually hold on until his working-day ended with the evening jog and he got back to his living-quarters in the gatehouse.

Thin and sex-hungry Sally Mason was always ready for him. Keith seemed to have got over whatever problem had kept him indoors for a week and he was out and about most of the time. Which made things very convenient for Sally.

Some days when Toby got back to his own room he found Sally waiting for him on his bed, naked, with her legs wide open and a broad grin on her face. She'd be stroking her slack little titties and plucking at their pink bobbles, to make sure she was ready for him when he rushed into his bedroom and jumped on her.

Some days she couldn't even wait for him to get upstairs and pounced on him in the entrance-hall. She wrenched his shorts open the second he was through the front door and went down on her knees to get her mouth round his stiffie before he could say a word. After his day with the girls and the evening jog surrounded by pert little titties bouncing under clinging tee-shirts, Toby was more than ready to do Sally fast and hard.

There were also the mornings when Sally took Toby a

morning cup of tea after Keith got up early and went out. Drinking the tea had to wait till later – she would fling her short nightie off, whip the bedclothes back and impale herself on Toby. He'd given up wearing even pyjama bottoms – his twanger was always standing up ready for her.

No doubt about it, Sally was having the time of her life. With an athletic man at her disposal every day, it was as good as being on honeymoon. And as for Keith, he wasn't being neglected either – on the mornings he didn't wake up early and go out Sally woke him with her hand around his dick. She knew what to do to make a flopper grow into a stiffie she could spike herself on and ride.

All three of them were happier than they ever had been before. Keith because he felt he was being sexually abused by gangs of pretty sixteen-year-old girls, besides being raped by Sally three or four times a week. It excited him to think of it in those terms – that he was being raped, by the girls and by Sally. He loved it.

Sally herself couldn't imagine a more satisfying arrangement than the one she had with the two men in her life. She was having Toby every day and Keith two or three mornings a week. Her chuffie had never been put through its paces so regularly before, not even when she was a sex-mad eighteen-year-old.

As for Toby, he was sure that being Sports Coach at Lechlade Ladies' College was by far the best job he was ever likely to have. He meant to hang on to it, whatever it took.

He was on the tennis courts in his little white shorts showing a class the finer points of putting spin on a return when he saw the commotion where Sharon Pomeroy had tripped and fallen. She was an attractive woman, with long blonde hair she tied back most of the time, slender and with well-shaped titties that looked interesting under her clothes. Toby fancied her and had tried more than once to strike up a friendship.

Sharon would chat amiably but she didn't seem to have any interest in him. He knew what went on in the college between the women teachers and between some of them and the students. That being so, it was likely that Sharon had a bed-friend and wasn't interested in men. Which was, he thought, a pity.

He would dearly love to have Sharon's knickers off and lay her down on her back. His guess was that she came very quietly, with hardly a sigh – just a trembling of her legs, very genteel. The thought excited him and made him even more anxious to have her on her back. All considered, it was fortunate he was being well taken care of by Keith's wife.

When he saw Sharon being helped off the court he realised that she'd hurt herself. He handed his racket to the nearest girl and asked the class to carry on without him. He hurried after the group helping Sharon to hobble toward the main building.

'Thank goodness you're here, Mr Dundale,' Hilary said primly. 'Miss Pomeroy has strained her back and she can't stand up properly. It's not one of Miss Gregson's days today, so we don't know what's best to do for her.'

'Let me have a look,' Toby suggested. 'Stand still for a moment while I check her back – it won't hurt. Let go of her slowly, girls, so I can see how she stands on her own.'

Sharon groaned when Hilary and Orline released her and stepped away. Toby eyed her carefully – she was bent over forward and to one side. He put his hand flat on her back, just above her bum, and slid it slowly up along her spine to her shoulder-blades. She wore her white shirt loose outside her shorts and he could feel the warmth of her body.

He put his hand under the shirt and moved it up her back once more, to enjoy the feel of her smooth flesh. While he was stroking Sharon under the pretence of locating the damage, he was looking directly at Hilary. He went down on one knee and slipped both his hands under Sharon's loose shirt while he stared at Hilary's long thighs.

Her tennis shorts were shorter than they should have been; many of the young ladies were wearing shorter tennis and running shorts since they'd seen how brief Toby's were. He was sure the Principal had taken note and disapproved strongly, but so far she had not approached him again on the subject.

Hilary's shorts had practically no legs at all, leaving her long slim thighs uncovered almost to her groins. And where her thighs met there was a delicious little mound under the thin material of the shorts. This was what Toby was staring at while he was stroking Sharon Pomeroy's back and ignoring her faint moans.

He knew just what Hilary's kitty looked like – he'd fingered it lots of times on the massage table. It had fair hair and soft lips that opened easily to his touch. He felt a great urge to strip her tennis shorts down her legs, pull her down on the grass and ram his hard-on right up her. He'd told her more than once that he'd do her one day and she always smiled at him and contradicted him. But he meant it.

'Just *there*,' he said to Sharon, touching the painful spot on her back. 'I can feel where the trouble is – I think you might have torn a muscle or pulled a tendon or even displaced a disc. I'd have to make a proper examination to be sure.'

'We told Miss Pomeroy that you're a trained physio,' Orline said with a sly smile. 'She's in such pain – it's a great pity you're not allowed to help her.'

'Yes,' Toby agreed quickly. Behind Sharon's back he shook his head at Orline to warn her not to give the secret away. But Orline wasn't going to be put off, and the other two girls were grinning at him.

'I wonder if that's right, though,' Orline went on blithely. 'We know that you're not allowed to treat students – but does the same rule apply to teachers?'

'I really don't know,' Toby said curtly.

He was nervous in case Orline gave anything away in front of a member of the staff. If Sharon Pomeroy became suspicious of his activities she might report her fears to the Principal – which could be disastrous.

'We must get you indoors so you can lie down flat while we

get a doctor for you,' he said to Sharon. 'Slip your arm over my shoulder and Hilary will take the other side. We'll walk slowly.'

'I'm in agony,' Sharon said after a few steps. 'I must lie down. Help me down on the grass, please.'

'Not a good idea,' Toby said, shaking his head. 'If you lie down here you'll get chilled, even though it's a hot day. You were sweating on the court and if you let it dry on you, your back will seize up completely.'

'What can I do?' she asked desperately. 'You're the expert, so tell me what to do . . .'

'That's right,' Hilary said. 'You can't leave her in agony – you have to do something.'

'Forget about the silly rules,' Orline said. 'This is an emergency.'

'But . . . but . . .' Toby stammered, at a loss.

'You have my consent to break the rules,' Sharon said breathlessly. 'I will take full responsibility.'

'Well . . . if that's how you feel about it,' Toby said with a display of reluctance he didn't feel, 'let's get you to the treatment room and see what can be done. Walk slowly now, let me take your weight.'

Before ten minutes were up the whole group were in the treatment room, Sharon standing by the massage table supporting herself with both hands on it. She looked sideways at Toby and grimaced unhappily.

'We'll need to have your shirt off,' he told her.

'I'll help you, Miss Pomeroy,' said Hilary.

She reached round to unbutton Sharon's shirt and eased her arms out of it. Orline was ready with a suggestion.

'Better have the shorts off too,' she said, undoing the belt and zip. Toby stood back, wondering what Hilary thought she was up to, while she and Orline stripped Sharon down to her bra and briefs – and very brief they were too, he noted.

'I want you to sit on the side of the table facing me,' he said. 'Help her up, girls.'

In her tiny pink bra and briefs Sharon was near-enough

naked. And with a man standing not four feet away! But the ache in her lower back overrode her normal reactions and she let herself be helped up to sit on the edge of the massage table with her thighs very wide apart. Hilary, Marjorie and Orline watched wide-eyed while Toby moved in close to stand between Sharon's long thighs.

'I want you to put your arms round my neck,' he said, his own hands on her bare hips. 'Let your muscles go loose while I rotate your body just a little – it won't hurt.'

She did as he said, her chin on his shoulder and her arms round his neck. He stepped in closer still and heard the girls standing about the table sigh faintly. They could see that his belly was touching Sharon's bare belly and her titties were pressed against his chest. He knew what they were thinking – he was in the perfect position to do Sharon.

Truth to tell, his twanger was as hard as iron inside his tight jockstrap and he thought he could feel the warmth of her kitty right through her thin little briefs. He wanted desperately to do Sharon, but that wasn't what she was there for. He tried to put the thought out of his mind.

He held her hips loosely and began to swing her rhythmically from left to right, rotating her body just an inch or two on the pivot of her bum. As he'd said, the movement didn't cause her any pain; she let herself relax gently against him. He had her trust and she had lost her shyness. Her titties brushed against his chest as he swung her.

'Good,' he said confidently. 'That's it, just let your muscles relax completely with the swing.'

Sharon's body was so warm and soft against him that he was afraid he would shoot his load inside his shorts in another second or two. He had to finish the treatment before that happened. He clenched his teeth and on the next swing his hands clamped tight on her hips and he forced her hard round to the left. He heard the click in her back a second before she shrieked loudly.

'Got it,' he said cheerfully.

He had stopped all movement and was holding her body loosely against himself. He was sure she could feel the prod of his dick against her belly, even through his shorts and jockstrap.

'There was a displacement that had to be put right,' he explained to her. 'I want you to lie down flat now and rest.'

There was a stunned look on Sharon's pretty face – she hadn't as yet recovered from the sheer agony he'd caused by realigning her spine. She tried to lie down and winced.

'I want you to lie face down,' he said, 'with your arms folded and your head resting on them. Help her, girls.'

Behind Sharon's back Orline stuck her tongue out at Toby and pointed with her forefinger at the bulge under his flies. The three girls moved up to the table and between them turned Sharon and lowered her until she was lying face-down.

'Is that how you want her, bum-up?' Hilary asked cheekily.

'That's fine,' he told her, trying not to sound excited.

The girls retreated grinning to the side of the room and stood waiting to see what would happen next. But Toby didn't touch Sharon right away. For a long moment he stared down at her, noting that she had an exciting body with a long back, a round firm bum, shapely thighs. He sighed and moved her long blonde hair from the nape of her neck.

Under his fingertips her neck was very tense. He dug his fingers into it and heard her moan. He massaged her with skill, loosening the muscles and slowly working his way down her back toward her shoulder-blades.

'This is going to take some time,' he said to the three girls who were watching him eagerly. 'Off you go – Miss Pomeroy will be all right when I've done with her.'

That made Orline giggle.

'Shouldn't we stay and help her back to her room after she's done?' Hilary asked, tongue in cheek. 'She may be exhausted from it.'

'No need,' Toby said, pink-faced, 'I'll look after her.'

The girls grinned at each other and then grinned at him

before they left. They'd all been under Toby's hands on the table in the past week and they were certain that he was going to give the geography mistress the thrill of a lifetime when he massaged his way down from her back to between her legs.

Left alone with Sharon, Toby took his time, his fingers working down her spine to free all the tension. She moaned faintly from time to time and he knew that the sensations he was giving her were one-tenth pain and nine-tenths pleasure. It was an irresistible combination, very soothing, and he could feel her tension vanishing under his fingers. When he reached the damaged part of her back he left it alone and moved his hands further down, to the firm round cheeks of her bum.

He squeezed them and rolled them under his palms and then he pulled her little white briefs halfway down her thighs.

'Sorry about this,' he said casually. 'Your underwear was in the way – nothing to be alarmed about.'

As his fingers were digging into the flesh of her bum, she moaned again in pleasurable pain at the manipulation. The tenseness he'd felt in her when he eased her knickers down disappeared. And as for Toby, the feel of her flesh under his hands was so exciting that he was finding it very difficult to breathe normally. His hard-on was jerking in his shorts so furiously that he was amazed he hadn't come already.

With reluctance he moved on from Sharon's pretty bum and worked his way slowly down the backs of her thighs, letting his hand slip between them from time to time, but not touching her kitty. He was certain he'd shoot his cream when he turned her over to massage her front, but until then he could enjoy the throbbing sensations in his twanger and belly.

He gave special treatment to her calves before he held her ankles in both his hands to rotate them. He clasped her slim feet and eased them backward and forward. By the time he was pulling gently at each of her toes in turn, she was so relaxed that she was half-asleep.

Toby straightened his back and looked down eagerly at her long body and the neat cheeks of her bum. How badly he wanted to slide his stiffie into her and do her! The need was urgent, very urgent, even though he'd come once already that day – early that morning Sally Mason had rushed into his bedroom to throw the bedclothes off and straddle him.

To be honest about it, Toby was getting tired of being made use of by Sally every time she felt the need for a dick inside her. Which was often. She had a husband – she could just as well jump on him in the mornings.

Toby didn't know it, but Sally *was* straddling Keith for a ride two or three mornings a week. Including that very morning. The first thing she did when she woke at seven o'clock was to pull her nightie up round her thin waist and diddle her kitty till it was slippery and ready. Then she rolled the sleeping Keith onto his back and awoke him by dragging his pyjama trousers down his legs.

Keith had been having a dream about being tied naked to the trunk of a tree and sexually abused by a gang of girls wearing only knickers. As a result his twanger, conveniently for Sally, was stiff as a broom-handle. She threw a leg over him and sat across his hips, her hand sliding firmly up and down his hard-on. With the ease of regular practice she impaled herself and Keith reached full consciousness to find himself being briskly done. He reached up to take Sally's titties in his hands and closed his eyes.

After she'd ridden him and drained him dry, Keith got up and dressed and went downstairs. As soon as the front door closed, Sally leaped out of bed and made for Toby's room. By seven-thirty she was straddling him for her second ride of the day. He wasn't asleep when she arrived, he'd woken up earlier and was waiting for her.

While she was sliding up and down his iron-hard shaft Toby was sighing in delight at the slippery softness of her kitty. It was very warm and wet – she was even more aroused than usual, he thought, not knowing that Keith had been up there before him.

But now in the afternoon, with Sharon on the massage table under his fingers, Toby began to resent being used by Sally in the early mornings. One look at Sharon Pomeroy's long luscious body and round titties and he couldn't understand how Sally Mason managed to excite him when she took her shortie nightgown off and flashed her lean frame at him.

Toby eased Sharon over onto her back on the table. She lay perfectly still with her eyes closed, breathing slowly, three-quarters asleep from the skill of his massaging hands, the pain in her back forgotten. He started with her neck again, and this time his touch was feather-light. He took his time; it was five minutes before he progressed from her neck as far as her titties.

While she'd been lying on her face having her back massaged, Sharon hadn't noticed her bra-strap being undone. When Toby turned her over he eased the bra away completely and dropped it on the floor. His palms glided round and over her bare titties, so lightly that she was hardly aware of the touch. Even when after a while his fingertips rolled over her little pink bobbles, the touch didn't alarm her. After a very few seconds her soft little bobbles grew firm – and even then she accepted the thrill as part of the massage. By the time Toby left her titties to massage her belly with slow circular movements, her mouth was open and she was visibly aroused.

Her tiny briefs were still halfway down her long thighs. The patch of curls revealed was a neat blondish triangle against her creamy skin. Toby ran his fingertips through the curls and heard her gasp. She was ready to come, whether she knew it or not. And he was so far gone now that he doubted if he could go on with the massage without shooting off in his underwear. When that happened he wanted to have his fingers in her kitty, between the lips, touching her secret nubby.

He slid her briefs all the way down her legs in a movement so relaxed that she hardly noticed what he was doing. He arranged her legs apart on the table – not widely, just enough to give him a full view of her fair-haired kitty. She gasped and trembled when she felt his fingers between her thighs.

'What are you doing to me?' she asked drowsily.

'The sort of accident that puts a back out often causes groin strain as well,' he said, trying to sound expert and under control. 'I want to make sure there's no damage there.'

He had both hands between her legs, his fingers probing into her soft groins, exploring and stroking, only an inch away from her kitty.

'I can't feel any strain there,' she said, her voice shaky.

'We'll soon know,' Toby told her. 'Let your legs go limp.'

He took her by the ankles and raised her legs slowly off the table, then moved his arms apart to spread her thighs, his hands firm and confident. Sharon's eyes were blinking and her mouth was open, sighing loudly. Toby held her legs wide apart while he stared in fascination at the long pink lips between. They were moist and slightly open – his massage had definitely aroused her and she wasn't far from the big thrill.

'No problem in your groins,' he murmured.

He lowered her legs gently to the table – still wide apart. He wasn't even pretending to massage her any longer, he was playing with her. His fingers eased her kitty open and he bent down to breathe warmly on the little pink nubby that he'd exposed.

He couldn't help himself. He ripped the zip of his tennis shorts down and let out his straining, pulsating twanger. Sharon lay exactly as he'd put her, with legs spread wide and arms limply down by her sides. Only the rhythmic rise and fall of her titties revealed her sexual agitation. In a flash Toby was on the table and on top of her, hard-on in his hand to steer it between the moist lips of her kitty.

He pushed in. It was a close fit but not uncomfortable.

'Oh, no, no,' she sighed in faint protest when she felt his shaft pushing up into her, 'I don't let men . . .'

The rest of her explanation was lost completely as Toby's rapid in-and-out slide pushed her the last inch over the edge and she came under him. She didn't scream or thrash her legs about, she didn't arch her back or drum her heels on the table. Genteel tremors ran though her body and she gave half a dozen little sighs.

In fact she did it much as Toby had always imagined she would, and the effect on him was instant. He moaned and convulsed as he felt his cream shooting – but at the very last half-second he realised what disaster could follow if he let it surge into her. He moaned as he dragged his wet and jerking twanger out and shot his sticky load onto her bare belly in long powerful pulses.

When it was all over he climbed off the massage table and did up his gaping flies. He wiped Sharon's belly with a handful of tissues from a box on a side cabinet. He'd been so excited that he'd shot as far up as her titties, he observed.

She opened her eyes when she felt herself being wiped. And not just her belly – her legs were still wide apart as Toby took another handful of tissues and gently wiped the wet lips of her kitty.

'I don't know what to say,' she murmured faintly. 'What you've done to me is inexcusable – I must have been mad not to stop you.'

'Inexcusable,' he agreed at once, 'but breathtaking and overwhelming – you have to admit that.'

'I admit no such thing,' Sharon answered. She sat up, grimacing at a twinge of pain in her back.

'Steady,' Toby said. 'No sudden movements. I'll help you dress and get you safely to your own bed.'

He slipped his arm round her bare waist and helped her sit on the edge of the table while he collected her clothes from the floor.

'What then?' she asked him.

He pretended to take the question seriously.

'The walk will make your back stiffen up,' he said in his best professional manner. 'When you're in bed I'll give it five minutes massage to settle you.'

'Only my back,' she said firmly. 'Nothing else.'

'Of course,' he said. 'Trust me, Sharon.'

He wasn't telling her the truth, of course. He fully intended to do her again before he left her to rest and sleep.

Chapter Thirteen

One of the college domestic staff, Mrs Avis Treadle, was busy vacuuming and tidying up the common room of Sawby House when she made an unusual discovery. A Polaroid photo had fallen under one of the arm-chairs. Avis picked it up and put it up on the mantelpiece over the fireplace, for whoever dropped it to find the next time she was in the Common Room.

Avis didn't really bother to look at the photo. The girls were always losing things. She propped the picture against the chimney-breast and turned back to her work. Then it dawned on her what she had just seen. She turned off the vacuum-cleaner and picked the photo up again for a close look.

There was no mistake, it was a photo of a standing twanger. Taken close-up. With light-brown hair around the root and the hood rolled back to expose a shiny pink-purple head. Avis had seen plenty of hard-ons in her time. She was in her thirties, twice married, once divorced, once deserted.

Three nights a week she walked down to the Jolly Roger pub and sat in the saloon bar to see which of the local lads would buy her a drink or two before offering to walk her home. It was understood that between leaving the pub and reaching her home they'd walk down Lovers' Lane, behind the church. On dry summer evenings Avis would lie down on the grass with her legs open and her knickers off, so the lad of the evening could climb on top and give her a seeing-to.

In winter when the ground was wet and cold, she'd put her

back against a tree for a knee-trembler, her coat unbuttoned and her skirt up round her waist. Avis was very popular with the regulars at the Jolly Roger – unmarried lads and married men alike, she was always willing to drop her knickers. Over pints of ale the lads would give each other a nudge and say *She's always ready for a good seeing-to, is our Avis*.

There was nothing out of the ordinary about the dick in the photo she found under the chair. Since she'd turned sixteen she'd seen and handled a lot of them and she knew. The one in the picture was five to six inches long and solid-looking. The best thing about it was that it was stiff as a steel poker. That was how Avis liked them, standing up ready to give her a proper seeing-to.

There was no means of telling who it belonged to, but if it was any of the local lads, the odds were a hundred to one it had been up Avis. And more than once. It might be an old friend, she told herself, or it might be a total stranger.

Either way, she'd never heard of anyone having a photo taken of his twanger before. Not that she had any complaint about that – it might be a souvenir of a happy occasion. What she found objectionable about the picture was where she'd found it. This was a college for young ladies. It wasn't the right place for photos of men's dicks. What was right for a woman of her own long experience wasn't appropriate for seventeen-year-old girls being got ready for Oxford University.

No matter that Avis had been thoroughly seen to the evening before in the meadow at the bottom of Lovers' Lane by both the Mottram twins, Vince and Bobby. She was indignant to think that the students of Lechlade Ladies' College were looking at photos of stiff dicks. So she put the picture in her overall pocket and took it straight to the Principal's office.

Enid Uppingham told her she'd done the right thing. And after Avis had gone back to her work, Enid looked at the picture carefully, through a magnifying glass. She studied the standing *thing* and the tangle of light brown hair it jutted up from, as well as the area of bare belly and tops of spread-apart legs that the photo included. She could make out green grass between the thighs – indicating that the man concerned was lying down in the open air.

Other than that, there were no clues to either the time and place or the participants in this disgraceful business. Common sense told her that at least two people must be involved – the man lying on the grass and the person who took the photo. Bearing in mind where it had been lost and found, there was no doubt in Enid's mind that a Sawby House girl was responsible for taking the picture.

As to the owner of the *thing* portrayed, the suspicion in Enid's mind that it was Toby Dundale exposing himself so shamefully amounted almost to a certainty. He was the only man on the teaching staff – it had to be him. It never entered her head that it might be the one other male at Lechlade, the caretaker.

Enid prided herself on not being a snob, but she found it quite impossible to believe that any young lady in her charge would have the least interest in the sexual parts of a member of the domestic staff.

That was how she regarded Keith Mason. As an educated woman she'd read Lawrence's novel about Lady Chatterley condescending to allow herself to be hand-mauled and penetrated fore and aft by her husband's gamekeeper, but she dismissed the book as a working-class fantasy.

Sitting at her desk studying the photo of the hard-on through her magnifying-glass, it seemed to Enid that she finally had in her hands the means to rid Lechlade of Toby Dundale. After this scandalous episode the Board of Governors would never again appoint a man to this traditionally all-female seat of learning. Her objections would be vindicated.

She locked the photo safely in her desk-drawer and walked out toward the tennis courts, joyful revenge in her heart. A group of girls stood watching Toby give Penny Carlton and her friend Nesta Wade a lesson in ball-control. He was wearing the same skimpy white shorts Enid had found highly immodest and had complained about to him. There were hardly any legs to the shorts at all and his golden-haired thighs were completely exposed.

He'd been Sports Coach for less than a term, Enid reflected, but he'd already been a very bad influence on the girls. Take Penny Carlton, for instance, a young woman with a very overdeveloped bosom. It was obvious that she wasn't wearing a bra under her shirt. Her heavy titties swung every time she hit the ball. When she ran, they bounced almost up to her chin. *That was for Toby Dundale's benefit*, Enid said to herself, tight-lipped and jealous.

She shuddered when she saw him putting his hands on the girls. Now he was standing right up close to Nesta Wade's back, with his arms round her to guide her forehand smash. Enid was sure he was rubbing his *thing* against Nesta's bum. Tall fair-haired Nesta was the girl Enid most wished to get her own hands on. She stared at Nesta's titties in her shirt – which was unbuttoned halfway down – and saw that Nesta was as braless as Penny.

She studied Nesta's long bare thighs as she leaped for the ball, noting that her tennis shorts were as disgracefully short as Toby Dundale's. She caught a flash of curls where Nesta's thighs met inside the skimpy shorts and realised that the girl had no briefs on! Enid stood open-mouthed, hoping for another glimpse of that hidden kitty with the blondish curls.

She wanted to feel Nesta and kiss those secret lips between her legs. She wanted to lick Nesta until she shook and moaned and came. But Nesta only had eyes for the Sports Coach, this *man* with a big horrid *thing* between his thighs. She was flaunting her beautiful young body at him because in her innocence she wanted to lie on her back for him . . .

It was Toby's fault, Enid said to herself. He wasn't to be trusted anywhere near young girls. Men were all the same, wild beasts lusting to get their hot hands on young girls' bodies. He had to be got rid of – she'd known that from the day he first came to the college.

* * *

There was a message for Toby when he finished coaching for the day – the Principal wished to see him in her office that evening at eight o'clock. He shrugged as he screwed the note up and threw it in the nearest waste-paper basket. He'd seen her watching him from the side of the tennis courts and his guess was that she was going to moan at him again about his shorts. He'd give her the same excuse about looking for longer ones in the summer vacation.

He made a point of arriving exactly on time. She was not at her desk, she was sitting in an armchair by the fire-place, with a half-full glass in her hand. She'd changed into a dark-green sleeveless dress that outlined her heavy titties. Her black hair had been brushed to a high gloss, pulled back to cover her ears and fastened behind her head. The thought ran through Toby's mind that she had dressed to attract him.

He was looking good himself, he thought, in his striped red and black blazer and white trousers, with a silk cravat tucked into the open neck of his shirt. Athletic, handsome, blond and wholesome – a sight sure to make every female heart beat a little faster. If Enid took her dress off and lay on her back for him, he'd give her the thrill of a lifetime.

If he could have read her mind he'd have received a nasty shock. Enid was certain that the photo Mrs Treadle had brought her marked the end of his career at Lechlade. After she'd confronted him with it she was going to inform him that he was suspended, pending a disciplinary hearing by the Governors. She would insist that he pack and leave the college first thing in the morning, and she never expected to see him back there again.

The prospect of all this was so great a pleasure that Enid didn't want to hurry through it. She was going to savour her revenge to the full and make this miserable male person squirm and writhe, like the wretched worm he was, before she kicked him out. She was very pleasant when she asked him to sit down.

'Mr Dundale,' she began, 'during the few weeks you have been here—'

'Oh, please call me Toby,' he interrupted, flashing Enid his best boyish smile.

'Very well, then,' she said with a gracious smile of her own, 'as I was saying, Toby, in the time you have been here at Lechlade we have not always seen eye to eye. There are certain matters I have brought to your attention, on which you have not felt completely able to accept my point of view.'

She sounded so friendly that Toby was tempted to meet her halfway. If she intended to seduce him, he'd go along with it and his worries would be over – she could never get him sacked after he'd had her.

'You mean my swimming gear,' he said with a little chuckle. 'It's not that I wish to defy your judgment – all I have with me is six pairs the same. But I promise that in the vacation I shall look for something more in keeping with your wishes.'

'I went to the trouble of shopping in Oxford for a suitable pair,' she said mildly, 'but you chose not to wear them.'

'There was a problem with the size,' Toby reminded her cheerfully.

'Leaving aside for the moment the extraordinary fact that when you are coaching our young ladies in the pool only a few square inches of your body are covered,' Enid went on, 'there is also the question of your unsuitable tennis shorts.'

Toby was hardly listening to her. He remembered what happened the last time they had this conversation about sports clothes – it had ended with Enid diddling him. At the time he thought she was playing some sort of power game to humiliate him, but later on he reached the conclusion that she'd done it for pleasure. Her own pleasure. That seemed obvious now that she was dressed to attract him.

'Let's forget about my sports gear,' he said, a touch of insolence in his tone. 'We both know that's not the reason you invited me here.'

'You're quite right, Toby,' she said very pleasantly, 'it's entirely another matter we have to settle between us today.'

Toby grinned at her. During their conversation she had slumped back in her armchair until she was almost lying on it. From where he sat in the chair opposite he had a fine view of her thighs – the skirt of her green dress had slipped up over her knees, and the knees seemed to have drifted apart.

'Let me guess,' he said. 'You don't want to talk about the clothes I wear when I'm coaching...'

'Correct,' she said. 'We've gone far beyond those little items now.'

Enid was enjoying leading Toby on and making a fool of him before she destroyed him. She was getting her own back for being made miserable when she saw him rubbing himself against Nesta's pretty bum. She slipped lower in her armchair until she was sure that Toby could see her pale green knickers.

Their chairs were set not far apart. If he dared he could lean forward and touch her chuffie. Or more exactly, he could touch the nylon-covered mound under her knickers. His ever-ready twanger was standing stiff in his trousers and he very much wanted to reach out and feel between her legs. More than that, he wanted to pull her knickers down to see if the curls underneath were as black as the hair on her head.

She looked away from him and then back quickly, to catch him peeping. And she did – he was staring straight up her skirt.

'If you're not interested in what I wear, you must want to talk about taking clothes off,' he teased her.

'That's right,' Enid said with a smile as toothy as a shark. 'I asked you here because I wish to talk to you about taking *your* clothes off.'

By now she was almost horizontal, with her knees spread as wide as her dress allowed. With a grin on his face Toby slid forward off his own chair, onto his knees, and put a hand on each of her plump knees.

'What on earth are you doing!' she said in outrage.

Toby ran his hands up her thighs under her dress and tried

to pull her knickers down. Her face turned pink. He'd got them only a little way down her sturdy thighs when she landed a resounding slap on his face that rocked him back on his heels.

For a second he saw her black-haired chuffie, the lips long and pink between the curls. Then in a flurry of movement she yanked her knickers up tightly, clamped her thighs together and pulled her dress down over her knees. She sat up straight-backed in her chair with a frown on her face and Toby realised that he'd made a bad mistake.

'You are a sex maniac,' she said. 'How dare you assault me – if it was anyone else I'd send for the police and have him arrested for attempted rape. But I refuse to bring scandal to the college, so I shall continue as if nothing had happened. Sit on your chair and listen to me carefully.'

Muttering apologies and wondering what had gone wrong, Toby got back on his chair and rubbed his face ruefully – she'd landed a heavy smack.

'I said I wished to speak to you about taking your clothes off,' Enid said in a steely voice, 'because there has come into my possession a photograph of you in a state of nudity.'

She had the Polaroid in a white envelope tucked down the side of her chair. She got it out and held it up for him to see. Toby reached out to take it, but she snatched it back.

'You've seen enough,' she said. 'It is obvious you have persuaded some poor misguided girl to collude with you in this act of indecency. I want to know who took the picture – I want her name.'

'But I've no idea,' Toby said. 'Why ask me?'

'This photograph is of you,' Enid accused him. 'You needn't bother denying it. I shall request an emergency meeting of the Board of Governors and show it to them. You will be summarily dismissed – and good riddance.'

Toby was indignant, knowing that he was wrongly accused.

'That is *not* me in the photo,' he said firmly. 'I suppose that with your lack of experience of men you believe that we're all built the same.'

'Lies can't help you now,' Enid said, smiling in triumph. 'You are now revealed as the sex-crazed beast you are, corrupting young girls. If it weren't for the publicity the Governors would have you prosecuted in addition to dismissing you.'

Toby was not to be put down so easily, not when he knew he was in the right.

'Dear Enid,' he said pleasantly, 'even though you actually handled me yourself the last time I was here in your office, you obviously learned nothing – you can't tell one dick from another. I can prove that's not me in the picture – and what a fool you'll look before the Governors then.'

'What do you mean?' she demanded. 'I don't believe a word of it – you're lying to save your neck.'

'Take a good look at the photo,' he urged her. 'Note the proportions of the stand – it's thickish for its length.'

Enid held the picture up and studied it.

'Now mine, as you have every reason to know since you have personally diddled it,' Toby said, 'is longish for its width.'

'What obscene rubbish!' Enid exclaimed. 'You're trying to deceive me.'

'You're an intelligent woman,' he retorted, 'you understand geometry and arithmetic. The thickness to length proportion of the stand in the photo looks about one to three. Agreed?'

'This is mere time-wasting and evasion,' she said, frowning.

'Whereas the length to width ratio of mine is more like four to one,' he said as he stood up and slipped off his blazer.

'What do you think you are doing?' Enid asked sharply when he unzipped his trousers.

'Demonstrating my point,' he answered, pushing his jockstrap down over his hips to bare his flopper. It had been stiff when he thought he was going to do Enid, but the smack on the face had shocked him so badly it had shrunk and hung limp and small out of his flies.

'Compare them carefully,' he said. 'You'll see the difference in the relative proportions.'

'I see nothing of the sort,' Enid said coldly. 'Put it away and stop this buffoonery at once.'

'I see there's a problem,' he said, glancing down in disappointment, 'but that can soon be put right.'

He took his dangler in his hand and jerked it vigorously up and down to make it stand. But becoming aroused under the cold stare of the disbelieving Principal was not as simple as he'd thought. After a minute or two of useless diddling he closed his eyes and imagined Sharon Pomeroy's naked body stretched out for him to massage. That did the trick – his dick soon stood thick and hard in his hand.

'There,' he said triumphantly, letting go of it to give Enid the full view, 'see what I mean about proportions?'

'To be candid with you,' Enid said in a disparaging tone, 'I can see no such thing. You are attempting to hoodwink me.'

Once again she was enjoying the opportunity to shame him. She leaned forward in her chair and held out the photo beside his hard-on while she compared the two.

'Feel it,' Toby urged her. 'The difference will be obvious to you.'

'I shall do no such thing,' she said coldly while her eyes swivelled back and forth between photo and hard-on. 'Control yourself.'

The inconvenient truth was that Toby was correct about the proportions. Furthermore, the curls around the twanger in the photo were light-brown and his were much blonder. Enid had to acknowledge that the *thing* that had been photographed wasn't the same *thing* that was poking up strongly before her very eyes.

Being a fair-minded woman, she accepted that she had falsely accused Toby. Her face blushed a dark red as she began to murmur apologies.

Toby took it well. With a smile of victory he readjusted his jockstrap and zipped his trousers. He sat down again and accepted the drink Enid pressed on him, a whisky and soda.

She went into explanations of the heavy responsibility laid on her for the moral well-being of the young ladies of the college.

Toby nodded and assured her that he agreed with all she said and then asked if all the Lechlade teaching staff had the same responsibility. He'd heard rumours, he said, that some members of the staff formed close friendships with students.

The suggestion embarrassed the Principal – she knew it to be true and she knew which of her teachers diddled students. But she wasn't going to discuss that with a *man*. She told Toby he ought not to listen to malicious gossip.

She poured him another drink and he embarrassed her again by saying he'd heard of an incident that took place in the gym – a teacher playing with a girl sitting on a vaulting horse. And then slipping her own knickers down while the girl knelt on the floor and tongued her.

He didn't think it necessary to tell Enid he'd seen all this with his own eyes through a glass panel in his office door – Eleanor Redruth playing with Linda Knight's ginger-haired kitty – because at the time he was rubbing himself against Orline Ashby's bum and he'd been so excited that he came. If the Principal got even a hint of that she'd get him sacked in double-quick time.

Enid tried to dismiss the story as mere rumour, though she suspected it was true. She filled his glass again and they went on talking in the same vein for a long time, she defending while he suggested. The combination of several glasses of Scotch whisky and his exertions that day made Toby feel sleepy. In the lunch-break he'd given Sharon a thorough massage, on the bed in her own room. Her back was more or less better but she'd become used to his attentions and expected daily therapy.

After she'd come for the second time during the massage, he climbed on top and did her very satisfactorily. He didn't have to pull his twanger out at the last second this time because he always carried a packet of johnnies with him now – black, see-through, ultra-sensitive.

That wasn't his first time that day. Sally had jumped on him at seven-fifteen in the morning, after Keith had gone out to check the hot-water boilers. She mounted Toby for the usual ride, but he entertained some rebellious feelings toward Sally these days and he rolled her off before she started bouncing up and down.

She was too surprised to resist when he turned her face-down on the bed and hoisted her bare bum in the air. He rammed his hard-on into her chuffie from the rear and rode her until she took the big jump squealing.

It was one of Debbie Gregson's days at the college, so no girls could ask him for a 'finger massage'. But jogging with twenty girls at the end of the teaching day had revived his interest and raised a stand in his shorts, as always – the sight of all those young titties flip-flopping up and down in tight tee-shirts did it to him every time.

When he got back to the gate-house to shower and change, Sally was waiting for him with her knickers in her hand. She pushed him down on his back on her kitchen table, dragged his shorts down round his ankles and did him with her mouth.

While Enid was defending the reputation of the college and its teaching staff, she saw Toby's eyelids droop and refilled his glass. She didn't know about his activities that day with Sharon and Sally and strongly suspected that he'd tired himself out doing students.

The fact that she'd come off worst over the photo hadn't discouraged her. There were other ways of getting him sacked – her mind was very active with the possibilities as she watched him nodding off in his armchair.

When Toby woke up again the room was pitch dark; he was disoriented. He was lying on his back with a blanket over him, but he was partly-dressed. His blazer and cravat were gone, his shoes were off, his flies were unzipped all the way down and his flopper was out. Someone lay against him, pressing close.

At first he thought it was Sally waking him up for an early

morning romp. Except Sally never lay beside him, she jumped straight on top. As he gradually reassembled his memories he knew it couldn't be Sally because just before he fell asleep he'd been with Enid Uppingham.

Enid had been lying back in an armchair, letting him see right up her dress to her knickers. Pale green, he recalled, stretched tight between her thighs. He'd very nearly had those knickers off and done her on her own chair, but she lost her temper because she wanted to talk about a silly photo which she thought was of him.

Don't understand that woman at all, Toby thought. *Can't make out what she wants – have me sacked or have me do her. Maybe both.*

While all this was going on in his head, he rolled on to his side and explored with his hands under the blanket. The figure pressed close to him was female, no mistake about that. His hands slid over a pair of big bare titties. Then down a plump belly to a thick thatch.

It's Enid Uppingham he said to himself. *We must be on the sofa in her sitting-room. She took my jacket and shoes off after I dozed off. I was sitting in an armchair drinking whisky – but how did she get me across to the sofa? She's taken all her own clothes off – I suppose I must have done her, though I don't remember it.*

The woman next to him stirred a little and clasped his limp flopper in her hand. What she said when she spoke took him by surprise and made him wonder how drunk he really was.

'It's me, Penny,' she whispered in the dark. 'I couldn't help myself, I had to come back for more after this morning.'

Lovely Penny Carlton, Toby thought. Eighteen years old and the owner of the biggest pair of titties in the whole college. Twice a week she came to him to be massaged – she adored having her bouncers stroked and played with. She was a dark brunette and the curls around her kitty were nut-brown. When he pressed his finger inside and diddled her, she came very easily. Once was never enough for her, he had to do it twice before she was satisfied. But she hadn't come for massage that morning, because Debbie Gregson was using the treatment room all day.

'Don't understand,' Toby murmured. '*What* this morning?'

He hadn't yet entirely tumbled to it – his companion on the sofa was Enid Uppingham and she was playing a devious game. Her aim was to trap him into admitting that he'd had some of the girls. When she had a name or two, Enid was going to question the girls ruthlessly until at least one confessed that she'd been taken advantage of by the Sports Coach. After that it was plain sailing – he could be fired without notice.

Enid had picked Penny to impersonate in the dark because she'd seen Toby giving Penny and Nesta a tennis lesson earlier in the day. She'd seen him stand close behind both girls in turn, his arms round them to guide their strokes. She was sure he'd rubbed his *thing* against both Nesta's bum and Penny's. And it was surely stiff at the time.

'On the tennis court this morning,' she said, pretending that she was Penny. She had the right-sized titties and by whispering she disguised her voice.

'You want to play tennis at this time of night?' Toby said stupidly.

Enid's clasped hand was sliding deliberately up and down his twanger, and it was long and hard now.

'No, silly – I want you to do what you did in the pavilion. You can't have forgotten how you pulled my shirt out of my shorts and felt my titties and I wasn't wearing a bra.'

'Ah,' Toby said thoughtfully.

He had no recollection of doing anything to Penny or any other girl that particular morning – he'd been done by Sally before breakfast and he was saving his strength for Sharon in the lunch break. Anyway, he'd never actually *done* Penny, much as he'd like to. He'd felt her big plump titties on the massage table and diddled her kitty with his fingers, but that was all.

On the other hand, he never turned down an offer. Lying on the sofa in the dark, he pressed his middle finger into the chuffie that was apparently being offered to him and it was slippery. His companion was lying on her side facing him; he put his hand under her top thigh and lifted it over his hip.

'You *must* remember what you did to me this morning,' she said, still pretending she was Penny. 'Tell me you do, Toby.'

'Well . . .' he said – and Enid held her breath.

This was it, he was on the verge of admitting to her that he'd done Penny Carlton.

'You did Nesta as well,' she whispered to encourage him. 'I don't mind a bit because she's my friend.'

'I've been told you and Nesta do each other all the time,' Toby said, his fingers moving inside Enid's open chuffie.

'I like it better when you do it to me,' she whispered. 'Tell me how you did it to me this morning.'

'In detail, you mean?' he asked.

'Yes, yes, yes . . .'

Enid rubbed her bare titties against him and pushed her belly at him – all this to encourage him into the confession she knew was trembling on the tip of his tongue. He was going to describe how he'd done Penny Carlton. He was going to tell her he'd rammed this big thick *thing* she was holding up a young girl and ravaged her body with it.

She didn't think she'd get Penny to admit she'd been done, she was too independent-minded a girl to be pressured. But when Toby had admitted that much, it shouldn't be hard to get him to reveal the names of other girls he'd got his *thing* into. Little Linda Knight, for instance – if her name came up Enid was sure she could force a confession from her.

Enid's thighs were well parted, one pressed down on the sofa and the other over Toby's hip. She was completely exposed and he was feeling her – he was good at that, the wretch, she decided. But now he took advantage of the offer he supposed she'd made – he brought the head of his twanger to her open kitty and pushed it in.

'Was it like this, this morning?' he asked. 'Remind me.'

By now Toby had realised that his first impression had been

correct, it was Enid Uppingham lying on the sofa with him, not Penny. He couldn't think why she was trying to fool him, but it didn't matter. His stiff dick was sunk all the way into her and he was getting a fast thrill from sliding it in and out.

'What are you doing – stop it!' she squawked.

She tried to pull away, but his hands were on her big bum to hold her in place and his clamped arm kept her leg up over his hip. Suddenly he was jabbing into her hard and fast.

'Oh...' he moaned, 'oh, yes...'

Enid felt him jerk against her belly as he shot his cream into her. His fourth time that day – his personal record – it made him feel proud.

'No...' Enid cried out in dismay. 'Stop it...'

It was twenty years since she'd been done by a man – she was a nineteen year old student at Oxford when Marcus Burlington took advantage of her one afternoon in a punt on the river. It had happened almost without her knowing – Marcus suddenly rolled on top of her and she felt her kitty being penetrated and stretched open. He'd huffed and puffed for half a minute and that was it.

Afterward she'd decided that it was a waste of time – men weren't up to giving a girl real pleasure. Other girls were so much better at it. Now here she was being done by Toby Dundale – a man she despised. She could feel his beastly *thing* reaching right up inside her and jerking madly in its creamy release.

'No, no...' she gasped again.

She was wondering why she was gripping Toby and pulling him closer to her. Three seconds later she came herself – and her overwhelming emotion as she felt the big thrill was amazement.

Chapter Fourteen

Joy Locksley's affair with Debbie the physiotherapist lasted only a week or so after she'd introduced her to the delights of girl-to-girl sex. Then she passed her on to her friend Eleanor Redruth.

Eleanor really preferred younger partners. She often said, only half joking, that the best age to start them was sixteen, although for an outstandingly sexy girl she'd go as high as eighteen. But she didn't mind helping Joy out by taking the physiotherapist off her hands. She enjoyed all Debbie had to offer and then passed her on again – this time to Monica Howlett, the modern languages teacher.

Without realising how or why, Debbie was doing the rounds. This was a strange experience for a woman who until then had stayed with the same boyfriend since she was a schoolgirl.

When Monica had explored Debbie's possibilities in bed she passed her on to Claudine Stanhope, the junior history mistress who was the least popular teacher at Lechlade. Most people thought Monica was too serious, but as Debbie had absolutely no sense of humour of her own, she didn't even notice.

During Debbie's adventures at Lechlade her smooth-shaven kitty aroused a good deal of interest and gossip in the staff common room of Wexby House. 'It's curiously sexy' was Eleanor's verdict. 'Very exciting to feel' was Monica's comment. 'Marvellously kissable' was Claudine's opinion. All agreed it looked very young and girlish, though Debbie was twenty-seven. Another thing about her that aroused interest was how easily she came when she was fingered.

Joy didn't pass on the information that Debbie's virginal-looking bare kitty had been reamed and stretched and creamed into almost every day for the past ten years by Lawrence Baxter. It was entirely up to Debbie herself to tell her new friends about her experiences. Their concern was getting a hand up her white uniform overall and into her knickers for a feel.

They all appreciated Debbie's superb talents when she was naked and on her back, most of all Monica Howlett. Plump-tittied Debbie was very much to Monica's taste, perhaps partly because Monica's general unpopularity meant she had problems finding close friends.

The first time she had Debbie's knickers off and stroked her bare kitty she became wildly enthusiastic. Debbie was sitting in an armchair in Monica's room in Wexby House, with her heavy titties hanging out to be handled. Monica flung herself on her knees between Debbie's thighs and tongued her furiously.

Debbie gasped and stretched her legs wide open and came in less than thirty seconds. Monica ignored her whimpering and shaking and carried on licking her button. She made her come six times without a pause before Debbie begged her to stop.

'I can't,' Monica moaned, 'I've got to keep on doing you . . .'

On hearing these words Debbie, who was strong and trained in the manipulation of the human body, gripped Monica's shoulders and rolled her over onto her back on the sitting-room carpet. Holding her down with one arm, she stripped off Monica's skirt and knickers passionately and repaid the favour. From then on the two women were practically inseparable.

Debbie could hardly believe how her life had changed in the few weeks she had been employed at the college – it was less than a term. The old days when Lawrence used to finger her kitty for about ten seconds before he shoved his hard *thing* up her and shot his little lot now seemed very far away. The present was very different, because with her new friends she wasn't the passive recipient of somebody else's lust – she was an equal partner in hours of pleasure. She took now, as well as giving.

Originally Joy had initiated Debbie into the world of girl-to-girl sex as a means of keeping her quiet. That was after silly Annabel had spread her legs on the massage table and made Debbie suspicious about what had been going on at the college before her arrival. It would have been real Sunday newspaper front-page – if it had got out. Joy diddled the new physiotherapist for the sake of the college's good name. As a Head of House it had been her duty, or so she told herself.

When Debbie was no longer a threat, Joy felt she could pass her on. To be perfectly honest about it, Debbie's sturdy body and big bouncers were not Joy Locksley's ideal. She greatly preferred a slender playmate with small round titties. A body like her own, in fact.

Apart from the question of physical sexiness, Joy had a fairly strong suspicion that Debbie was still letting her married boyfriend have her. A chauvinist pig who had been abusing Debbie's big body for his own selfish male pleasure ever since she was a schoolgirl – that was how Joy thought of Lawrence. She also disliked the thought that the bare-lipped shaven chuffie she fingered and tongued had been rammed into by a stiff male *thing* the day before.

Although there could be no confirmation of this short of a full confession by Debbie, which was not forthcoming, Joy had been right in what she suspected. In those early days of Debbie's transformation she wasn't yet ready to give up Lawrence. He was what she'd known for many years – she knew what to expect when he put his hand up her skirt. These new experiences at the college might be a passing whim, not a long-term arrangement. And while it was nice to be diddled by Joy Locksley, Debbie wasn't completely convinced it was right to let her.

Then after a week Joy faded out of the picture and Eleanor Redruth took over Debbie's further education. Eleanor's skilfulness when she had Debbie on her back with her legs apart startled the physiotherapist, who till then had thought she knew all there was to know about physical massage. So she did, except as it applied to the most interesting part of the body – and that she picked up very quickly under Eleanor's expert guidance.

She began to realize that Lawrence could do nothing for her that even began to compete with the pleasure of being diddled by Eleanor Redruth. In any comparison between the use of his twanger to produce spasms of delight and the use of Eleanor's tongue for the same purpose, Lawrence's *thing* that he was so proud of was very definitely second-best.

Debbie found that hard to believe at first, but she decided that the truth of it was inescapable after the day Lawrence had the time to do her twice.

After classes ended at four-thirty that day, Eleanor and Debbie met by earlier arrangement at the back of the main sports pavilion near the tennis courts. Until then Debbie had always gone to Eleanor's room to be diddled, but the bold maths teacher liked change and the spice of danger and so had asked Debbie to meet her at this new place.

Actually it was new only to Debbie, for this wasn't Eleanor's first time behind the pavilion. She'd been there in the past with more than one girl – she liked outdoor sex, lying on the grass on warm summer days. The river bank was another favourite place of hers where she meant to take Debbie one day soon.

They lay together on the grass in the shade of the pavilion, each with a hand up the other's clothes, their fingers slowly teasing inside each other's knickers. Eleanor was taking the lead, as she invariably did, and had Debbie's white coat-dress unbuttoned from the top down to the belt and her plump titties out and bare. She was sucking at their dark-red bobbles at the same time they diddled each other.

Neither knew that they were only yards from the spot where the caretaker Keith Mason had been bound, gagged, blindfolded and interfered with by a gang of girls from Sawby House. This was where he'd been held down on his back with his jeans round his knees while the girls inspected his hard-on twanger.

Rachel Fermor took instant photos of it. Veronica Jameson sat on his face and rubbed her chuffie against his mouth until he was almost frantic with lust. And Tessa Bowland diddled him with a busy hand until she made him shoot his cream in the air to amuse them. If Debbie had known what had happened where she was playing with Eleanor, she would have been horrified and have hurried away from the spot with blushing cheeks.

But if Eleanor had known, she'd have thought it very funny the way the girls turned the tables on a Peeping Tom and would have had a good laugh about it. More than that, she'd have gone looking for Rachel Fermor and asked for a detailed account of the ravaging of Keith.

Happily for Debbie's sense of decency and propriety, the saga of the caretaker's fate was only just beginning to be told around the college. It hadn't yet reached the teaching staff, except in a distorted way the Principal, who assumed that the photo Avis Treadle found was of Toby Dundale – and to her consternation ended up being done by him while trying to trick him.

None of that disturbed Debbie and Eleanor as they lay on the grass near the spot where Keith had shot his bolt. At Eleanor's urging Debbie's thighs were apart. Her breathing was fast and shallow and her dark-brown fringe clung moistly to her forehead as her fingers fluttered inside Eleanor's wet kitty.

Debbie came first, shaking and panting. Seconds later Eleanor moaned and sucked hard at Debbie's right tittie as she came too. They had a rest and a breather, exchanged words of admiration, and then did it to each other again.

★ ★ ★

Not only did they not know about Keith being diddled in the long grass a few yards away from where they lay, they didn't know that the irrepressible peeper was spying on them at that moment from the same spot. Since his adventure with Rachel, Tessa, Veronica and the others, Keith had returned to the same spot every day. Hope of seeing the girls sunbathing topless was partly the reason – and also the hope of being jumped on and interfered with again.

The word had spread amongst the students, however, and no one came here to sunbathe semi-nude any more because of him. He'd been disappointed day after day and he'd decided that this was the last time he'd wait in the long grass in the hope of seeing bare titties. When he saw Eleanor Redruth and Debbie Gregson, the new physiotherapist, lie down together behind the pavilion he thought he must be dreaming.

They're really doing it he said to himself, only half-believing his own eyes. *They're fingering each other!*

His hard-on was straining inside his jockey-shorts when he saw Eleanor unbutton Debbie's white uniform coat, undo her bra and pull her heavy titties out. He had been lying face-down, close to the ground to avoid being spotted, but now he wriggled onto his side so he could unzip his jeans and release his throbbing twanger from its hot confinement.

Purely by chance he was well-placed to see up both women's clothes as they played together. He could see Eleanor lean over Debbie to lick the pink bobbles of her titties while at the same time she slid Debbie's little briefs halfway down her thighs to feel her chuffie.

Oh my god Keith moaned to himself, *it's beautiful*. In his desperate excitement he said it aloud. But luckily not loud enough to be heard by the women so pleasantly occupied with each other. His dangerous exclamation was due to a sudden glimpse of Debbie's chuffie when her little briefs came part-way down – it was pink and chubby and bare-shaven, as smooth as the palm of his hand.

He'd never seen a woman with a bare-shaven chuffie before. Even the sixteen-year-olds of the college had pretty little muffs between their thighs. He gripped his leaping twanger and stared pop-eyed while he waited for another look at this unique furless kitty – if only Eleanor would move her hand away for a moment.

Eleanor's own chuffie was on view now that Debbie had pulled the front of her knickers down to do her – with long strong fingers trained in massage of all kinds. Keith saw brunette curls in a small neat triangle between two long slim thighs. He had no interest in Eleanor's kitty, however, because during his career as the college's resident Peeping Tom he'd seen many like it.

Girls' kitties, glimpsed through windows – brunette kitties and blonde kitties, once or twice a ginger one, younger than Eleanor's, of course. Which meant they hadn't been fingered so much. Mostly they were so pretty that Keith wanted to kiss them and make the girls squeal.

He didn't think he'd kiss Eleanor's, even if she asked him to. She was thirty – much too old. Peeping at the two women on the grass his desire was focused on Debbie's plump bare chuffie. In the throes of pleasure she threw her legs up and apart and he couldn't stop himself gasping out loud when he saw it again. The lips were stretched open by Eleanor's fingers dabbling wetly inside.

Keith couldn't believe how quickly Debbie reached a climax. Only a minute after Eleanor had put a hand between her thighs, Debbie's back arched off the ground and she wailed, 'Yes, yes, I'm coming...'

It was too much for Keith – his straining hard-on jerked in his hand and he shot his creamy load in a long stream onto the grass.

At nine that evening Lawrence turned up at Debbie's flat – without any warning, as usual for him. Debbie had changed out of her uniform into a roll-top white sweater and jeans. The sweater clung round her heavy titties to make them look even bigger; the jeans were tight over the fullness of her bum. Debbie was a well-developed woman in all respects.

That may have been the reason why Lawrence started with her when they were at school together: from the age of twelve onward Debbie'd had titties that made boys nudge each other and wolf-whistle at her. By the time she was sixteen they'd filled out so much that grown men, including one of her teachers, were falling over themselves trying to get their hot eager hands on them.

Lawrence didn't believe in long foreplay when he came round to visit Debbie at home. A quick kiss was the only preliminary before he dragged her through the flat to the kitchen, gripped her by the waist and lifted her up to sit on the table.

'I've missed you,' he said, his hands up her thin sweater to undo her bra and feel her bare titties. 'You've been out the last three times I've been round – where have you been?'

'I've been very busy,' she said.

She liked his hands on her titties but she couldn't help thinking that he didn't handle them as well as Eleanor had, only hours ago, behind the sports pavilion. He didn't even play with them as nicely as Joy Locksley had done – and Debbie suspected that Joy didn't find big bouncers very exciting.

'Busy doing what?' Lawrence demanded, his fingers rolling over her bobbles and making them stand up.

'I've been doing extra hours most evenings at the college,' she said. And that was true as far as it went, although the evenings had nothing to do with physiotherapy, as Lawrence assumed.

'Hope they pay you overtime,' he murmured. 'Why do they need you more often than before?'

Debbie didn't want to go on answering questions about her activities at the college. She knew how to divert Lawrence's mind from the subject. He was wearing a navy-blue blazer and grey slacks; she reached down to run her hand over his flies. She could feel the bulge underneath and grinned as she pinched it between her fingers. His twanger was long and stiff, as she knew it would be. He only had to touch her titties to get a hard-on.

He responded by moving his hands from underneath her sweater to the crutch of her jeans. The fashionably washed-out jeans were so tight over her bum and belly that he groped awkwardly for the zipper and couldn't pull it down.

'Wish you wouldn't wear jeans,' he said. 'You know I like you to wear a skirt so I can put my hand up it.'

She didn't offer to help him – he wouldn't want that because he always wanted to be in control. She was his woman and it was his male right to do her when he wanted to. He got the zip down at last and felt inside her knickers to finger her kitty.

Before she took up with Lawrence, Debbie's only experience had been with her friend Franny. The two of them had played together for hours, tittie-kissing and kitty-feeling, pressing fingers inside to give each other a thrill.

With Lawrence it had been a shock at first that he didn't want to play with her as Franny did. He felt her for about ten seconds and then shoved his *thing* up her. Inadequate and crude though his technique might be, Debbie came so easily by nature that it was enough to carry her over the edge.

After a few repeats of Lawrence's *wham-bam* approach she began to like the feel of his thick hard-on stabbing deep into her belly more than that of Franny's finger tickling her button.

For ten years she accepted Lawrence's thirty-second battering as the genuine and only way of doing it. Until one afternoon when, by a curious chain of events, she found herself being diddled by Joy Locksley. Joy was good at it – what she did to Debbie bore no comparison to Franny's girlish fumblings. Debbie was amazed to find that being diddled by Joy felt nicer than being done by Lawrence. When Eleanor Redruth took over from Joy, the pleasure was even more captivating. What Lawrence had been doing to her seemed boring now.

Certainly it struck her as boring that evening, sitting on her own kitchen table while Lawrence groped and muttered as he tried to get her jeans off. He got them down to her ankles and then found he'd have to take her trainers off first. His twanger was throbbing hotly in his underwear, making him too impatient to tackle the laces properly.

He grew redder in the face, bending down to struggle with the knots, until it was too much for him and he wrenched the trainers right off her feet with laces still tied. Debbie put her legs together to let him get her knickers off, and he at least managed to do that without too much of a struggle.

In a flash he had her knees wide apart and was standing close to her belly with his hard-on in his hand. She braced herself with both hands behind her on the table-top, and he slammed his dick into her with one quick thrust.

'Been days since I did you last,' he complained as he held her by the waist and slid in and out. 'You can't leave me on my own like that, it isn't right. I've got to have you, Debbie – it makes me miserable and bad-tempered if I don't get to do you.'

You've always got your wife Debbie thought rebelliously. *I'll bet you've been doing her every night since you saw me last. So don't try to fool me with your moaning.*

She wanted to come – the feel of his hard-on inside her always made her want to. She was surprised she hadn't already, as he'd been at it longer than it usually took to push her over the top. He was shaking and sighing and she knew he'd shoot his bolt in a second.

But he was doing nothing for her. Not like this afternoon when Eleanor made her sob and go into ecstatic spasms by the touch of her fingers. Not just one quickie – they'd diddled each other twice behind the pavilion.

Lawrence groaned and jerked his belly hard against her as he shot off into her kitty. Debbie was left unsatisfied and disillusioned. When he'd finished he pulled out and wiped his dick and tucked it away in his trousers. Debbie slid off the table, put her jeans on and made them both a cup of coffee.

He normally kissed her goodbye at that point and vanished, but perhaps he guessed something of what was on her mind. Maybe he even realised that she hadn't been able to come, though he didn't usually take much notice of her feelings. Whatever the reason, after they'd drunk the coffee he took her jeans off again and lifted her back onto the table.

He slid into her wet chuffie very easily and belted away. It took him longer this time and Debbie became excited enough to come when he did.

For her that was still slow – she should be on at least her second or third thrill by the time Lawrence squirted into her belly. She gasped and dug her fingernails into his shoulders but the truth was that it wasn't as nice as when Eleanor had thrilled her.

By the time Eleanor passed her on to Claudine Stanhope, it was plain to Debbie that she really didn't need Lawrence making use of her for a quickie when he could get away from his wife. Claudine taught her how to play 'heads-and-tails' – Debbie was embarrassed the first time she found herself with her face between Claudine's thighs and Claudine's between hers while they tongued each other, but soon she began to relax and enjoy it.

Claudine was making purring noises deep in her throat while she kissed and licked Debbie's smooth-shaven kitty and pushed her wet tongue into it. Debbie was blushing pink and trembling all the way down her spine as she parted the long lips of Claudine's kitty with her tongue and flicked at the little button inside.

Claudine had explained to her that the object was for both of them to come at the same moment. But however often they tried they never managed to achieve that. Debbie came quickly when they played this little game, so by the time Claudine got her thrill, Debbie had climaxed three times already. After she got used to it, though, Debbie loved this way of giving and receiving pleasure.

Lawrence had never pushed his tongue into her kitty and she knew he never would. His way was *diddle 'em, do 'em, dump 'em*. It was time she dumped him, she decided. She invited Claudine round to her flat for dinner one evening, it being understood that she would stay the night and leave early next morning to get back to the college in time for breakfast.

Debbie had never had anyone stay the night with her before, not even Lawrence. She cooked a meal and opened a bottle of wine and she and Claudine ate facing each other across the table on which she'd sat hundreds of times with her knickers off and her legs apart for Lawrence.

She didn't mention this to her new friend Claudine in case it upset her, but she thought about it on and off while they ate and smiled secretly to herself. After dinner they cuddled up together on the sofa in the sitting-room, listening to music from the CD player while they kissed and stroked each other's titties.

Debbie had left off her bra, so her titties swelled big and heavy out of her shirt when Claudine unbuttoned it down to her waist. Claudine's own titties were of average size and shape, but with prominent dark-red bobbles. The two women played and whispered and kissed and pushed their tongues into each other's mouths until Debbie quivered and gasped and came.

Debbie had planned this encounter in her own home as her declaration of independence from Lawrence. To let herself become submissive to someone else, even Claudine, would undermine her new self-respect – although she knew that she had to come again, and the sooner the better. The instant she got her breath back she wrapped her arms round Claudine's waist and dragged her off the sofa and down onto the biscuit-coloured shag-pile carpet.

'Yes, do me, Debbie,' Claudine gasped, 'I want you to . . .'

She was on her back, plucking at her skirt. She was pulling it up her legs to uncover her knickers for Debbie to take down and tongue her. Debbie wriggled out of her own skirt to reveal that she was wearing small see-through knickers.

With a frown of concentration on her face she knelt astride Claudine and leaned down to suck the upstanding bobbles of her pale-skinned titties.

'Make me come,' Claudine sighed. 'You must – I can't wait.'

Debbie was at no one's beck and call any more. She sat up straight, slid forward over Claudine's wet-bobbled titties and sat on her face.

'Later, maybe,' she said with a grin.

She rubbed herself on Claudine's mouth to feel the warmth of her breath through the thin nylon of the transparent knickers. Claudine's mouth was open and she was gasping.

'Lick me,' Debbie commanded, 'I'm the one in charge now.'

Claudine stared up wide-eyed and tongued the smooth-shaven lips through Debbie's knickers until the flimsy material was soaked right through – wetted from outside by Claudine's tongue and from inside by Debbie's own sexual excitement.

'I'm coming now,' she said in a shaking voice. 'Don't stop, Claudine.'

She meant she was about three seconds away from the big thrill. It was the worst possible moment for an interruption – but there was someone knocking loudly at the door. Without a shadow of doubt she knew it was Lawrence. He had a key of his own, which he'd had since the day she moved in, so he could walk in and do her any time he felt like it.

This was the first day of Debbie's independence and she'd bolted the door after Claudine arrived. Lawrence was stuck outside, banging on the door with his fist and shouting.

'Don't stop!' she gasped to Claudine. 'Don't stop...'

The insistent knocking went on and on while Debbie sighed and moaned and arched her back and shook with delight. When her body went slack at last, Claudine twisted her head free from between Debbie's thighs and stared up at her in alarm.

'There's a man shouting outside,' she said. 'Who is it? What does he want? He'll break the door down in a minute.'

Debbie smiled contentedly and lay beside Claudine on the shag-pile. Her heavy titties hung out, her bare-shaven kitty was prominent under the dark wet patch on her see-through knickers.

'Do me again, Claudine,' she murmured, 'then I'll have you on your back and tongue you senseless.'

'Who is it trying to get in?' Claudine said anxiously.

'Nobody who matters. It's only my ex-boyfriend. I told you about him.'

'He sounds very annoyed – what do you think he wants?'

'He wants me,' Debbie said with a broad grin. 'He wants to stick his *thing* in me and do me. That's all he ever wants.'

'You said you'd finished with him!'

'I have, but he doesn't want to finish with me. I expect he's got a hard-on and he's looking for somewhere to put it.'

Claudine was staring at Debbie's pink-lipped chuffie with a look of dismay on her face. She put her hand over the wet patch on the knickers, as if in protection. The thumping at the door continued.

'I know you're in there,' Lawrence shouted. 'What are you playing at? Open this door, I can't stay long.'

'What are we going to do?' Claudine whispered anxiously.

Debbie smiled and moved her legs apart, wriggling happily under the warm hand covering her chuffie.

'I'm not going to do anything,' she said, 'I've nothing to say to him and he can't get in.'

'Well, I've something to say to him,' Claudine huffed. 'Who does he think he is, shouting and carrying on like that!'

She got up from the carpet quickly and went to the window. She opened it and put her head out to glare at Lawrence, who stood eight feet away still hammering at the door.

'You,' she called out, 'go away, you're not wanted here. Any more of this rowdy behaviour and we shall phone the police and report a break-in. So clear off.'

Lawrence turned from the door and stared at Claudine. He saw a flushed but intelligent face under smooth light-brown hair, ears with red-coral pendants, a determined chin and a long neck. Through the glass, he could see two bare titties hanging out of an unbuttoned pink silk blouse.

'Who are you?' he demanded as he took a stride toward the half-open window. 'Where's Debbie?'

'She doesn't want to see you,' Claudine said determinedly. She'd forgotten that her blouse was undone and she'd arrived at Debbie's wearing no bra, so she didn't realise she was showing this noisy man her titties – the bobbles still wet and shiny from when Debbie had licked them.

'I'm coming in,' Lawrence insisted. 'Unbolt that door!'

Claudine had been a teacher too long to be intimidated. 'Go away and stop disturbing the neighbourhood,' she said. 'You're not wanted here, are you so stupid you can't understand that?'

Lawrence was staring at Claudine's bare titties. A dread and almost incredible suspicion was forming in his mind. 'Who are you?' he asked again. 'Are you from the College?'

'What if I am? I'm a friend of Debbie's, which is more than you are. From what I've heard you're a crude, selfish male pig. Debbie's been abused by you far too long and she wants no more to do with you.'

Lawrence was two steps from the window, his eyes fixed on Claudine's titties. She looked down in the direction of his stare and saw what was attracting his attention. She blushed a dark red; it started at her hairline and ran instantly down her cheeks and her long neck, right down to her titties.

'You shameful, disgusting beast, you're trying to take advantage of me!' she said shrilly. 'I'm phoning the police now to report a pervert trying to force his way in.'

Lawrence didn't react to that – there was something else on his mind.

'What are you two doing in there?' he asked hoarsely.

'None of your business,' Claudine said briskly. 'Go away!'

She closed the window and locked it. She drew the curtains across with a broad two-armed sweep that set her loose titties swaying and bouncing. It was Lawrence's last glimpse of her.

Debbie wasn't on the white shag-pile. She wasn't on the sofa either. During the altercation at the window she'd picked up her skirt and left the sitting-room. Claudine went looking for her, wondering what she used to let her boyfriend do to her – besides the obvious coarse act that men always wanted to do with their long ugly *things*.

She found her in the bedroom. Debbie had stripped naked and was lying on top of the bed, her strong thighs well apart to display her smooth bare kitty. She smiled up at Claudine.

'What took you so long?' she asked. 'Get your clothes off – I'm going to do you to death tonight.'

'I don't know if he's gone away or not,' Claudine told her, sounding nervous. 'What if he stays there making a nuisance of himself?'

'I don't care what he does,' Debbie said. 'He can go home to Lorna and do her till he makes her belly swell again.'

'Oh!' Claudine's mouth pouted in disapproval of the very idea of any woman being stretched open and brutally penetrated by a male.

'You used to let him put his *thing* inside you?' she asked in horror.

'We all make mistakes when we're young,' Debbie said. 'Now get those knickers down before I rip them off your body.'

Chapter Fifteen

When she was free of Debbie, Joy started to make other plans. She liked Debbie well enough, but that sturdy torso and those meaty thighs were not her idea of beauty. Big-tittied girls never made Joy go damp between the legs, only girls with slender figures, with small pointed titties set high. It was sad, but treacherous Annabel had the perfect figure for Joy's taste.

It was out of the question to think of taking up with her again, after she'd demonstrated how appropriate her nickname 'Anybody's' was. Joy began to look around elsewhere and before long her thoughts turned toward another fair-haired and slender young student – Nesta Wade.

Joy started to observe her, without being noticed herself. She saw her in the swimming-pool with her slim body outlined by a wet and clinging costume. She saw her in shorts and a tee-shirt, coming back in a crowd of girls from an evening jog with the Sports Coach. Soft fair hair stuck to her perspiring forehead – Joy's knickers felt moist between the legs while she wondered if the hair on Nesta's kitty was equally fair and soft.

There was no doubt about it, Joy liked what she saw. She began to daydream about diddling Nesta. She imagined herself stripping Nesta's tee-shirt off and kissing those high, pointed titties; she could almost taste the salty tang of the perspiration trickling down between them. She visualised her fingers stroking between Nesta's long thighs. She fantasised kissing her eyelids and the corners of her mouth, watching her face grow radiant with expressions of ecstasy at the ultimate thrill.

For three nights in a row Joy lay in bed and thought about Nesta while she diddled herself. Since the incident of the face at her window she'd taken to closing the curtains before she went to bed. Someone had seen her that day, lying on her bed naked, with her legs apart and her hand between them to finger her chuffie. It could have been one of the girls, but Joy suspected it was Keith Mason the caretaker.

These were hot summer nights, but the curtains were drawn across Joy's bedroom window. No one could spy on her now while she undressed and lay naked on the bed. She cupped her titties in her hands and tickled their pink bobbles. She stroked her belly with both hands and opened her legs to touch the dark-brown curls of her chuffie. She parted the outer lips and pressed two fingers between the moist inner lips.

There was an image of Nesta in her mind while she gave herself a long slow finger-wave. She'd seen Nesta in the gym, in white shorts and tee-shirt, leaping over a vaulting-horse, her hands on the handles, legs spread sideways to clear the jump. Joy pictured her going over it naked, thighs wide open to reveal the blonde curls and pink lips of her kitty.

The opportunity to translate wish into reality came at the end of an afternoon. In addition to her responsibilities as Head of Wexby House, Joy taught a class in English literature. At four-thirty the bell rang and the girls gathered up their textbooks and notepads and made their way chatting out of the room. Except for Nesta Wade. She dawdled behind the others until they had all gone, then advanced to the tall desk where Joy sat at the front of the room.

'You have a question, Nesta?' Joy asked, pleased she had this chance to be alone with her for a moment. 'Something not clear to you in *Paradise Regained*?'

'Yes, I've a question, Miss Locksley, but it's not about Milton's poem.'

'Then what?' Joy asked.

She was thinking to herself how desirable Nesta was, her pretty face, her slender figure and sexy long legs. According to

222

Eleanor Redruth she had a permanent friendship with Penny Carlton, her room-mate last year but not this. Penny was a strapping big-tittied girl and Joy found it impossible to believe there was any physical attraction between the two of them. She ought to have asked Eleanor if she'd ever had Nesta herself – but on second thoughts, she didn't want to know.

'What I want to ask you is why you've been following me about the past few days,' Nesta said, looking into Joy's eyes.

'Whatever gave you the idea that I'm following you?' Joy said, her cheeks a faint pink.

'Everybody's noticed it,' said Nesta, 'all my friends. Why are you doing it, Miss Locksley?'

In the empty classroom Joy's desk was not a barrier between the two of them. Nesta was standing beside Joy's chair.

'Can't you guess?' she asked Nesta, seeing it was useless to deny it.

Nesta smiled so sweetly that Joy rubbed her thighs together inside her skirt without knowing she was doing it. *This lovely sexy seventeen year old knows what I want* Joy said to herself happily. *How much simpler that makes everything!*

She put her hand under the girl's short grey skirt, between her knees, and slid it upward, enjoying the feel of sleek nylon and warm flesh underneath. Nesta moved her feet a little apart so Joy's hand could slide all the way up, to rest against that warm and secret place where her thighs met. Only thin tights and knickers now separated Joy's hand from the soft lips of Nesta's kitty.

'Yes, that's what I thought you wanted,' Nesta said.

'I've taken a great fancy to you,' Joy said. 'Does it embarrass you, Nesta, to be fancied by a teacher?'

Nesta shook her head and smiled prettily.

'I think you're very elegant, Miss Locksley. Everybody does. It's sexy to be fancied by you.'

Joy turned her hand between the girl's thighs to bring her fingertips to bear on her kitty. She stroked it through the two thin layers of nylon. Nesta's mouth opened wide in a sigh – the

223

stealthiness of the situation was exciting her as much as the physical contact.

'Shall I make you happy now, Nesta?' Joy asked. 'I can make you very happy, you know.'

Nesta knew 'happy' was a way of referring to the big thrill. 'I know you can, but do you think you should?' she teased. 'I mean, suppose somebody saw what you were doing – we'd both be in trouble.'

Joy's exploring hand slid under the waistband of Nesta's tights and knickers, her palm flat against the girl's smooth young belly. 'What a pity not to be happy, though,' she said. 'I'm ready to do some very thrilling things to you.'

Her fingers reached Nesta's kitty inside her knickers and she began to stroke the soft lips. 'You'd like me to make you happy, wouldn't you?' she asked.

'Oh yes,' Nesta said softly. Her face was flushed a pretty pink and her eyes half-closed. 'I'd like it very much – and I'd like to make you happy, Miss Locksley.'

'You know my name, it's Joy. Will you lie on your back with your legs open while I tongue you?'

'Oh, yes – but we can't do that here,' Nesta sighed, moving her feet a little further apart on the parquet floor.

'How sad – I shall have to play with you standing up,' Joy told her. 'I'll give you a nice knee-trembler. You've had that lots of times before, I'm certain.'

While they were whispering to each other Joy pressed her middle finger between the lips of Nesta's kitty and touched her nubby – it was already moist. She stroked it, making Nesta sigh and tremble. Not much was needed to take her to the verge of coming.

'This isn't the place for what you want to do,' Nesta said. 'If someone comes in we'll never hear them till too late.'

'Don't worry about that,' Joy said reassuringly as her finger teased inside Nesta's chuffie. 'I'll look after you.'

'Can't we go somewhere else?' Nesta sighed. 'You can do me all you want, but it's not safe here.'

Joy stood up from her desk and took her hand out of Nesta's knickers. She held the girl's hand to lead her to the class-room window nearest to them. The tip of her finger was slippery on Nesta's palm, and the girl gasped to think it was her own excitement that made Joy's fingers wet.

They stood side by side looking out of the long window, hidden from the waist down to anyone watching from outside. The view was across the back lawn and the flower garden to the sports-field beyond.

'There,' said Joy. 'Now you can see anyone coming this way and warn me in good time – does that put your mind at rest?'

'What if someone comes in at the door?' Nesta objected. But she stood close to Joy and stroked her hand.

'Lessons are over for today. No one will think of coming in here until the cleaners start at six. I'm beginning to think you don't really want me to make you happy, Nesta.'

'Oh, I do – really I do! I'm all hot and bothered – put your hand in my knickers again and you'll see.'

Joy moved behind Nesta and pressed against her while she reached round to put both hands on her titties through her white school blouse.

'Keep a sharp watch, Nesta,' she said with a grin the girl didn't see while she unbuttoned her blouse all the way down.

She felt behind Nesta to unhook her bra and slipped her hands inside the blouse to cup her bare titties. Nesta gave a little gasp when Joy's forefingers glided over her little pink bobbles.

'If somebody walks past now they'll see my titties,' she sighed, 'but I don't care. Do you think I've nice titties?'

'You have the most beautiful small and elegant pointed titties, Nesta. When we can be someplace where it's safe to take our clothes off, I'm going to play with them and lick them until I've given you the biggest thrill you could ever imagine.'

Still standing behind Nesta and pressing tightly against her, Joy could feel the girl's body trembling with pleasure. They

225

were both staring out through the big window but they saw nothing, neither the deserted garden nor the girls dashing up and down the field in the distance, playing a fast game of hockey. Joy and Nesta were too involved in each other and lost in sensation to hear the far-off cries and shouts or the shrill whistle as the Sports Coach called off-side.

'Are you going to feel happy, Nesta?' Joy asked very softly.

'Oh, yes,' Nesta breathed, 'in another second I'm going to.'

Joy eased her hand out of Nesta's knickers and carefully hitched the girl's short grey skirt up to her hips. She rolled Nesta's tights down her thighs and her knickers with them.

'What are you going to do?' Nesta sighed.

Joy moved to the trembling girl's side and sank slowly to her knees. Her side was against the wall below the window to support her as she turned Nesta half-sideways.

'Are you keeping watch outside, Nesta?' she asked with a chuckle. 'Is anyone creeping up on us to get a look at your bare titties? One of the girls, maybe – or have they all seen them in the shower?'

Her hand lay on the soft fair curls between Nesta's thighs, and then touched the lips of her kitty, pouting and moist. Gentle fingers opened them wider and exposed the little pink nubby.

'Oh, you're making me come,' Nesta sighed.

Joy put her mouth to the girl's warm chuffie and pushed her tongue inside to flick at the firm nubby. Nesta knew a great deal about this – she had it done to her most days, very often by Penny, but by many other girls as well. She knew an expert touch when she felt it, and soon decided that Joy was very good at tonguing.

'That's fantastic,' she breathed, 'I'm going to come now.'

Joy's tongue worked faster. Nesta made little gasping noises and hung on to the windowsill to stay upright when her legs went rubbery. Her whole body shuddered at the moment the big thrill jolted through her.

'I love you, Joy,' she moaned, 'love you, love you . . .'

After that afternoon approach in the empty classroom everything turned out well. Joy invited Nesta to come to her private sitting-room whenever she had time to spare from her lessons and games. They lay on the grey sofa together, knickers off and titties hanging out of unbuttoned blouses, and Nesta proved to be very nearly as expert as Joy at fingering a kitty to bring on the big thrill.

Joy Locksley had changed a great deal in a few weeks, from the rule-bound Head of House who at the start of the term would never even consider diddling a student, to the sophisti-cated player of sex-games with young girls she had lately become. She thought it very likely that Nesta told her friend Penny everything that happened to her on Joy's sofa.

Girls being girls, and in particular born gossips, it seemed all too likely that Penny and Nesta told all the others about the latter's deep friendship with their Head of House. *Every girl in the College probably knows by now that I'm diddling Nesta regularly* Joy said to herself. *And I don't mind a bit.*

She and Nesta had been treating each other to thrills for about a week or ten days when Joy was invited by the Principal to have coffee and a glass of brandy with her after dinner. It wasn't the first time she'd been invited, as each Head of House was given coffee and a drink and an encouraging chat by Enid once every term.

As it happened, Joy had already had her meeting with Enid soon after the term started. They'd had a long chat about prospects for university places for the second-year girls. She couldn't imagine why she was being asked a second time.

They sat facing each other in chairs on either side of the empty fireplace, each with a small cup of coffee and a small glass of brandy to hand. Joy was looking suitably elegant in a short black dress with an elaborate jet-bead pattern on the bodice. Enid wore a dark-green dress Joy had seen her in several evenings that term. It exaggerated her titties, which were anyway too heavy for Joy's taste.

Joy had no way of knowing that only about a week earlier Toby Dundale had been sitting in the same chair she sat in now. Or that on that occasion Enid was wearing the same dress, but was slumped back in her chair until she was almost lying on it. Toby had a view of her thighs, and as her dress rode up over her knees, a glimpse right up to her knickers.

That particular evening had not turned out as Enid planned. She'd expected Toby to resign to avoid being sacked in disgrace, but instead he'd got his twanger up her and she'd been done on her own sofa. She still didn't understand how it had happened and hadn't spoken to him since.

'Joy,' she began – she was on first name terms with Heads of Houses – 'you know I have a high opinion of your abilities. But sadly there is something I must mention to you.'

'Really? Are you worried about Wexby House exam results?'

'I am not worried about that,' Enid said firmly, 'but I *am* concerned about another matter. For a week or so now you've been trailing after a girl in your House. You know who I mean, Nesta Wade. It's pointless to deny it – I've seen you watching her in the pool and on the tennis courts. You clearly feel inappropriate desires for that girl.'

Oh dear Joy thought, *I must have been very obvious – Nesta noticed me herself and asked me why, though she knew why all the time. Enid knows less than anybody what's going on in the college, so if she noticed me, then everybody else must have seen me mooning about after Nesta.*

'I'm not a fool,' Enid went on. 'I know what happens between girls all the time. And I know that some of the teaching staff have intimate friendships with girls. But I am not pleased to find that a Head of House is involved with a girl.'

Joy was no fool either. She was asking herself how Enid had managed to detect her watching Nesta. And how Enid could imagine what Joy had in mind when she observed Nesta's smooth young body in a thin wet swimsuit or a tight clinging tee-shirt. Could it possibly be that Enid was watching the girl herself? That Enid wanted to get her own hand into Nesta's knickers?

'Nesta Wade,' said Joy, smiling pleasantly. 'What a very pretty young woman. Soft blonde hair and a slender figure – long thighs. A pair of elegant little—'

'Joy!' Enid interrupted, her cheeks pink. 'You mustn't talk about one of the students in those terms – it is unsuitable.'

'Have you seen her in the showers?' Joy asked with a smile, trying to sound innocent.

'Well,' Enid said slowly, 'I may have noticed her by chance. But that is not the point. As I understand it, Nesta has been involved with Penny Carlton all the time the two of them have been here with us. That seems to me normal and appropriate. I imagine it provides them both with the satisfaction healthy young bodies crave. But this term Nesta appears to have become the centre of adult interest.'

'You mean me, I take it.'

'If it were only you, Joy, I might close my eyes to what is going on. This is Nesta's last term at Lechlade – in September she and Penny will be at university. But some of the interest in her is deplorable and I find it hard to remain silent.'

'I don't follow you,' Joy said, her brow wrinkled in puzzlement. 'Are you saying there are other teachers involved with her? Eleanor Redruth, perhaps – but surely you must know that Eleanor dabbles with every girl in the college who'll let her. No one takes that amiss.'

'I'm referring to the Sports Coach,' Enid said, tight-lipped. 'There was an occasion recently when I happened to be passing by the tennis courts and saw him pretending to coach Nesta. He stood much too close to her for decency and he put his arms round her from behind. It sounds unbelievable, but I very much fear he was rubbing himself against her.'

'Perhaps you saw more than was really there,' Joy suggested. She was sure now that big-tittied Enid wanted to diddle Nesta.

'The event cannot be dismissed out of hand like that,' Enid

said. 'It was obvious that Nesta was not wearing a bra under her shirt. The coach's hands were very close to her unguarded bosoms at that moment and I am not at all convinced that he didn't feel them.'

Joy smiled to hear Enid say 'bosoms' instead of titties. It was one more sign that the Principal was hiding a desire to get her hands on Nesta's body. Joy tried to picture the scene in her mind: Nesta sucking the pink bobble of one of Enid's big bare bouncers and Enid fingering Nesta's wet little kitty. The picture did not please Joy.

'I've noticed a trend among the girls to go braless this term,' she said casually. 'Why do you suppose they do so?'

'They are doing it to attract the attention of the Sports Coach,' Enid said, refusing to speak the name of the man who had slipped his *thing* up her and made her come – she still couldn't get over that.

'Surely not,' Joy said, playing innocent.

'I'll tell you something else,' Enid said sternly, 'and this shows how far things have gone – while that man was fumbling at her, Nesta had no briefs on under her shorts. You may be sure many other girls are not wearing them either, since Nesta and Penny are the trend-setters for Wexby House.'

'How do you know she had no knickers on, Enid?' Joy asked. 'Did you follow her into the showers and watch her strip?'

'The girl's shorts were indecently short – more evidence of that man's pernicious influence. Every time she reached up high to return the ball I could see right up to where her legs joined – do you understand?'

'You saw the hair round her kitty, is that what you mean?' Enid nodded. She didn't trust herself to speak.

'And are her curls blondish?' Joy persisted, knowing very well they were, having played with them all the past week.

'I regard you as a friend,' Enid said shakily. 'May I speak openly to you, Joy? Since Maureen Plessy damaged her knee and had to give up her job I've had no one to confide my deepest thoughts to.'

230

'Speak as freely as you like,' Joy said in an encouraging tone. 'What you say will go no further. If I can help you in any way, it will be a pleasure to do so.'

'It was only a brief glimpse of Nesta's curls, but it had a disturbing effect on me,' Enid confessed. 'All sorts of very unsuitable ideas came into my mind.'

Joy looked down at Enid's lap and saw that she was gripping her thighs with both hands, her fingers spread. Enid was sexually aroused and determined to conceal it.

'Ideas such as wanting to see more,' Joy prompted her.

'I couldn't stop myself following her into the showers. I saw her naked, soaping herself, giggling and talking to Penny. I saw her pointed little titties and her blonde-haired kitty. I would have stared all the time she was there if I'd dared. But I forced myself to move on, before my presence gave rise to comment.'

'That night when you went to bed,' Joy sighed softly, 'I'm sure there must have been pictures in your mind that stopped you falling asleep.'

'I couldn't wait till bed-time,' Enid said, her face scarlet. 'Seeing Nesta naked under the shower put me in such a state that I came straight back here and sat in this chair and gave myself all the relief I could.'

'Oh, I see,' Joy murmured. 'You sat there and gave yourself a finger-wave. Did you take your knickers off, or did you just slip your hand down them?'

She was getting bold now with her questions, certain she'd broken through Enid's natural reticence. Their new friendship was going to be very useful to Joy's future career.

'I slipped them off,' Enid whispered. 'They were damp. I sat here with my skirt pulled up and played with myself till I came hard. And even then I couldn't get the memory of Nesta's naked body out of my head – I had to do it to myself again.'

Joy half-closed her eyes to picture Enid sitting in the armchair with her skirt round her hips and her hand down between her thighs. The curls on her chuffie were sure to be very dark – the hair on her head was glossy black. How was it when a big woman like Enid reached the climax? Joy wondered. Did she come hard and noisily, or did she announce her thrill with little whimpers?

'You diddled yourself twice,' she said. 'That sounds nice. What about that night, when you went to bed?'

'I had to do it twice more before I could go to sleep.'

'My dear Enid, all this worry about Toby Dundale feeling the girls is having a dreadful effect on you,' Joy said. 'Girls diddle girls and teachers diddle girls. It is unfortunate if a male is doing the same to them, but it's not that important and you mustn't let it distress you.'

'But suppose he is doing more than that,' Enid said hastily. 'Suppose he is actually *doing* them – what a disaster for the college it would be. When I think of how he was pressing himself against Nesta and rubbing against the cheeks of her bum, I'm sure his *thing* was standing stiff at the time. Naturally I ask myself if he takes her somewhere private and gets it out, then pushes it up her and *does* her till he shoots off.'

'Oh lord, what a thought!' Joy exclaimed. 'My impression from seeing him in his skimpy little drawers in the pool is that he has a large and long *thing*. Not that I know much about them, of course, I've only seen a few and I've never actually had one inside me.'

'Your observation is accurate,' Enid said grimly. 'He does have a large, long *thing* – far too big for a young girl, I'm certain it would cause harm to her. Even a grown woman might find it too much to cope with easily.'

Joy was listening in silent amazement. Enid obviously knew more about Toby Dundale's male *thing* than she pretended. She must have seen it and she'd perhaps held it in her hand, to be so descriptive of its size and thickness. Could it possibly have been inside her chuffie?

The thought seemed highly improbable to Joy at first. No one who knew Enid could easily believe that the Principal of Lechlade Ladies' College had been flat on her back for a man. But the idea arose naturally from what she'd said about Toby

Dundale's twanger. She knew too much about what a woman would feel when it was inside her. So had Toby actually had Enid's legs open and *done* her? Had she let him shoot his load into her plump belly?

And where did all this happen, if it did? In the gym, behind the tennis courts, here in her sitting-room? And how often had he been allowed to do her? Was it a one-off or did they get together three times a week? These were fascinating questions and Joy was dying to know the answers. This wasn't the time to ask them, however. It would be better to return to them on another day, when Enid had total confidence and trust in her.

'Enid, you are letting yourself become obsessed with Nesta and Toby,' Joy said. 'I don't know if she's ever let him do her, but I can assure you that he's not doing her now. You are under too much high stress, Enid, that's the real problem.'

'But what can I do?'

'Massage,' Joy said at once. 'Deep body massage. All your tension can be relieved that way. Debbie Gregson has wonderful relaxing hands. I am on good terms with her, I shall explain the problem and arrange for her to treat you daily for the rest of this term.'

'Do you really think that will help me, Joy?' Enid asked hopefully.

'I guarantee it.'

As it happened, Debbie was to be at the college the next day. Joy was at the treatment room at nine o'clock to talk to her before she became involved with others needing the touch of her skilled hands. They kissed, and because they were still very good friends they stroked each other's titties for a moment outside their clothes. Joy explained the position with the Principal and Debbie declared she'd be happy to give all the help she could to a woman she respected highly.

Enid didn't want to be seen going to Debbie for massage in case the situation was misunderstood and she was talked about. And it was out of the question for Debbie to be seen anywhere near her bedroom. So Debbie presented herself in Enid's sitting-room at ten-thirty.

The session got off to a slow start, for Enid was slightly flustered at the prospect of showing her near-naked body to a stranger. At Debbie's urging she slipped off her black-and-white day dress and her shoes and tights, though her face went pink when she rolled the tights down her legs. She stood barefoot and shy on the carpet in her large-cup white bra and knickers with an embroidered edging.

Debbie eyed her body up and down, the heavy breasts, the plump belly, the sturdy thighs. 'There's no need to feel shy with me,' she said with an encouraging smile. 'Off with your underwear – I want you naked.'

'Oh,' Enid breathed, her cheeks blushing red. She sat down on the sofa and reached behind her back to undo her bra.

'Do you have to watch me so closely?' she asked.

'Why not?' Debbie said with a chuckle. 'Bare bodies are my business – in a minute I won't just be looking at you, I shall be handling you.'

Enid shut her eyes in embarrassment and pulled her bra off. Her chubby titties flopped out and dangled heavily, the pinkish bobbles looking too small for so large an expanse of pale-skinned flesh.

'Bigger than mine,' said Debbie with a grin, 'and I've had men trying to grope me since I was twelve years old. Did they try to get a feel of yours when you were a girl?'

'Men are lustful beasts,' Enid said with conviction. 'They only want one thing and they have no regard for women. We are better off without them pawing at us.'

'I wouldn't have agreed with you once, but I do now,' Debbie said with another grin. 'Take your knickers off, please.'

Enid pressed her plump thighs together and raised herself an inch from the sofa while she slid her knickers down her legs. She stopped when they were round her ankles and glanced at Debbie as if unsure whether to proceed.

'Give them to me,' Debbie said firmly.

Enid removed them completely and handed them over. With Debbie's hand on her bare shoulder to spur her on, she turned sideways, swung her legs up on the sofa and lay down on her back. Her legs were still pressed together; Debbie smiled to herself when she saw how big a patch of coal-dark curls Enid had at the base of her plump belly.

'Hands under your head,' she said, arranging a cushion to make Enid comfortable. 'That's it, now close your eyes and relax. Think beautiful thoughts and we'll soon have you feeling very well indeed.'

Her hands were occupied first with Enid's big loose titties, rolling them round and lifting them and cupping them in her palms. Her fingertips played over their little bobbles until they stood up proudly.

'Oh,' Enid sighed, 'I'm starting to feel better already.'

She didn't keep her eyes closed. She wanted to watch the full-figured Debbie in her white uniform bending over her and how her titties hung as she bent. Where the dress was buttoned at the top there was a glimpse of cleavage between round fleshy titties.

Debbie was now stroking Enid's belly round and round, a slow deliberate motion that sent tremors of pleasure through her. Debbie ran her fingers through the glossy dark curls where the Principal's thighs met.

'Open your legs, please,' she said. Enid gasped, but complied and slid them apart.

'Ah yes,' Debbie said softly, staring at Enid's plump-lipped chuffie in its birds'-nest of black curls with an interest that was more personal than professional. 'Very nice.'

Enid trembled when she felt fingers between her thighs, stroking the soft lips and then pressing between them. She wanted this, but it seemed so unfeeling to lie down and be diddled by someone she didn't know, someone who wasn't a friend.

'Must you do that?' she murmured.

'We're coming to the most important part of the massage,'

235

Debbie said, her broad face split by a grin. 'Close your eyes and just let the sensations flow through you.'

Debbie didn't know that the last time a stranger's fingers were inside Enid's chuffie they were Toby Dundale's. And he hadn't stopped with just his fingers, he'd dragged her legs apart and sunk his stiff twanger into it. Enid's mind was full of that unwelcome memory while Debbie diddled her with an expert touch.

At least Debbie had no hard dick to slide into her. Under her dress she had a big warm chuffie like Enid's own. None of the teaching staff confided in Enid, so she didn't know that Debbie's was bare-shaven. But she knew that the physio-therapist had no thick hard shaft to stretch a chuffie wide open, and that was the most important thing, Enid said to herself; Debbie's skilful fingers were the right instrument to bring on the tremendous thrill she was panting for.

'Ah, we're nearly there,' Debbie murmured, her fingers gliding quickly over Enid's slippery little nubby. 'Do you feel ready for it?'

'I do, I do,' Enid gasped, her chubby belly shaking.

Debbie put her hand under Enid's knees and raised them till her heels almost touched her bum – with a young girl they would, but Enid had too much flesh on her thighs and big round bum for that contact to be made. She parted her knees as wide as they would go, offering herself to Debbie without restraint.

'Big is beautiful,' Debbie said.

She had the lips of Enid's chuffie wide open and diddled her with three fingers of one hand. Enid was twitching non-stop. She stared round-eyed at Debbie's smiling face and decided that she was not a stranger, she was a new friend. Soon she would be a close friend.

Enid's mouth gaped wide and she gave a long trembling moan as she came, her whole body shaking like jelly.

'Come, come, come,' Debbie urged her, fingers fluttering in the warm slipperiness of her chuffie.

After that it took Enid a good five minutes to recover enough to speak again. Debbie wiped her with a paper tissue and straightened her legs to make her comfortable on the sofa.

'There,' she said cheerfully, 'I'm sure you feel much better now – you look stress-free for the first time since I met you weeks ago.'

'You and I can become close friends,' Enid told her. 'I haven't really felt so on top of the world for ages. When can you massage me again?'

'It's best to do it every day,' said Debbie, 'but tomorrow is not one of my days here. Joy Locksley explained to me that these are exceptional circumstances, so I'll be back to do you again this afternoon about four, if that's convenient.'

Enid put her hand over her chuffie to make sure it was still there and all right after the fantastic sensations that had surged through it five minutes ago. It felt very much all right, warm and relaxed and still slightly damp.

'Oh yes,' she breathed, 'four o'clock will suit me very well. And we'd better extend your contract with the college to have you here every day, if that suits you. What do you say?'

'I like the idea. I'll see you tomorrow at the same time.'

'Yes,' Enid said happily, 'and this afternoon at four. While I'm in this high-stress condition I feel I need to be massaged twice a day.'

Debbie grinned at her and pinched her chubby belly lightly. 'This afternoon I'll give you my very special massage,' she promised. 'Some people find it's too much for them, but you'll love it.'

'Yes,' Enid sighed, eyes closing in bliss, 'I know I shall.'

Chapter Sixteen

On the last night of term Eleanor Redruth staged her secret naked net-ball game in the gymnasium. She'd been thinking for weeks which girls she could persuade to take part and equally important, which girls she would most like to observe leaping about naked.

She settled for two from Wexby House, matched against two from Sawby House. The Wexby pair were Hilary Landor and Linda Knight. The Sawby House couple were Tessa Bowland and Rachel Fermor.

Besides their prettiness and their enthusiasm for girl-to-girl games, Eleanor also chose these four for their contrasting body types. Rachel had black hair and well rounded titties and a thick black fleece between her thighs. Tessa was a long-haired brunette with pointed little titties on a narrow frame and very little body hair.

Hilary was tall and fair-haired. She had the prettiest little titties imaginable and could well be an international model if she chose not to go on to university to read law and become a barrister. Linda had small soft titties that dangled just a little, but she also had the famed ginger-haired kitty that drove Eleanor into sexual frenzies.

The four contestants met Eleanor in the gym at midnight, when all was dark and silent throughout the college. The gym was well away from the main buildings and no one was awake to see the lights go on. Eleanor set up the net while the girls stripped down to socks and trainers for the match. She set the net high, the top edge eight feet above the floor, because she wanted to see their bodies stretching up for the ball.

The girls had thrown the jeans and tee-shirts they arrived in on the bench by one wall. Eleanor stripped off too, both to keep them company and to be immediately ready for another kind of game at the right moment. The girls lined up while she reminded them of the rules of the game – it was a sight to make her feel moist between the legs, four lovely naked girls, all arms and titties and long sleek thighs.

While she was enjoying a good look at them, they were eyeing her with equal interest. She was twenty-nine and kept herself trim with constant tennis and swimming. And private indoor games with any girl she could get her hands on. She had a nice pair of titties and a kitty that pouted its lips through neatly-trimmed brown hair.

Besides ginger Linda, she'd also tongued Rachel and diddled Tessa. And she'd nearly had Hilary in the showers after they'd both been out on one of Toby Dundale's evening jogs. But they heard someone coming in – or so Hilary claimed – and then the moment was gone. Eleanor intended to make up for that failed try tonight.

'There'll be no whistle,' she said, 'and no shouting by you. I'm sure we can't be heard over in the main buildings but we don't want to risk it. When you think you've scored, stand still and wait for my decision. Sawby House will start the first half and Wexby the second.'

The two pairs took up position with the high net between them. Eleanor lobbed the ball to Rachel, who caught it one-handed and jumped high to slam it over the net. Hilary reached sideways to get to it before it hit the floor and the game was on. It was every bit as exciting as Eleanor had imagined – lithe bodies in rapid motion, dashing and leaping, stretching out for the ball, bare titties bouncing, thighs flashing, bum cheeks rolling. Eleanor forgot about refereeing and stood open-mouthed.

In was supposed to be fifteen minutes a half. Eleanor had

kept her wrist-watch on when she undressed but was too entranced by the game to check the time. And the girls were so obviously enjoying the freedom of hard exercise in the nude that it was a pity to stop them. The score was at 15-12 in Wexby House's favour when Eleanor glanced down guiltily at her watch and called *half-time!*

Though the lights of the gym couldn't be seen from the main college buildings, they were visible from the gate-house. Or at least that side of it where Toby Dundale's bedroom was. He was half-asleep when a light flickered through his window. He got up to see what was going on, and away in the distance he saw the gym blazing with light. It was after midnight; this he had to investigate. He pulled on a sweater and jeans and made for the stairs quietly with his trainers in his hand – he didn't want to disturb Keith and Sally.

He was fumbling at the chain on the front door when he heard a step behind him. Then Sally pressed herself against his back and put her arms round him, groping for his flies, while she asked where he was going.

'The gym's all lit up,' he said. 'Nobody should be there at this time of night, so I'm going to see what's going on.'

He turned round in her arms to get her hands off his flapper before she made it stand up. She held the cheeks of his bum while she rubbed her belly against his. Even in the near-darkness of the entrance hall he could make out that she was wearing a short flimsy wraparound dressing-gown over a nightie that was even shorter.

'Who could it be?' she asked. 'Burglars?'

'Burglars don't turn lights on. It's the last night of the term and some of the girls might be playing a prank. But I have to make sure.'

'I'll come with you,' Sally murmured, her kitty warm against his thigh through her cobweb-thin nightwear. 'Keith's fast asleep and he'll never know I'm gone.'

She didn't bother to say that she'd had Keith on his back

twice that night and ridden him to a standstill, but Toby guessed as much. He took her hand and they trotted silently across the grass to the gym. Twenty yards away from the big lighted windows he made her stop and they went the rest of the way on hands and knees. The windows ran from ground-level to roof the whole length of the building. Toby and Sally lay flat on the grass a few feet back and looked in.

It was the half-time break. The girls, who had brought towels with them and bottles of Vichy water, sat in a row on the bench by the wall to wipe perspiration from their faces and necks and titties. Linda had spread her legs to wipe between them – and perhaps to draw attention to her pretty little ginger kitty.

She'd prefer Eleanor's attention, but any of the girls would do. She'd been diddled by Hilary lots of times, but by neither of the Sawby House girls. Linda thought she wouldn't mind being fingered by either of them.

Hilary stood up and put her foot up on the end of the bench while she retied the lace of one of her trainers. She was bending over to reach it, but not enough to hide her fair-haired kitty. Eleanor had it in view and could see drops of perspiration trickling down Hilary's belly toward the curls.

Eleanor was sitting two along the bench. She leaned forward to stare past Linda at Hilary, her hand clasped between her own thighs.

'I know what you're looking at,' Hilary said casually. She hadn't got her breath back completely yet from the fast and furious first-half.

'Hilary darling...' Eleanor sighed, almost giddy with desire for the girl's slim young body.

Hilary left her lace alone and straightened up with one foot still on the bench. She put her hand to her kitty and stroked it while she grinned very knowingly at the girls watching her. Eleanor, especially, was fascinated by the blondish hair and the moist pink lips.

'I've tongued her lots of times,' Linda confided to Eleanor.

'Look all you want to,' Hilary said with a smile. 'I know what you do to girls, Miss Redruth. Everybody knows – because you've had nearly every girl in the college. You tried to do it to me under the shower.'

'Yes,' Eleanor sighed, her hand clamped between her own lean thighs, 'of course I want to do you.'

'I stopped you by saying somebody was coming in. You daren't be seen doing it, but that doesn't stop you looking.'

Eleanor was trembling. She pulled her hand from her thighs and opened them to show her brown-haired chuffie. She pressed both hands over her small bare titties – her face was scarlet.

'Why do you talk to me like this, Hilary?' she stammered.

'Because,' Hilary answered bafflingly.

Eleanor knew a challenge when she heard one. She got up from the bench and took the three steps needed to reach Hilary, dropped to her knees and pressed her mouth to Hilary's chuffie.

'Oh – look at that!' Linda said to the Sawby House girls.

Hilary stood firm, one foot on the floor, one on the bench, her thighs held apart by the stance. Eleanor's cheek lay against Hilary's thigh, smooth skin on smooth skin. The cheek was flushed and hot but the thigh was cool.

'I didn't think you'd dare in front of an audience,' Hilary said in surprise.

Her hand was on the wall to keep herself upright while little tremors ran through her from the flick of Eleanor's tongue against her nub. She looked down at the top of Eleanor's head and there was a smile on her pretty face.

'I know I'm worth kissing, all my friends say so,' Hilary said. 'You made it obvious you wanted more than a look, but I wouldn't let you. Do you know why?'

Eleanor moaned and moved her hands from Hilary's thighs to grasp the taut cheeks of her young bum.

'You can't even guess,' Hilary said.

Outside on the grass Sally had pushed Toby onto his side to

get at his twanger – it was hard as steel when she dragged it out of his trousers.

'You see what she's doing to that girl?' she gasped. 'Is that what you meant by a *prank*?'

She pressed her mouth to Toby's without waiting for an answer and pushed her tongue inside as her hand raced up and down his hard-on.

In the gym Rachel and Tessa got up from the bench and stood close to Eleanor to get a better view of what she was doing to Hilary. Linda sat on the bench next to her and played with herself while she watched the tonguing. The three girls whispered to each other and smiled slyly.

'The reason I've never let you feel me is because you're so sure you can have any girl you want,' Hilary said.

'She can have me any time she likes,' Rachel announced, 'I think she's absolutely super.'

'I'm special,' Hilary went on dreamily. 'I decide who I'm going to let tongue me, I don't let myself be had by everybody who fancies me.'

From where she sat on the bench, Linda reached up to stroke Hilary's perfect little titties.

'You've let me diddle you dozens of times,' she whispered. 'Does that mean I'm special too, Hilary?'

'Oh,' Hilary gasped. She was trembling from head to foot. 'Oh, that's nice, I shall come in a minute! Stop it, stop it, you're trying to make me lose the second half.'

'I don't mind if we lose the match,' Linda said, 'I want to see you coming.'

Eleanor's arms were round Hilary to support her through the big thrill when it came. Hilary's thighs opened wider – the wet tongue tip that fluttered over her nubby was driving her hard into orgasm. She squealed and came, rubbing her soft chuffie against Eleanor's mouth.

Toby was on his back on the grass now, with his jeans round his knees and Sally flat on top of him. She'd spiked herself on his twanger with one flick of her hips – her chuffie was so wet that it instantly slid all the way up her. She opened her thin wraparound and he put his hands up her short nightie to get hold of her slack little titties while she did him with more energy than anyone would expect from a look at her skinny body.

She pulled her tongue out of his mouth to gasp, 'I'm coming, Toby . . .' He bucked under her and shot his warm cream into her.

Five minutes rest and a drink of spring water were enough to revive Hilary so the second half could start. Eleanor watched with a smile on her face – she'd planned the evening of a life-time and brought it off. She'd realised her dream of watching young girls playing naked netball. She'd tongued Hilary at last and before they went back to their rooms she meant to have the other three girls.

The match ended with Sawby House winning 27–19. Eleanor by then was stroking her own titties and desperate to get her hands on Linda's ginger-haired kitty. She didn't give her a moment to rest – she took her arm and dragged her over to the thick mat where martial arts were taught, pushed her down on her back and told her to spread her legs.

Rachel and Tessa sat down on the wooden bench and reached for their bottles of spa water. Hilary stood in front of them, wiping her titties and underarms with her towel.

'It was a good match,' she said, 'but we'd have won if Eleanor hadn't done me at half-time and weakened me.'

'Don't think so,' said Rachel lazily. She was leaning with her back against the wall and her legs stretched out in front of her. Hilary looked at the long slender body spread nakedly before her, noticing how Rachel's titties were heaving with each breath.

'Yes we would,' she said firmly. 'Is it true your friends call you "Monkey"?'

Rachel looked back at her through half-closed eyes. Her glance travelled very slowly down from Hilary's flushed face to her titties and then to the blondish little bush between her legs.

She smiled and said nothing. Hilary dropped down on her knees between Rachel's outstretched legs and stroked her kitty.

'It's because of this, isn't it?' she asked.

Rachel still said nothing, but she began to move her hips and belly in a slow thrusting motion, only an inch or so back and forth but enough to slither her kitty against Hilary's hand.

'Because you won unfairly, you owe me something,' Hilary said, 'and I'm going to have it.'

She reversed her hand so it was palm upward, then drew her middle finger up between the lips of Rachel's kitty to part them.

'You're wet,' she said, touching the little nubby.

She held her hand still then and let Rachel rub herself against the fingertip inside her. Rachel's head was back against the wall, her eyelids still only half open while she slid herself back and forth in a cunning little rhythm.

'I'm not diddling you – you're doing it to yourself,' Hilary sighed. 'You're giving yourself a thrill on my fingers. You're going to make yourself come, aren't you?'

Hilary's free hand was between her own thighs to touch her blondish little fleece. Her finger probed the lips and slipped inside, where the wetness lingered from Eleanor's tonguing.

'I'm going to make us both come together,' she gasped.

Toby had rolled over to stare through the gym windows again. He could see Eleanor Redruth lying on the mat with Linda, the teacher's head poised over the bright ginger thatch of the girl's kitty. Eleanor's groping fingers pulled the lips open and Toby saw her plunge her tongue into it.

Linda started bucking her belly upward as the tongue slithered over her nubby. Eleanor's hands were all over her, gripping the cheeks of her bum, rubbing her belly, rolling her titties and plucking at the bobbles.

The sight of Linda being done made Toby's limp flapper grow long and stiff again. And what Hilary was doing to Rachel on the bench stiffened it even more – he moaned under his breath when he saw how she diddled the black-bushed girl and herself at the same time.

He pulled Sally up on her hands and knees, with her head toward the window, then flung her short nightie up over her back to bare her bum and forced her knees apart on the grass. There was no need to fumble with his hand between her thighs, she was wet and open. He got behind her on his knees and his hard-on was pointing where it wanted to go.

He put the head to the loose wet lips and gave a push – and he was in and up her. He held her by the hips as he repeatedly slammed into her, all the while staring at Hilary doing Rachel in the gym. Sally was as eager as he was, jerking her bum back at him to meet his jabs and drive him deeper into her.

'Oh, look!' she gasped. 'That girl's coming – look at her – do me, do me, Toby...'

'I'm coming too,' he moaned. He was on the short strokes and ready to shoot his creamy load.

'Yes, yes, yes,' Sally wailed.

EROS
in Town

Anonymous

When the aristocratic Sir Franklin Franklyn and his half-brother Andy arrive in London to claim their inheritance, they find not the respectable family home they expected but the most lascivious of brothels. Frank takes things into his own hands and transforms the town-house into the most luxurious, romantic house of pleasure in all London. Here, every desire is catered for, any amorous wish met.

Not to be outdone, Frank's saucy sister Sophie declares that women are as much slaves to desire as men, and to prove her point she establishes a stable of lusty lovers patronised by the most elegant ladies in the land.

Thus both brother and sister indulge themselves in an orgy of sensuality that surpasses even the wildest flights of erotic fantasy . . .

FICTION / EROTICA 0 7472 3199 0

SWEET FANNY

The erotic education of a Regency maid

FAYE ROSSIGNOL

'From the time I was sixteen until the age of thirty-two I "spread the gentlemen's relish" as the saying goes. In short, I was a Lady of Pleasure.'

Fanny, now the Comtesse de C---, looks back on a lifetime of pleasure, of experiment in the myriad Arts of Love. In letters to her granddaughter and namesake, she recounts the erotic education of a young girl at the hands of a mysterious Comte – whose philosophy of life carries hedonism to voluptuous extremes – and his partners in every kind of sin. There is little the young Fanny does not experience – and relate in exquisite detail to the recipient of her remarkably revealing memoirs.

FICTION / EROTICA 0 7472 3275 X

A selection of Erotica from Headline

BLUE HEAVENS	Nick Bancroft	£4.99	☐
MAID	Dagmar Brand	£4.99	☐
EROS IN AUTUMN	Anonymous	£4.99	☐
EROTICON THRILLS	Anonymous	£4.99	☐
IN THE GROOVE	Lesley Asquith	£4.99	☐
THE CALL OF THE FLESH	Faye Rossignol	£4.99	☐
SWEET VIBRATIONS	Jeff Charles	£4.99	☐
UNDER THE WHIP	Nick Aymes	£4.99	☐
RETURN TO THE CASTING COUCH	Becky Bell	£4.99	☐
MAIDS IN HEAVEN	Samantha Austen	£4.99	☐
CLOSE UP	Felice Ash	£4.99	☐
TOUCH ME, FEEL ME	Rosanna Challis	£4.99	☐

All Headline books are available at your local bookshop or newsagent, or can be ordered direct from the publisher. Just tick the titles you want and fill in the form below. Prices and availability subject to change without notice.

Headline Book Publishing, Cash Sales Department, Bookpoint, 39 Milton Park, Abingdon, OXON, OX14 4TD, UK. If you have a credit card you may order by telephone – 01235 400400.

Please enclose a cheque or postal order made payable to Bookpoint Ltd to the value of the cover price and allow the following for postage and packing:

UK & BFPO: £1.00 for the first book, 50p for the second book and 30p for each additional book ordered up to a maximum charge of £3.00.

OVERSEAS & EIRE: £2.00 for the first book, £1.00 for the second book and 50p for each additional book.

Name ....

Address ....

....

....

If you would prefer to pay by credit card, please complete:
Please debit my Visa/Access/Diner's Card/American Express (delete as applicable) card no:

Signature .... Expiry Date..............